# Hardly Beach Weather

## BERNARD COHEN

*flamingo*

An imprint of HarperCollins*Publishers*

**Flamingo**
An imprint of HarperCollins*Publishers*, Australia

First published in Australia in 2002
by HarperCollins*Publishers* Pty Limited
ABN 36 009 913 517
A member of the HarperCollins*Publishers* (Australia) Pty Limited Group
www.harpercollins.com.au

**HarperCollins*Publishers***
25 Ryde Road, Pymble, Sydney NSW 2073, Australia
31 View Road, Glenfield, Auckland 10, New Zealand
77–85 Fulham Palace Road, London W6 8JB, United Kingdom
Hazelton Lanes, 55 Avenue Road, Suite 2900, Toronto, Ontario, M5R 3L2
*and* 1995 Markham Road, Scarborough, Ontario, M1B 5M8, Canada
10 East 53rd Street, New York NY 10022, USA

National Library of Australia Cataloguing-in-publication data:

Cohen, Bernard, 1963–.
   Hardly beach weather.
   ISBN 0 7322 6430 8.
   1. Automobile travel – Australia – Fiction. 2. Man–woman
   relationships – Fiction. I. Title.
A823.3

Cover and internal design by Darian Causby, HarperCollins Design Studio
Cover photographs: road by Getty Images; car by David Lange
Author photograph by Wong Kan Tai
Typeset by HarperCollins Design Studio in Sabon 11.5/16
Printed and bound in Australia by Griffin Press on 80gsm Bulky Book Ivory

5 4 3 2 1          02 03 04 05

FOR MY MOTHER

# DAY ONE

Maria is travelling lightly. This means she is bringing the same amount of stuff as usual, but is in a relentless good mood. I am travelling heavily. The contrast is the story of my relationship with Maria: I set out with good intentions, and she ruins everything.

I am sitting in my car as the back seat slowly fills with Maria's soft bags full of underwear, her picnic utensils, bottles of drink, hefty camera bag. Maria's a photographer, she says. She's sold a few photographs. A few. To be fair, my suitcase takes up most of the boot, but I'm not disposed to be fair: the back seat will soon overflow with Maria's things, for which I feel unjustifiable contempt.

1

I am sitting in the car because my relationship with Maria has progressed beyond simple obligation. I did not offer to help her with her luggage and (goes without saying) she didn't ask for my assistance. She waved from the door when I drove up, in lieu of inviting me in. Thus I learnt that our relationship has also progressed beyond entering each other's houses. This is the latest of many sometimes tiny, sometimes almost imperceptible steps in the unpicking of her life from mine.

For a while after our break-up, we talked on the telephone every few days. I tried to be heavy in a light sort of way, and she laboured over her lightness. I'm sure it was tremendously healthy, to work through things as we did, and I'm certain it did me no end of good, having all that time to relive and reflect on what had gone wrong, to mull over the last months of our time together, and to apportion blame to Maria.

Maria seemed unable to benefit from this process at all, always trying to sound cheerful, but underneath it just too defensive to admit anything. I apologised to her, all the time. I asked what she'd like me to apologise for and I apologised for it. I admitted I'd been less than ideal at times. She never admitted anything, no matter how often or how clearly I pointed out her failings. After a time, our conversations became shorter and shorter until hardly existing at all. This was also Maria's doing. She says she's one for visible progress and, whether bloody-mindedly or not, she was unable to discern any improvement in me. So, she was always on her way out, or in the middle of something, or busy with 'other matters in her life'. In this manner, she helped neither of us.

All the time, I tried to rescue our relationship, to build annexes to what had been, to invent other directions, other possibilities. I wanted our mutual return of keys to take on a ceremonial aspect, or at the least to involve a few drinks and some reminiscence, whereas Maria wanted only to 'stick them in the post'. I hoped and suggested we might continue to share our mutual interests in reading and music. Maria wanted to return the three books and four compact discs I had chosen for her as presents, and for me to give back 'the shelves full' she claimed she had merely lent me. I wanted to introduce her to any new friends I might make; Maria insisted that her social life had very rapidly recovered and exceeded its former state, and that she was so busy making new friendships and strengthening old ones that if she were to take up my suggestion, she would spend nearly every waking moment with me.

This, thought Maria, would be too much.

While I found Maria's general negativity disheartening, I nonetheless continued my efforts towards her. Negativity was an attitude; maintaining an attitude did at least indicate a relationship existing and, I reasoned, a negative relationship is no worse than one which has failed and dissolved; a negative relationship must be preferable to a negative non-relationship. Waiting for Maria in the car on this hot December afternoon, it occurs to me: the worth of my persistence will be measured during this journey.

As if my thought patterns were providing cues, finally Maria climbs in to the passenger seat, looks across at me.

'Are you okay?' she asks.

'Do I look like I'm convalescing?' I demand. 'There's nothing wrong with me. You don't have to use that tone.'

'Calm down, it was a straightforward question. Jack, seriously, would you rather I went by bus? I still have time to get the overnight one tonight. I'd rather you said so, anyway, if that's what you mean.'

'It's fine and I'm fine,' I say. 'I'm just impatient to go. It's hot.'

'Okay, okay. Good. Let's go then.'

I start the engine, pull away from Maria's house and head towards Parramatta Road. We're setting off much later than I had predicted, and I would have predicted we'd run late. Through a combination of additional cups of coffee, half-hour waits for news reports on bushfires en route (not good) and short telephone calls of minor deferral, mid-morning has become mid-afternoon. I accept some of the responsibility: I drank, I listened, I telephoned. For her part, Maria waited for me. She did nothing to speed the process. It's past four o'clock by the time I turn left onto Parramatta Road, away from the city.

'Sorry,' I say (see what I mean). 'I just started to feel kind of queasy. The heat, I guess.'

'It's okay. Thanks for the lift.' She grins and winds open her window. She pulls a tube of sunscreen from her shirt pocket, and massages it onto her face and left arm. She offers the cream to me, but I decline.

'Maybe a little apprehensive too,' I confess, after a moment to decide that the admission will act more as a licence than a weakening.

'I'm glad you said that. I am too.'

'Yes, it's a positive start,' I comment, 'the two of us bonded in mutual fear.'

Sydney's postwar boom stretches before us, fifty kilometres of suburban backyards, arterial roads lined with battered shopfronts from the pre-supermarket era, massive billboards (encircled, like arenas, by floodlights) commending to us American underwear, European mobile telephones and avuncular news reporting, every few hundred metres another promise of car parking or fast food or self-service petrol, tens of thousands of vehicles to pass between here and the city's western boundary, three or four lanes of traffic in both directions though, clearly, most of them are headed the opposite direction. Soon we'll pay our dollars and be on the tollway, forty-five minutes from then and we'll have left the city, and it will be Maria and me. I will know no one but Maria.

'It's completely wrong to be driving west,' I remark. 'It goes against all the training of my youth. It's a beach afternoon, it's obvious.'

She squeezes some cream onto her left hand, rubs it into her right forearm.

'What do you say?' I joke-insist.

'It's too late. We're committed. There'll be no turning around for us,' she declares, laughing, allowing the ironies to reflect on the journey ahead, but also on everything which had brought us to this point.

Of course I laugh too. What else could I do?

*

Despite the coming apart of our former love relationship, we are in my small car. We are driving. To be more accurate, I am driving. How much more accuracy and precision can one man provide? I am driving her — well, why not? — I am to drive Maria fourteen hundred kilometres.

Surely this is only because of my good nature. We can be friends, I said, and she said it too, at least for a few weeks. (She said it first, to be honest, but that would have been because she also said we were no longer lovers.) I really thought we meant it. Otherwise I wouldn't have offered. And (would-go-without-saying-if-it-hadn't-been-said) she wouldn't have agreed. I imagined our former love transforming into a further viable relationship, tried to picture what intervening phases there must be. I imagined overcoming those weeks which seemed like epochs of anger, disappointment and indifference, and somehow finding something else beyond: comradeship, helpfulness, an easy, flirtatious way of being with each other. The glossy magazines claim this process is a good thing, that an ex-lover can be recycled into a reasonably useful sort of being. From Maria's point of view, there couldn't be too many better uses for a discarded boyfriend than to drive his discarder halfway across a continent — though to be fair (as always), she's never been the magazine reader; that's my department.

Of course, the magazines are gender prescriptive: they speak only of ex-boyfriends as helpful souls. I try to imagine parallel purposes to which I could put Maria, but can think of very few. Reassurance is pretty much all I can imagine demanding from her, and that would hardly be her natural role. If I were to find a successor girlfriend, and she were also to dump me, perhaps Maria could usefully offer a few words of comfort. For example, 'I'm sure you weren't entirely at fault, this time.'

Or she might assist me with the ageing process which looms before me, now that I must face the future alone: there I'd be, concerned about my receding gums, telling her that I've read that constant toothbrushing can stimulate regrowth, but that I can see how close this is to madness, how easily it could lead to the obsessive and compulsive brushing of the madman who stands in the hospital car park a few blocks from Maria's home, and who never ceases the brushing: although he obviously must have been susceptible to such disorderly behaviour, could receding gums have been his trigger? No doubt Maria would calmly advise me to see a dentist, would tell me that I didn't seem that mad to her, not even at my worst. Will I thank her? Yes, because according to those same sources, politeness is at the heart of friendship.

The worst is that I don't actually want to be nice, relaxed and friendly, not in Maria's vicinity. Or I don't know if I want to, but I'm not deluded enough to believe myself capable of such extreme control in response to her ever-supple and confident openers: 'Hello, ex-darling, how's life without my civilising influence?'

'It's great, but I'm a little down because all my friends despise me since you poisoned their minds against me.'

'Yes, I was mad at you then, but I don't hate you any more.'

'Thank you for being so frank.'

'You're welcome. Shall we have a few drinks and a cup of coffee and some ice cream as a sign that we both like drinking and coffee and ice cream?'

'I'd love that. Could you help me sew this button on?'

'I'd love that too. Thanks for the champagne on my birthday yesterday.'

'It was fun to choose, oh beautiful person for whom I can still recall my desire.'

'Hee hee.'

I can't see Maria sticking to her part either. For the moment, though, we're side by side, amiably enough, having successfully set off. I suppose 'friendship' remains the best word for our relationship, even if in general the term speaks more to the poverty of language than to our stable and mutual good feeling. 'Acquaintanceship' is too inexperienced. 'Friendship' is a better word than 'undefined', more precise if less accurate. It's a pity only that Maria is not my friend.

Behind us, actually and metaphorically, are two beginnings for this drive. There is Sydney, and there is our relationship, before Maria claimed to have 'friendshipped' it. Our moment of happiness. If this journey were to be weighed with significance, the proper place to have begun it would be the Harbour. We should have left Maria's, driven around Bennelong Point, gazed at the Opera House on its prosthesis of reclaimed land. This would have been a promising beginning. (We would have needed to erase or bracket the meaningless journey from Maria's to the city, as I here parenthesise and abridge my own preparations — which, briefly, involved emptying my two drawers of clean clothing into a battered suitcase and throwing my laundry bag in beside, rounded off with a daypack of several books and road maps.)

Still, if I needed to plot Sydney as our setting-off point — rather than a small square of poorly kept suburban lawn — I guess we also should have met and fallen in love beside the water rather than in a mutual friend's suburban lounge room, in a pub, in my bed and Maria's bed, in kitchens. We should have organised our own beginnings better, discovered depths before entwining ourselves in them, overcome tremendous obstacles to bring ourselves together. Significance seems not to have been fated, nor planned.

Ahead, two unpromising endings, one containing the other. There is Adelaide and, within that city, that dual centre of the Arts and of violent criminal perversion, there will be Maria's new lover, as yet nameless and undescribed.

But these endings are not yet in vision, not ready for my modest assessment. Before facing curtailments, we have this journey to enjoy or endure. In the week since my invitation, my week of alternating dread and lust for this small future, it is beginnings which have occupied me. The week has filled with daydreams of immediate revelation, of Maria's confessions of regret, my own worthy statements of acceptance. In my mind, we will have concurred in the parameters of these miles.

Instead, even this false, poorly marked commencement of our great journey is overcome with anticlimax and interruption. Not only do we set out from the wrong point, but we are not even touched by the spirit of impending revelation. I experience no immediate discoveries of a personal or landscape nature. I cannot see the future stretched out along the road ahead. I cannot discern reconciliation as lovers or reconciliation to some lesser, more 'useful' relationship. So far as I can tell, Maria, also, is untouched by either enlightenment or the sense of its imminence. Ahead, in vision, there is smoke haze, arrhythmic flashes of brake lights, the ticking over of road markings.

Perhaps I am expecting too much, setting myself up for failure, to paraphrase another magazine (or, possibly, the same one). Yet, I cannot entirely imagine a journey I would want. Perhaps it indicates yet another of my plentiful shortcomings, but I cannot picture the two of us sharing anything other than minor agreements and arguments.

This is immediately borne out. We barely have attained the six-laned momentum of Parramatta Road with its promise of highways endlessly westward, when we mutually decide that we're hungry.

'Have you brought anything to eat?' I ask her. I've made a couple of uninteresting sandwiches, but assumed we would eat them immediately. 'I guess we should stop at bad truckstops all the way?'

'Mm, country-frozen crabsticks. Who says there's no Australian cuisine?' Maria laughs.

We decide to stop for food. Maria's smiling, whether from emerging travel excitement, non-specific personal happiness, or from the renewed pleasure of being with me: being with me, that is, where there is little chance of my becoming morose or argumentative in front of our friends, where the novelty of our journey offers a chance to break away from the landscapes of our former relationship. As I change lanes, I allow myself to believe that she is happy because she is in this car with me. At this moment, it seems the most likely reason. I don't ask, however, don't grant her the possibility of denial.

I join the queue to turn right up Norton Street. I am the last car through on the green arrow, surely a good omen. A moment later I have a parking spot, right outside the greengrocer's, and have reversed into it with one simple, smooth, double-turn of the steering wheel. Maria is smiling, I am lucky and talented, and anything is possible.

*

In the fruit shop, a young greengrocer stacking fruit gives us a big happy smile. I smile back, why not? I'm a friendly guy. He strolls across to where I'm counting pears into a plastic bag, exhales: 'You guys look so relaxed together. So *together*. It's great. I just had to say something.'

This absurdly inaccurate misreading silences me, but Maria delivers an aspartamic 'Thank you.'

'You're welcome,' he says. He pauses, waiting for one of us to continue — is he expecting a revelatory love story? — but we don't.

'I'm in love too,' he continues, 'but you should have been through what I went through!'

'Oh?' asks Maria, who seems to have intervened to claim the conversation, somewhat flirtatiously in my view. 'Would I have wanted to?'

'Definitely not. It was utter torture. She wouldn't live with me. I begged her to. I pleaded for weeks. I asked her for reasons. I promised to make myself better, to do whatever she wanted.

' "Why won't you live with me?" I begged.

' "You are too unromantic," she claimed. It was terrible. I felt so desperate for her.'

'I've found that pleading can be counterproductive,' I mutter. Maria keeps her eyes carefully fixed on the fruiterer, who continues with his tale.

*

But I like you, and you — well, you've got nothing to complain about. We're okay.

That's just the attitude which is why I won't live with you or even near you.

Because I'm content?

Self-satisfied is more the word.

I'm satisfied with you as well as with me. I'm satisfied with many aspects of my life and of the world.

I'd like occasional senseless spontaneity.

I can provide that. Look, I can jump in the air and turn a full circle.

That's very athletic, but not what I meant.

Oh.

Sorry.

Me too.

How about if I do something romantic?

Like what?

I don't know.

I know you don't.

I'll do anything you ask.

You want me to suggest a romantic action for you to take?

Yes.

Get your bicycle and find me the perfect mandarin. I'm hankering after the ideal piece of fruit. Cycle as far as you need to go to find it for me.

And then you'll move in?

Romance is unconditional.

Are you sure? I'll have to change my mindset, you understand?

Try.

I'm on my bike!

*I returned a week later.*

Hi, you've found it?

Hello. Oh my, I'm all out of breath. Here it is: a rich orange colour, peel neither too loose nor too difficult to remove; healthy but not overwhelming amounts of pith; evenly sized though clearly individual segments; not too many pips for comfortable eating, but a few because it's from a healthy plant intent on self-propagation; a good, medium size, neither small and bitter nor large and watery; and the taste: sweet, yet not sugary. And I've learnt from the search, which took me into fruit-growing areas north, south and west of suburbia. I've discovered that the ideal fruit is a matter of balance and moderation. Here! Take it!

Thank you. Please, have a section.

No, no, it's fine. I'm thoroughly mandarined out, really. Shall I pack your things while you eat?

Oh no, it's much too soon for that.

I'll come back in an hour, if you like. Go off and have a shower. A bit of romantic tension, eh?

14

Not really what I meant. How about this: come back when you've brought me a thimbleful of water from every ocean.

Serious? You'd like me to bring you small amounts of sea water. For why?

Pure gesture.

And if I do that, then I'll have been romantic?

You will have, hopefully, yes.

So, oceans. Atlantic, Pacific, Indian, Arctic and Southern. Any others you can think of? I'd hate to go all that way, and get back and you say, 'You left out the Bering Sea' or something.

Those'll do.

What about two out of five?

See you later.

Three?

Mm, you're right. This mandarin's delicious.

Three would definitely be a gesture.

Goodbye.

*We were separated for three long months before I returned.*

Hello.

Hello.

You'll be pleased to know I have brought you five thimblesworth of oceanically differentiated salt water.

Thank you. I'll treasure them.

Will you live with me now? Can I move in with you?

The mandarin was truly succulent. The water is lovely. I agree you've made a genuine beginning.

But?

But no.

No?

Not yet.

Tomorrow then?

Bring me a shellful of sand from each of the continents.

Sand? My God! That'll take ages. Don't you know, some continents are beset by ice this time of year; some don't even have sandy beaches. They've got gravel all along the shoreline, or cliffs. I'll have to grind the rocks myself, take the place of epochs of erosion.

Sand won't be that hard to find.

And then you'll move in with me?

You haven't brought the sand yet.

I live in hope of promises.

I never break a promise.

I'll get the sand.

Goodbye.

I'm going already.

*Can you believe it was six months until we met again? Why should minerals take longer to gather than liquid? Without reason, they did.*

Hello.

Hi.

Sand.

Thank you.

Pack?

Done already.

I feel older.
I love you for ever.
I guess I am older.
Kiss me.

*

'So that's it,' he says triumphantly, then, with what's obviously supposed to be a meaningful look, he adds, 'But I don't feel bad about people who haven't been through anything at all for their love.'

This is an incredibly annoying thing to say, but for some reason I find myself smiling. Maria fidgets a couple of mandarins into a plastic bag.

'Oh. I wasn't referring to you two,' says the greengrocer, sensing the change of mood but grinning nonetheless. 'I have a feeling you're true romantics.'

Maria says nothing.

'Maybe I was,' I say. We've all got these big grins on our faces.

'Anyway,' he says, 'better get back to it.'

We buy our fruit and leave the fruit shop, turn up the road towards the delicatessen.

'That was fairly weird,' says Maria.

'At least he recognises a fellow romantic,' I say. 'And it was a beautiful story. What a cruel woman to put him through so much when it must have been obvious to her from the start that he was the one she wanted. If only you'd recognised me in the same way.'

'It's hard to be romantic when you're unable to do anything without complaining. You're one of the least romantic people on the planet, Jack,' says Maria.

'I am not. I only need to be brought out a little.'

She ought to pay more credit to my small victories. I then do something of which to feel proud: I refrain from using our journey ahead as ammunition. I think of saying: yeah, well I'm not complaining about driving you HALFWAY ACROSS A CONTINENT, AM I?

But that might be self-defeating, so I hold that one back.

Instead I focus on attacking the other guy's manner: 'A bit of verbal overflow there.'

'He was very pleased with life,' agrees Maria, 'in an insistent kind of way.'

'Yes. Not sure if I prefer that or the more traditional grey-bearded, glittering-eyed pessimist.'

'The fruit shop event as a whole — setting and telling — was spellbinding in its own way.'

'I wonder if he tells his story to every pair who go in there, an innovative way of building customer loyalty among local lovers, developed in consultation with XYZ Marketing Service Providers: business solutions for every size of enterprise, including yours.'

She laughs. 'So cynical, Jack, even for you.'

'Pity his interpretive powers were so limited.'

'How so?'

'Well, he hardly got our relationship right, did he? What did he say? "You guys look so relaxed together. It's great"!

As though, there we were, a couple of off-duty film stars buying cheap apples. Not exactly spot on there, eh?'

'Sure, Jack. I guess not.' She sounds more guarded, no doubt fearing my occasional combativeness. 'At least we're trying to be friendly.'

'You should shout more.'

'You'd complain, in your quiet way.'

'I'd shout back.'

'Yeah, in that case maybe that guy would have got some insight into other people.'

'Unless he's just too permanently self-absorbed.'

'Poor bloke. We've really stopped being nice about him now.'

'I bet his girlfriend's really disgusting too.'

'Perhaps they're happily foul together.'

'Won't last,' I say, and we laugh again as we arrive back at the car and organise our bags of fruit among Maria's travel gear in the back seat of the car — laugh, having forgotten that we didn't last either.

I am pretty used to people unburdening themselves to Maria, or at any rate used to her claims about the frequency of those occurrences. When we were together she'd often tell some story or other of a stranger who felt obliged or compelled to tell her of a recent marriage failure or a childhood dream disappointed by poor luck.

Usually I wasn't a witness to it, and to be honest I'd discounted these stories as pick-up lines, probably because no stranger — no sober stranger, let's say — had ever bothered to seek my views on her or his developing crises. I guess it's not conclusive proof, but at the time it seemed good enough to me.

Also, what an eccentric and perverse tale to tell, this fruiterer's rare confession of happiness.

After all, and this is the fundamental overlooked by all the magazines and movies and easy-reading novels: there's only one way for a love story to finish up well, and so many variations on bad endings. I also overlook this. Despite the statistically obvious fact that zillions more relationships end than continue for eternity, at some level I too believe in inevitable betterment. I don't mind criticising what deserves criticism, or even self-criticism. This, many people (e.g., Maria) might see as a particular failing of mine, the necessity to criticise in combination with the compulsion to verbalise. I am, however, and deeply, an optimist. Good things will happen.

My way of seeing is well illustrated by my attitude to this journey, especially by contrast with Maria's. It's simple enough to set out our different motives for this journey.

I am, despite my control of the verbs — to initiate, to have (a car), to drive — observing. I undertake in order to see what will happen.

Maria, despite her claims to an observational vocation, undertakes in order to define or, more precisely, to delimit. She places us within a metre and a half of each other, to remain in this proximity over so many hours, to occupy intimate space, so as to clarify our separateness.

We will sit in this car, Maria, I, our numerous contradictions, our history of debate, our relationship once mutually definable and now splintered into competing renderings.

*

I am not a valuable person. Maria knows it. Her friends and family know it. Her replacement boyfriend, I am sure, knows it too.

Oh, and I know it, but only because Maria has explained it very carefully to me.

In summary, I am deficient in ways emotional, spiritual, personal and material. I am dependent, hardhearted, gullible, depressive, inappropriately happy, pedantic, shallow, sulky, needlessly and apolitically impoverished, insensitive and unforgiving. Sorry. I am very, very sorry.

At the expense of adding evidence for descriptor number six, I also need to point out that the last adjective in the preceding list is unfair. I often forgive Maria. Nonetheless, this is not the same as forgetting, or having the capacity to forget. Although Maria has always criticised me in an ad hoc manner — failing by failing, event by event, every word only in response to what she believed to be an immediate crisis, an immediately correctable inadequacy — I remember all as if they were utterly cumulative.

Still, I won't say she's wrong about me, about very much at all. I could quibble with her view of certain events, certain moments in the decline of our relationship. I can suggest minor re-tellings of various of our interactions over many months. I might even question her overall assessment of the likelihood of our future happiness at the moment she decided to remove the question altogether. But I won't claim any kind of personal goodness for myself, won't substitute a fine and sympathetic self-portrait for Maria's vitriolic unkindness. It's not just that I wouldn't dare. Also, from here, with nothing except the beginning of a journey, Maria and I, a car, the road, time … I'm in a situation which can only improve.

*

I think of the ways we might have fallen in love, had we not met through mutual friends or in a course or at a bar, had it not seemed as though it were impossible for us not to meet, had we lived in another time when a letter might contain shared glances and promised agreements.

*Dear Jack,*

*I can only imagine that to receive a letter such as this, inked in its by now unpractised cursive, would be as unexpected for you as it would me, but having met you in those same barely formal circumstances as are ubiquitous among those of our acquaintance, and being at this moment in the same gently contemplative, light-headed frame of mind as upon our encounter, I would wish for no other method to convey this mood to you; I therefore pray you will excuse all inadequacies in my attempt to fulfil this sincere if necessarily hopeless desire to convey such sense to another, be as it may one whose sensibilities seem profoundly sympathetic.*

*It is a winter day, the temperature here undoubtedly much the same as at your abode not three kilometres distant, but I wonder if we also share the same clear light effects, inflected through five well-grown eucalypts beyond the rear fringe of my small back garden? Do not answer this question, but another!*

*In the several days since our meeting, I have carried our quiet if somewhat rushed conversation with me, reflected upon our coinciding views regarding several subjects and the interesting nature of those points at which we disagreed, and continue to value, or it seems, increasingly value the connection I feel between us, fleeting as it may appear.*

*By my having written, you will at least infer, I hope, that I have drawn friendly judgment on you, liberty though this might appear; I must believe, for example, that you will accept the good faith of this letter, and that you will do so also on the strength of our short encounter. Were this a letter of another era, you would perhaps hope for more than the following request; as it is of the present, and having argued my way thus far, I can only seek your permission to telephone you, which I would do with the intention of arranging a further meeting.*

*I hope this finds you well.*

*Respectfully,*

*Maria*

Dear Maria,

Well, phew. Whoo. Hmmn. Umm. Erm, yes, to say. Well (again), I have received your recent correspondence and assent to all its potential significations, to every implicit demand, overt request or tenuously deducible wish. Concluding (though early for conclusions!): I surrender. Do with me what you will.


Dear Jack,

Angels: how do they power their wings? Their hearts keep them aflutter, their chest cavities full of giant voluntary and involuntary muscles.

Rice: does it enjoy its cooking?


Dear Maria,

Extraordinary moments: the instant someone finishes a jigsaw, crossword; signs a contract (inhaling 'ffft'); finishes a long book. In between these events, I glance at the clock and it reads 12:12:12 or 5:55:55.

Remember striding along that jetty? From where I sat, behind a small yellow mound of sand, you appeared to walk out onto the harbour. Kiss me.


Dear Jack,

There was an ad in Saturday's Herald: 'Narrow-minded yob rqd to share sml 4 bdr hovel with 3 drunken bigots'. How good things will be between us!

*Dear Maria,*

*The clouds move too quickly to define. What are we to do with the hopes and intentions accumulated before our meeting, with the requirements of other relationships of whatever kind, or with files headed 'to be completed'? I shall lay them aside and shall think no further on them. For you, I am utterly without reservation. I am committed to you, to every moment with you.*

*Dear Jack,*

*I love your room, with narrow-slatted blinds of different hues and tints. I love your looks. I love how you clothe yourself in a kind of self-conscious mysticism. I love how difficult you can be when you feel threatened. I love that old sardine can you keep your loose change in. I love how often you remind me that you are fully insured. I love you, you're so shy that when we make love you say, 'This isn't life. It's just a series of improbable chemical reactions in the presence of unusual catalysts.'*

*Dear Maria,*

*Together, we were so full and so spacious, so total and yet so free, so straightforward and still so brimming with paradox. In the future I'll know better.*

*PS I've tried to remain interesting.*

*Dear Jack,*
*That's all there is. I'll telephone at some point to arrange redistribution of hitherto shared possessions and artefacts.*
*Until then,*
*goodbye,*
*Maria*

*

Unimaginable, is it not, that I once shared intimacies (touches, beliefs) with this uncommitted woman beside me? Yes. It is unimaginable, in all but my hardworking mind. Instead of the clear delineations set out by correspondence — in both senses, of exchanged letters and of silently agreed understandings — we have no clarity. For a moment, lettering across the tight pink T-shirt of a nearby pedestrian says it all: 'Dream On'.

We make our way towards the delicatessen. Time passes as though we were still together. We share occasional certainties. We both understand the value of the food we shall purchase, its superiority to good, solid country cuisine. We each understand this, in our different ways, Maria the undeclared snob, me the secret gourmet. The pair of us, together through the door, equally metropolitan from top to toe.

*

I am not a valuable person. That, I believe, has been well established. I know it and accept it. This greater public knowledge of my worthlessness has at times probably

26

constrained my behaviour or, at least, curtailed my tongue. This is not surprising, at least not for me, and it shouldn't surprise Maria either, not if she knows me as well as she should, and she should know me well. Otherwise she paid insufficient attention during our relationship.

I am silent but my mind is active.

Despite my irrepressible internal rhetoric — my intrapersonal medium, which must always interpolate comment, define and interpret — I am feeling positive about Maria, about myself, about the world, about our places in the world. Here we are. We will sit in my car together. We will achieve distance. Together we will progress. I will drive and she will drive. We will make a path across Australia and our path will continue to exist in our minds. We will speak words which make little north and south squiggles across our westward journey. As we make this path, I will think about Maria and about us. I will analyse what her gestures and words mean. I will drive and I will continue to classify. I cannot stop, as if by stopping I might risk ceasing to be.

Maria: ex-girlfriend, heartbreaker, weeping woman, poisoner. Me: victim, coward, peacemaker, lover.

Those are the definitions, though they're for domestic consumption only and should not be taken to reflect the manner in which I relate to external others. Maria might dispute the adjective 'weeping', but I have seen her. She has seen me too. We have seen each other. We have wept, mutually. We have wept in repose and wept running through the city streets.

She might dispute the word 'poisoner'. Now, I might assure her, is no time for disputation. I hold fast to that word. She may contest my peacemaking, but I will not be swayed.

We are going somewhere, Maria and I. First we will invest in our future appetites, and then we will set off. I have initiated something which now begins to happen. I feel good about initiation and about movement. I have much to feel positive about. My positivity itself is something to feel positive about. My attitude reflects the general trend, a kind of market-sentiment indicator of the self. How's my self-sentiment? Are the indicators ascendant? Oh yes, positively bullish!

\*

On this scale, I'd rate the assistant in the delicatessen 'bear' rather than 'bull'. He seems hardly capable of spooning three olives into a bag, moves more slowly than any shop assistant I've ever seen, and somehow manages to retain our sympathy. The words morose and despondent are inadequate to describe his mood. When Maria asks for some Turkish bread from behind the counter, he visibly gulps down a sob.

'Are you okay?' asks Maria, direct as usual. 'You look like you could use a break.'

'I need more than a break,' he whispers. 'I need a new life. I can't take this kind of work any more.'

'A delicatessen does this to you?' I ask.

'Oh yes,' he says, shaking his head. 'Walter has left me in work. I had Walter, and now I only have this.'

He sweeps his hand around, indicating shelves stacked with imported items, vegetables of all kinds made golden in olive oil, almond biscuits individually wrapped, black-ribboned chocolate boxes. The food might promise prosperity and individual fulfilment, but the seller's demeanour rebuts his employer's gift for display.

'Ah, Walter,' he sighs. He begins his tale with sotto voce chanting, slowly includes us in his telling with shy glances, then direct address, and finally with intimate disclosures of behind-the-scenes delicatessen knowledge.

*

I am trying. I am trying not to see.

I am trying not to see myself.

I am trying not to see myself as though...

I am trying not to transform everything I think into a chant of self-affirmation. With this new job, I have something to keep me occupied. I concentrate on my new job. I am slicing the meat. Neatly. The customer is trying to speak to me while I am slicing the meat. No. The customer actually is speaking. The customer walked in and very deliberately pointed to the meat and said an amount. The customer spoke and continues to speak. I am trying to slice the correct quantity. I am trying to please the customer so the customer will stop speaking and leave. I am trying things. While other people in the world take action, I am making attempts. I am trying to slice the meat without the customer's voice. I am trying

29

to slice the meat without the customer's voice reminding me of Walter. Walter's way of saying 'Toikish'. As a joke. In delicatessens.

When Walter and I used to... In between the jokes I imagined serious interchanges. Yet it is the jokes which constantly appear. Walter's sense of humour and my laughter. What a pair we were, walking along together. We would speak to each other and Walter would say something to crack me up and I would freeze until the convulsions stopped. This is the picture I conjure when I think of us walking together. It is an image of my helplessness. It interferes with my drawing of strength from within.

I am trying not to see myself. I am trying not to see myself as if I were a little test. In a chemistry class. What is the concentration of chlorides in this solution? How would one extract the sodium chloride from this beaker, the tears from my eyes? I am trying not to be too calm. This I believe to be important. Under my olive skin, I am trying to find. No. To strike. Yes, to strike. A balance between honesty and nothing. The latter. The latter has it all over the former, believe me.

The customer says the word 'Turkish'. I bite my lip. I am pouting and telling myself: 'This situation was inevitable. I knew it. I knew it. I knew it.'

In my head, I hear Walter's special delicatessen joke over and over. I pretend to ask myself: 'Why is that?' As if I don't know ... everything.

The olives are wrapped in white paper that I have attempted not to crease. I have tried to make a list of numbers on the white paper. At the bottom is the total. The customer is checking the total on his digital electronic calculator. I have tried to establish the correct total. I do not know if the customer is practising a delicatessen joke on me. I do not know if the customer's checking is a delicatessen joke. If I am the object of the customer's joke. He does not tell me. I do not know if I have made a mistake despite having tried to establish the correct total. He does not tell me if the calculator is somehow funny, and he does not correct or confirm my total. He hands me a ten-dollar note and I try to give him some change. The customer counts the change. I try to have feelings. Which hurt.

The customer's groceries are in a plastic bag on the counter. I have tried to put them there. So that the white paper packages do not collapse within the white plastic bag which would then slip onto the floor from the momentum caused by its internal avalanche, tearing the thinly sliced meat. The customer takes the package in hand. He nods to me. Once. He says 'Thanks'. He smiles nicely. With white teeth. The smile is more sensitive to my feelings than the calculator joke, if it was a joke. The customer could have said 'Tanks' but he did not. Walter would have said 'Tanks'. First he would have given me a little nudge in the ribs with his elbow and then he would have said 'Tanks' to the person serving, which would not have been me. I would have been a customer too, or at least on the customers' side of the counter. When we reached the footpath together he would have said, 'Now do you see why delicatessens are such ridiculous places?'

I would have laughed and said, 'I wish I understood you because then I would be crazy too.'

While I think all this, I begin to stare at the ceiling fan which is rotating so slowly as to have no effect. The customer left-turns on his heel. He walks out. An air current follows him out. It lightly disturbs the top sheets of the pile of butcher's paper. He has gone. I am alone in the shop with the ceiling fan mindlessly and pointlessly rotating. I am alone in the shop with the ceiling fan mindlessly and pointlessly rotating and with Walter's well-rehearsed joke.

Oh, WalterWalterWalterWalterWalterWalterWalterWal terWalterWalterWalterWalterWalterWalterWalterWalter WalterWalterWalterWalterWalterWalterWalterWalterWal terWalterWalterWalterWalterWalterWalterWalterWalter WalterWalterWalterWalterWalterWalterWalterWalterWal terWalterWalterWalter everywhere nor any drop to drink. That was my joke. But I stopped.

His name is not funny once a person has become used to it. He told me that people are surprisingly adaptable, but I do not feel even unsurprisingly adaptable. I do not feel as though I am capable of the least measure of adaptability. Walter became normalised as the label for someone who walked into delicatessens and made secret jokes which were only for me. It was just Walter is Walter. If I were just me, then I would not work in my new job in the delicatessen.

The customers would not walk through the door and point at the meat and I would not serve them and wonder if they were making jokes. I would not be offended if I were not working at the delicatessen. I would be honest instead of nothing and I would be okay. I would not eat sandwiches at lunchtime with sausage or cheese and pickles. I would be clear to myself. I would understand all my motivations. I would be as sweet and obvious as a Turkish delight.

Today there is a special on dips. Guacamole, hummus and taramasalata. Tahini and French onion. They are cheap as the month of May. The customers come in and buy tubs of dip. They do not make jokes which I would not understand. The dips are two dollars for a small tub and three dollars for a large. There is no special on crackers and corn chips. This is where the profit is. I am sure of this. I am paid by the hour. Nonetheless, I do not point out to the customers that they might find cheaper crackers elsewhere. I am a valuable employee. I have a ... what? I have an income. (Whoo! I nearly said 'a vocation'.)

Oh no!

The hummus is running low.

There is more hummus out the back. I do not want to go out the back to get more hummus because Walter's uncle is there. Walter's uncle is making French onion dip by deep-frying onions in safflower oil and pouring the oniony oil into vats of sour cream. I have my doubts about the quality of the dip produced by this method, but it is probably best not to express these. I do not eat the French onion dip which I recommend highly to the customers who are attracted in off the street by the sign which reads 'Special! Dips $2 sml $3 lge'. This delicatessen belongs to Walter's uncle. That is the reason I have this new job: because Walter asked if I could have it. If I go out the back Walter's uncle will ask me something about Walter. Walter's uncle thinks Walter and my friendship is a very good idea. I do not wish to agree with him on this subject. Walter's uncle doesn't understand anything except for jokes. At least he smiles a lot.

Now, the empty pot of hummus. The empty pot which used to contain hummus makes me think of Walter.

It's not fair. I could conjure an image of Walter from the shape left on the pitted surface of the Jarlsberg. If the Shroud of Turin were strewn across the counter instead of butcher's paper, you know whose face I'd see.

Oh Walter, please stop being the phantom driver of every car I overtake on the malicious suburban roads. No longer appear in my dreams nor invisibly participate in all my conversations. Stop your walk resembling the walks of figures on distant pedestrian crossings. Return the limbs, digits, features I've lent you over the years. Take me from on the shelves and in the cartons where I imagine you keep my pieces and let me become whole. Hide your voice from the wind so that it no longer blows past and startles me. Explain to the branches and leaves that their touch must no longer be like yours. Bleach and leach your scent from unexpected street corners. Oh, Walter, erase your body's deep print from beside me on the bed, reconnect your shadow to yourself so it no longer haunts me, stop tapping on my window and creeping across the ceiling at two in the morning, ringing the doorbell at three until I awake. Stop wearing the clothes of anybodies in restaurant windows, remove your traces from the radio, from particular times of the day, from moonrises over cliffs in November. Disclaim the city so I can walk about in it purged of you. I'm trying, Walter, I'm trying so hard. I am trying not to see myself as dependent on you. Aspect by aspect I'll clear you out.

When I speak to Walter's uncle, I can only manage one syllable at a time.

'No. More. Dip,' I tell him.

Walter's uncle is staring at me. I am holding the hummus container stretched out in front of me, but it is upside down. I turn it up the right way and, drawing all my coping strategies to the surface, I add, 'Pleeease.'

I am coaxing the word to fill the proper duration.

*

'Sorry about the bread,' whispers Maria, possibly her first-ever apology.

'Not your fault.' He forces a smile.

I hand him some money and don't count the change. We're all looking down and glancing up. Maria and I are backing away, a farcical end to a royal visit. We now have bread and bananas. An intense shopping experience, I'm thinking. Today everyone has something to say about love.

'One thing?' he asks, pausing the retreat.

'Mm,' I say, or perhaps a single 'M', keeping the communication as brief as possible; it's already too much.

'It's that you seemed to be selecting food for a journey, and if you're heading west, um, could I get a lift with you?'

'Sure,' says Maria. 'How far are you going?'

I am dismayed at her eagerness, but worse follows immediately.

'Bathurst,' the lovelorn young man replies.

'We might not get that far,' I claim.

'Of course we will,' says Maria.

'I'll just get my things,' says the delicatessen man, showing his teeth for the first time. Two hundred kilometres of romantic complaint. Good one, Maria.

The man skips through the rear door.

'He could be a madman,' I say, spitefully. 'And you could have asked me.'

'You'd have said no?' she asks, reflecting my tone back. 'It's hardly an inconvenience.'

'It is inconvenient,' I say. 'We're supposed to be travelling together.'

'We are,' she says, 'but we're giving a poor upset man a lift for part of it.'

Soon an older man emerges to replace the delicatessen's assistant. He stares at us sceptically and interrupts our purposeless argument.

'You have to take him in the middle of work?' he says. 'Ach.'

'We are merely the means of transport,' I say.

'Haven't you heard of six o'clock?'

It's almost five, but I think of French onion dip and decide not to pursue conversation.

'Bathurst!' I hiss at Maria. 'All the way to bloody Bathurst! What about our time together for talking?'

'We'll have time,' she insists. 'He needs the lift more than we need to be alone. In fact, we don't need to be alone at all.'

'You still could have asked me first.'

'Yes,' says Maria, with the type of faux-apology which is her specialty. 'I should have asked you. Sorry. But it's done now.'

He returns with a small sports bag.

'Thanks for this,' he says, and before I carry through with my momentary misconception that the gratitude is directed towards me, the old man replies, 'Yeah, well make sure you're back by Thursday. The weekends are important this time of year.'

'Sure thing, Uncle,' he says flatly, probably lying. 'I'll only be a day or two.' And to Maria: 'Okay, let's go.'

*

I'm in this car with a head full of ideas, most of them directed towards Maria and my proximity to her. I have to say things, but there is a sad delicatessen's assistant in the back seat. Perhaps, like the fruiterer, he believes in our happiness. Perhaps he believes our assumed happiness will provide him with relief. We head westward once more, the three of us. Maria's overblown sense of good fellowship and humanity has recast our journey, deferred by many hours its potential as a vehicle for direct communication. We are no longer correspondents, merely travellers heading in the same direction. I seem to have become angry.

In theory I could speak, saying what I may dare to say if we were alone, revealing intimacies no matter how embarrassing to Maria and our unintroduced passenger. Or rehearsing our quarrels, making a show of it.

He might say: 'I had no idea I'd be intruding.'

I might say: 'You know now' or 'Oh? Did Maria neglect to mention our difficulties?'

Maria might say: 'It's nothing. Don't worry.'

He might say: 'I think I'll leave you to it.'

I could say: 'That's decent of you. Sorry about that.'

Maria: 'You're welcome to stay. Jack can be uncharitable.'

Me: 'You forget who booted whom.'

Maria: 'You overlook your shortcomings.'

Me: 'I can't, because of your lucid articulation of them.'

Him: 'I'm not asking for charity, only a ride.'

But nothing is said, so we'll have four hours with Walter's ex. I can only hope he has already performed his monologue.

I start the car and we pull into the traffic.

As always, I am silenced by Maria. Maria knows that I am driven to speak. We have been through this. My drive to speak — this is how I've explained it to Maria —

originates with others. My parents are demons. My school was full of shabby waxheads with woeful 'live for the moment' sayings they believed counted as statements of philosophy. At university I hung around with too many dope-smokers who had too much respect for two a.m. thoughts ('wouldn't it be cool if … ?'). My former workmates wrongly decided I was a man of ideas and occasionally consulted me. Certain people fell in love with me, almost always after conversation. Could this litany of human interaction account for it?

Perhaps and maybe. These were possible explanations. I am not one to draw final judgments on my motives. How could I? What irrefutable tools would allow me to claim that my views are unimpeachable? As an opiner, the bloke in the driver's seat is entirely non-professional. I have my faults — many they might be, well-known and much-repeated within this vehicle and elsewhere — but with regard to motive-judgment I am no impostor.

The millennium begins not with new bouts of messianism (not in Sydney, at any rate) but surrounded by professionally formed opinions, an era in which all civilisation depends on cultures of people paid to judge motives: law, psychology, media. Entire industries and economies rest on this. Against it I am an amateur, not even an amateur — who in this matter must, by definition, 'love' judgment. I do not love judgment. I prefer life without it. I could apologise again at this point, but here it will affect nothing. In my unselfjudged and unselfjudgeable state I remain, inexplicably and ignorantly, unable or unwilling to take conscious action or seek professional assistance to repress the vocalised exhalation of half-formed, ill-considered, weakly expressed, temper-triggering, conflict-provoking, atmosphere-altering, bloody stupid ideas.

Others may choose a clear side of the fence to fall into. I'm utterly open-minded.

Maria cannot stand me when I'm like this, and I could accuse her of grasping the first opportunity to circumvent it.

We drive. Signs promise that Sydney ends and that other named places exist beyond.

'I haven't decided which way to go yet,' I tell her, 'but let's go a real way, not straight down the Hume Highway.'

Maria spreads a map of south-eastern Australia across her legs.

'I guess we can't anyway,' I add, flicking my eyes towards Mr Misery behind.

'The Hume's boring,' she agrees. 'Bathurst is the best way anyway.'

Backseat says nothing, though we could have ended his journey before it began. He may be one of these superconfident people who believes he'll always get what he wants simply by being, or he may be someone who goes with the flow, as happy to hop out in Wagga Wagga as Bathurst. He may be nervously hoping and/or praying that we won't force him back to his meat counter. I cannot tell anything about him from the silence.

'Over the mountains, then decide between West Wyalong and Broken Hill?'

'Sounds okay,' she says. 'The bushfires are probably exaggerated.'

We pass the Hume turn-off. Maria waves at it.

'I'm sure that responsible emergency services teams will confine all fires to the National Park and other less economically useful areas,' I say. 'And fire's latest evolutionary role is to keep the paths clear for tour groups. Bushfires have adapted perfectly to contemporary civil needs.'

'And our contemporary civil need is to drive along a road.'

'Australia's wonderful like that. Here's a plan: we'll survey the fire from a lookout over the Grose Valley, appreciate the grandeur...'

'Could be a photo in it,' she says.

'...ingest thousands of tiny ash particles, inhale smoke, spend twenty minutes rubbing our eyes...'

'Sounding more like a barbecue than a noble vision now.'

'...and wonder what extinguished the fire between us.'

A sigh from the back: deep empathy with me, I'd guess. Maria tries to stamp it out.

'Ignore him,' she instructs. 'You put that in just to annoy me, Jack. I hope you're not going to map our relationship over the entire bloody country, centimetre by centimetre.'

'Maria, if you inspire me to it, I will map. Every molecule of bitumen will correspond to a regret.'

She laughs. (Give her credit where due.)

'What is going on with you two, if I may ask?' inquires Sad Sack.

'Nationalistic rekindling of an unsalvageable relationship,' I explain, and continue, 'We'll meet in Sydney, talk, kiss without stopping from Leichhardt to Penrith, fall in love, be incredibly passionate emotionally, intellectually and sexually all the way across the Great Dividing Range, cool off by Bathurst, then argue from there to Adelaide, with occasional sidetracks to Dubbo and Melbourne to make up, wipe away tears and provide pinnacles from which we can sink into argument once more.'

'Sounds like I'm in for an unusual journey,' he says.

'I sometimes exaggerate, but it's too early to say.'

'I'd plot it differently,' Maria says, without any explanation other than, 'And Melbourne's much too out of the way.'

'How about Broken Hill?' I say. 'Our love, seemingly mountainous, insurmountable, now a fractured, busted, rent, splintered and Broken Hill. Yet, even here, advances in environmental and relational technologies mean that reclamation and renewal are now attainable goals.'

I'm wondering if I'll hear more of Maria's proposed journey, or will just have to live through each event or sight interpreted according to her reactive impulse.

A sign prepares us to subsidise the partly privately built highway and we veer around to the right onto the wide smooth road.

A solitary man in a once stylish suit stands on the verge of the expressway, watching the cars accelerate as they curve onto the straight. We pause at a red light and suddenly the road is empty of vehicles. He gazes across the bare asphalt. His form is echoed by lampposts. Is he, like them, waiting for nightfall to prove himself useful? Is he some minor item of statuary left over from the nearby site of the Olympic Games? Behind, strips of cloud, or perhaps it is haze from the fires in the mountains, from horizon to horizon. The man could be posing for a photograph or some kind of outdoor life-drawing group. No one else, though, is in sight.

Ah no, he is moving slightly. If he's posing for anything, it's for a time-based medium. I find myself scanning the scene for TV or film cameras. Perhaps we'll find ourselves and my car as extras in an insurance advertisement with the voiceover: 'Many call me eccentric, and I'll admit my job is unusual. Some would say dangerous. But I love the intense smells of petrol and of rubber, blurring colours as commuters hurtle past me. It's the poetry of modern life. And someone has to do it.'

The legend would fade up in white serif lettering: Jeffrey Martin, Traffic Flow Supervisor, Strathfield Council.

His voice might continue: 'Sometimes, though, I do worry about my family. The job has its dangers. It only takes one reckless or mad driver. We've all read about "road rage". I am without fear for myself, but who would support them if I was injured or worse?'

Switch to shot of children and wife in suburban backyard. A second voice intercedes: 'Jeffrey is smart. He does not rely on luck alone. He has protected his family with [Brand Name] Life Assurance. You can't always be safe, but you can avoid being sorry.'

The lights change and we soon leave this sentinel of urban boundaries, a marker of the border between city and the utopian nowhere of smooth black road. Although we are still within the mapped boundaries of Sydney, once on the wide tarmac we are no longer in lived Sydney. The expressway with its cars speeding in both directions is its own region.

To our right now is the Olympic Stadium complex, once the site of the largest garbage dump in the southern hemisphere. This great wasteland was layered over with plastic sheeting, then covered with tonnes of clean fill in the shape of rolling green hills. It's pretty but (thanks to the impervious plastic) it doesn't touch earth. The so-called *Sydney* Olympics took place on a completely new continent. That's my theory, but Maria's already heard it and I don't feel like sharing my thoughts with Droopy behind me.

On the left, a queue of trucks creeps forward at the last exit before toll gates. I change lanes across to the right: speed is everything. We are racing forward at fifteen hundred metres per minute, in silence apart from the hiss of tyres on engineered road surface, and we continue in this manner until huge gaudy signs repeatedly and emphatically warn me to slow down and pay.

'I've got it,' calls Backseat. I wait at the booth while he gropes for change. He must want involvement with this trip. I'm hoping he won't be a talker. Or that he will, and that Maria will realise her error.

He hands forward the coins, I pay the toll and on we go.

'Actually,' I say, back on the relationship theme, 'it'd be impossible to map a relationship in the manner we were discussing before.'

'I wasn't discussing it,' says Maria. 'I was only contradicting you.'

'Never mind,' I say. 'Your contradiction was, for you, a pretty good effort at discussion.'

'Thanks a lot.'

Our conversation pauses once more; lanes of traffic merge and diverge around us, vehicles weaving between others, their drivers and I all understanding how not to collide.

'But I do have an alternative,' I say, 'more in the line of self-contradiction.'

'Self-contradiction is pretty much a way of life for me,' says the back seat.

'Just listen up!' I shout, mock-exasperated. 'Maria, this drive will be a continuum from Sydney to Adelaide, possible for any half-decent detective to follow the traces of tyre-track without a break. We don't suddenly disappear in Bathurst and show up in Waikerie. Whereas our relationship was all over the place, often went along completely irrational paths, depended entirely on two people's independent states of mind. I don't understand what worked and what didn't. Relationships are nothing like journeys, nothing like landscapes.'

'I'm glad you think that,' says Maria 'and I'll remind you from time to time if you seem about to forget.'

'That's lovely. I'll always remember where we were when you said that.'

'Where are we?'

'Wallgrove Road exit. Near Eastern Creek.'

'Is that a suburb? I thought it was a racetrack.'

'It's the place where our journey lost sympathy.'

'Aw. And so early on.'

'Yes,' I acknowledge. 'I say things for a joke and they turn out too true.'

We both agree.

'You people are more difficult to respond to when you're not being customers,' comments our guest.

'She's a complicated woman and I'm sensitive beyond measure.'

'Thanks,' says Maria.

The back seat recovers silence.

But with all the objectivity I can muster, our relationship was ordinary. It followed the regular patterns relationships follow. How could it not? People have to meet. They have to have various firsts. Rare couples remain paired, but when lovers do break up, dissolution is preceded by various crises and/or realisations.

With our relationship, so-called realisations were all Maria's and crises tended towards me. I had been right that we couldn't map our past relationship across the present and future journey. Instead, we would have to re-order history.

*

The expressway ends at the base of the mountains. The road narrows. The smoke haze that fills the Sydney basin becomes much heavier here. I flick on the headlights.

'Promising,' says Maria.

'Yes. It looks like we made the right decision about this route,' I say.

'Well, we're about to find out.'

'I'm with you all the way,' comes the voice from behind. 'Solidarity!'

'Thanks very much.'

There's a large car tailgating us, unnerving at this speed. I see five large figures in it, two in the front and three in the back. I tap on the brake to flash brakelights at the driver. I know this will annoy him. Slow unpredictability. The tactic succeeds immediately and he gestures rudely at me.

'I got two fingers from the yobbo behind,' I inform Maria. Deli-man begins to turn around, but then obeys my command, 'Don't look.'

The car pulls out to overtake us. It draws level, pauses for a couple of seconds while its occupants check us out. We hear incomprehensible snatches of noise through their open windows: probably more comments directed at us, 'get an effing horse' or equivalents. They pull away, accelerating more than should be possible considering we're already going along at the quite decent uphill rate of eighty kilometres per hour. The blokes in the back seat seem to be engaged in some sort of blokish argument, bumping shoulders and waving their hands in the available space.

In the other direction, Maria smirks.

'Goodonyer, boys,' she comments.

The car changes back in front of us and we see a bumper sticker insisting that a particularly bad commercial radio station supports the now-defunct Sharks football team, and explicating through its persistence beyond that sad team's demise that the car-owner suffers both from remnant football sentimentality and poor taste in music.

'That's great! Carna Sharks,' cheers Maria. 'Take it up the middle. Hit hard. Knock 'em down so he stays down. Come on, ya girl, get up.'

'This is an aspect of you I've never seen,' I say.

'All those nights at the movies wasted, when we could have saved the money and put in cable TV.'

The other car begins to put distance between it and us. We see the bloke on the left of the rear seat — who'd been sitting with his arm extended along the seat back — cuff his neighbour across the back of the head.

'Fucking hell,' I say. 'There was force in that.'

We burst out laughing.

'That's true love among men,' says Maria.

'I've seen better,' intercedes Deli-man.

'Hello, mate,' she continues, in a yobbo voice, ignoring him. Then she punches me not lightly on the arm and repeats, 'I said, hello, mate.'

And then we become them, to the best of our abilities.

*

'I said, hello, mate.'

'Right. That's a sentence you could be proud of.'

'That's not an answer.'

'True.'

'A problem here?'

'There's no problem here, no problem that can't turn around and go away as quickly as it arrived.'

'Sorry?'

'You heard.'

' "It", mate? You calling someone "it"?'

'End of conversation before it started is what I'm saying.'

'You're saying "it" again.'

'I'm too busy, mate, I really am too busy to waste time talking about nothing with you. I have to put up with your odour here, I spoke to you earlier because I'm a good bloke, and that's all.'

'You were unbusy enough then, and now you're saying "it".'

'There are three other people here, all of which like you slightly. Bother someone else.'

'Here's a warning. Don't come the white pointer with me, mate.'

'Aw, that'd be about right. About bloody right for you. I tell you how you fuck on about nothing and you start fucking on about sharks.'

'A white pointer isn't a shark, mate. It's a machine and it'd chomp through your sort of bullshit before you could say "breakfast".'

'Sure. You put a shark in a tank with a saltwater croc and see which comes out best.'

'A crocodile? You've got to be kidding, mate. There wouldn't be any of it left in two seconds.'

'That's not true either. Sharks have no brains at all. A crocodile can out-think a shark any day of the month. A shark wouldn't stand a virus's chance in a snowstorm.'

'Do you know how fast a shark swims, mate? Have you read anything about sharks at all?'

'Yeah, I've read plenty and then some. Anyone knows they're fast, but so are fleas. It's irrelevant. They simply have no brain. A crocodile would have zip problems putting paid to even four or five sharks at least.'

'It wouldn't stand a chance against a quarter of a white pointer. An eighth. A white pointer or even a nurse would tear a crocodile to shreds with its eyelashes. Sharks are a hundred times smarter than any stupid, crawling reptile and that's including salts and freshies. Sharks are incredibly smart. And they can hunt solo or in packs, so you are wrong there too.'

'You put a decent-sized croc beside a pack of any sharks you could think to name, and I guarantee you they'd look like a shoal of sardines.'

'That's capital-C crap.'

'You've never even seen a saltwater croc. So what would you seriously know?'

'I at least know that if you stuck the jaws of a white pointer in your toilet, they would not only swallow the toilet bowl and the cistern, but the whole bathroom including the vanity unit. They are very, very big.'

'And a crocodile wouldn't?'

'It wouldn't come close. You have to understand that a shark is a monster which does what it sets out to do, but a croc is only a jumped-up lizard.'

'Crocodiles are cunning beasts and sharks are dumb fish. The shark spends its time with stomach-ache from accidentally swallowing too much seaweed.'

'More horse manure, mate. You could poison a crocodile with a lead pencil. A shark'd gulp down ten kegs of DDT just to freshen its breath. The white pointer is not a delicate little skink waiting to drop its tail if you say boo. Crocs sit around all day with their mouths open, waiting to eat flies.'

'I think that's where you make your fundamental error.'

'Well, if you think it, it must be shit.'

'I'm just trying to tell you that you know nothing about crocodiles whatsoever.'

'I can't respect anything you say.'

'That's because you've got no brain to speak of.'

'And you're such a genius.'

'Your mouth opens and shuts like a goldfish's.'

*

If I'd been feeling ungenerous towards Maria, I feel better now, probably through having insulted her so thoroughly. She, likewise, has insulted me, punched me as I have driven, and satirised all men. The yobbo car which provoked all this has gone, though after another five minutes we see it again, stopped on the road's shoulder in front of a car with a blue light, a policeman leaning against the window while his colleague remains in the police car, presumably to check for outstanding warrants on the in-car computer.

This leads to more displays of wit. 'I don't know what happened, officer, suddenly the accelerator stuck as we were ascending the hill and when we flattened out, the car just about took off. I couldn't do a thing about it. Frankly, I was terrified. Weren't we, boys?'

Chorus of blokish agreement.

Another five minutes and they're with us again, first drawing up behind us, then pulling out to pass. There's a slap as an orange hits the column between the driver's and rear windows. Our passenger inhales sharply, exhales at length.

Both windows are open against this heat, so it is a near miss and I jump with the sound. It would have hurt.

'Coulda been worse,' says Maria, maintaining the tone despite the proximity of actual contact. 'Next time won't be fruit we chuck.'

The three yobs in the back seat have turned around to check our reactions.

'I'll get my camera,' says Maria, not moving.

'In case they show us their arses?'

'That's a lovely thought. Thanks for that.'

The brakelights illuminate and the yob car slows, but the driver's too impatient to play the game for long and speeds off again. One of the back seat blokes waves bye-bye as the car moves rapidly away.

'This damn brick,' says yobbo-Maria. 'Who superglued it down there?'

Deli-man and I yobbo-laugh, forced and grunting guffaws.

Two bends further and we catch up with them for a third encounter: we reach a serious-looking traffic jam and they are two cars ahead and, like us, not moving. For the next hour we watch them change lanes back and forth, trying to advance past yet another car, anything to overtake. I turn on the radio and it immediately advises avoiding the Blue Mountains, where poor visibility and frequent reassessments of fire risk due to sudden wind changes have caused road closures, diversions and severe traffic delays.

We are moving, if slowly. The divided road ends and we are in two-way traffic. The hoon car squeals a U-turn into the eastbound lane and disappears towards Sydney.

'There goes the entertainment,' I say.

*

I am not a valuable person. It is important to recall this fact from time to time. Maria's frequency of reminder has dropped, perhaps due to the presence in our back seat. He has a value. No, two. His even, rasping sleep-breath marks time as we move through the bushfire-affected traffic.

It is evening, after seven o'clock. We have driven much less far than planned. We have been determinedly relaxed. By now we expected to have driven more than twice this far. We have shopped. We have sat in a traffic jam. We have driven less than one-fourteenth of the way there. We are not counting, not at this point.

I drive slowly on through the forest, burnt black in the last days. The twilit air is red, and red reflects back from the clouds, like a flickering, bush version of city lights.

Another smile to myself for this thought: a good journey needs misinterpretation. Perhaps that's one to share with Maria? I decide against. Certainly I'm avoiding one interpretation of the journey, the one with lovely Maria and her lovely Mr Nameless and Undescribed attaining a lovely domestic ending while I drive a solitary return journey, reflecting sadly.

For the moment I also shun anything which adds to the sum of owed penitence. So how to misinterpret this divine excursion through the gently scorching New South Wales summer, Maria, me, side by side, a hanger-on snoring away behind, postcard-perfect Australia burning all around us? Selective omission, I suspect, is the best way forward.

The air is red. Around every streetlight there's a little halo; each lit-up house bounces a few photons back from the sky. It's the same, bushfire or no; over every settlement linked into the power grid, and over some which suck away at generators

— those noisy, industrial age relics — there's an arc of incandescence. The difference between a bushfire evening and a clear evening is this: when it's clear, you can sense Sydney from a hundred and fifty kilometres away. Tonight we're driving the wrong way, and the smoke has intensified the luminous presence of every village along our route.

I am reminded that the world is made of villages. Despite the extent of the urbanisation, there's no such thing as a city. Large population centres are merely an accumulation of overlapping villages, communities of attitude and occupation, communities which share interpretations of politics and behaviours. All that wasted luminance flying up to the sky, the light of dozens of communities of meaning, that's all cumulative, that's what engenders belief in the idea of the city. Maria and I live in the same village. That's all. We are the only two occupants, joined for the moment by a sleeping tourist, and this small village is pushing its brilliance ahead of it, not too fast.

I glance at Maria who never looks back. We have the windows open wide to encourage the smoke to blow through. Ash settles on my hands holding the steering wheel and I shake it off. Our eyes stream. The headlights push yellow tornadoes through the smoke as we creep past joke holiday destinations: U-Turn Bay and Traffic Island.

I've got the radio on again, am scanning across the AM band from 530 to 1700, looking for songs to tear our hearts out, to tear Maria's heart out. I'm winding, winding, rotating the dial through the fuzz of the semi-urban broadcast night, but there are only other people's songs, pop songs to make a fourteen year old weep for the hopelessness of love in the future, country classics for the lonely truck drivers, and advertisements interspersed to reunite us over our nostalgia for breakfast cereals we ought to have eaten in childhood had our unsentimental parents got the brands right.

Other people's songs are foreign languages, audible but incomprehensible. Maria digs through the glovebox in search of cassettes, finds only those we had shared, from which we had made shared meanings. She opts for dance music, overriding my attempts at melancholy connection.

*

We turn off near Wentworth Falls so Maria can take photographs. I've been here on a clear day, seen the 100-foot sandstone cliffs, felt the warm eucalypt scents washing up from the valley floor. This evening the smells are of smoke and ash. Our passenger wakes, coughing, and gets out of the car.

'Whuh?' he tries to ask.

'Rest area, photos,' I explain.

'Uh.'

I close the car windows and rummage around the floor behind my seat for her tripod, then lock the doors. What are the chances of a thief running from the bush to an otherwise abandoned lookout beside the road, sneaking up to the car undetected, opening the doors, sorting through the detritus to identify and take all our valuables? My car-functions must still be in wild and dangerous Sydney.

Maria's already staked out a position with a long view into the valley, nicely framed by not-yet-burning eucalypts in silhouette. Very classical, I guess. Perhaps she has other special effects in mind.

'Here, here,' she points, and I set down the tripod at the precipice. She's holding the shutter down and waving the camera around. Repeat. Repeat. Then screws the camera to the tripod.

'I won't be too long,' she reassures me.

I hold a blanket over her and her camera body to keep out the soot while she changes lenses. My eyes are running.

'I think I'm allergic to this,' I tell her, making a joke, complaining gently.

She grunts and presses the cable release. I hear the shutter click open-two-three click shut. She winds on and presses the release again: this time, a count of eight. She's bracketing — very professional. She's taking herself seriously. She's much more involved than we were together, much more professional. With us, casualness underpinned everything. It's not that we merely drifted together, spent some time together, then drifted apart, like a random encounter between two planets. On the other hand, I can't remember thinking, well, I think I'd like to embark on a relationship with this Maria person, who seems a damned good sort of person to spend plenty of time with.

I wanted to be with her, but it's possible that by the time I knew this I already was with her, so that I only wanted to continue to be with her, which is a poorer decision, or it seems so from a decisive, moral viewpoint. Who's to say whether setting out to have a relationship would have made the relationship last longer, if it's truly finished, as Maria and I have both agreed from our different angles? Who can tell whether, had I made strong decisions at the start of the relationship, I would have been a better person, a valuable person? Most likely, people who think that I'd have been a better human being for having made strong decisions at the commencement of our relationship are the people who think that anyone who makes strong decisions at any time is a worthwhile person, so the value system itself is self-perpetuating and nothing to do with me or my relationship with Maria.

Maria, for all I know, may claim to have initiated and nurtured our love along, though she no longer uses the word 'love' within my hearing, and I'd be surprised if nowadays she uses the word in relation to me within anyone's hearing, or would whisper it even in an unpeopled forest as the trees come crashing down.

I like to think we were content together, and that we knew when we met that we would be content. Some people might turn up their noses at the idea of contentment, but those would be people who imagine contentment as a quiet, passive thing. Our contentment was sometimes quiet, sometimes raucous.

I was content hanging around and I was content when Maria came up with her idea to become a photographer, to buy all this equipment, to go to places the day after news stories and photograph aftermaths.

This was her project, and it was the beginning of the rearticulation of our lives. Suddenly Maria was doing something, and she immediately wanted to know what I was going to do.

I found that talking about the things I usually did as though they were 'tasks' was a temporarily effective strategy. My primary project was to avoid work; sub-projects involved such goals as to have a good time, to meet people, to talk a lot. Maria may have harboured doubts as to the societal or personal value of these, but she didn't say anything against them. I thought, okay, so this is after all my project, and I aimed to work at it a little each day.

We were happy, I was happy, even when I was in a bad mood, even when Maria clamped and clammed up, which she'd do from time to time, and stayed that way for hours. Then we'd be back as normal again. That sort of thing, from what I've seen of other people's relationships, is okay. It's just okay, neither praiseworthy nor terrible.

Maria, however, began to think this was not all right. She thought we had to work at our relationship. I had no clue what she meant. In retrospect I should have noticed a deeper change in her: this idea of tasks, of projects, of working through, working at — her bandying about of the word 'work' — signalled a more significant alteration in her way of thinking. What it meant was that she wanted me to change, to become a toil-oriented boyfriend instead of a layabout. In other words, she wanted me discontented.

If only I'd been more aware, more awake to the implications of her newfound vocationalism, I might have been able to save us, to make sure she saved space for me, for my quiet and unfocused pleasure in life. I know that it's pointless building up these regrets; regrets are only becoming for farmers (if only I'd planted two days later; if only that storm had blown two miles, two damn miles north, we'd have come through...) and students (fucked that up). For a while I was sure Maria and I would be fine, with me as the words person and Maria undertaking all the deeds. I realise that words don't acquire the same level of social cache as doing stuff. Words are, after all, mere. I didn't care and I don't care about my community standing — it seems absurd even to use the term. But Maria... She wasn't a photographer when we met, and I can't say when she became one, but all of a sudden, without transition, there she was with this new professional attitude: planning, composing, setting time aside, doing material projects, finishing things.

After a few months, Maria's own discontentment became obvious. We tried to work at it. Maria said she thought something had changed, something had shifted and she no longer felt the same way. She had goals. I said I admired her goals and thought that her idea of taking photographs of places and events which were not news was a good idea. She said she wanted shared projects, a sense that we were moving somewhere together.

I tried explaining that I was the stable one. This was not the correct strategy.

Beside the clifftop, our passenger wanders over. In the valley, firefronts move perceptibly away from embers and towards fuel.

'What's up?' the deli-man asks, friendly. I nod to Maria's involved tasks.

'Getting there,' she calls, without moving from her camera.

It's sad but probably inevitable that Maria's self-imposed labours, tasks and projects have distorted her vision. Gone is her way of being casual in the world, which was the greatest part of what made her so charming and attractive. It's obvious in everything about her that Maria's changed for the worse. It's in the way she carries her equipment, the organised way she looks at a burning bush, the way her new walk articulates sense of purpose and, what's the most dispiriting — tragic, I think — her attitude to me. There's even a role set aside: I'm cast as The Driver. Nice. As usual, she has kept the best part for herself. This is what I've never liked about her.

'You forgot to load it,' I say, waving an empty film canister. I believe I succeed in keeping the nasty tinge out of my voice. Passenger begins to smile, but stops himself in time.

Oh yes, say her straight-line lips, Jack's irredeemable.

I can't remember having roles when we first got together, as our relationship grew into a relationship, as we moved into a house and room and bed together. Whether in this lack of role allocation she was behaving dishonestly, falsely presenting herself as a reasonable, pleasant person, or perhaps she was genuinely charmed away from her need for formalised preset limits — charmed by me, that is — or whether this whole professional role, time-related goal sort of thing is a temporary aberration, some kind of disorder from which she will recover, I can't say.

She tries some more angles. She points the camera rig this way and that, up and across. I hear the buzz of the timer, then the shutter clicks shut again and there will be more little firefly marks, more ash trails, across longer and longer strips of negatives. The air is thick with glowing embers. She's putting me at risk for her art, but I keep this to myself. I think this is the built-in contradiction. My primary role is to be silent. But I am a man of my word; I must speak. Without speech I do not exist.

I cannot recall the evolutionary chain which led to this, my extinction, the extinction of our love, cannot remember with any precision the successively more stringent regimes Maria imposed through force of will, through the overarching triumph of her projects and through her never-admitted undermining of the value of contentment. Strangely, I am not angry with her. I'm standing out here in a rest area between a clifftop and a depressive shop assistant, swatting at imaginary insects and leaf-shaped ashes which disperse into dust at a touch. It's Maria who has ceased to meet my eye, and I'm looking at her apologetically, sorry for the bad joke which stands in for my malicious thoughts. I think Maria should snap out of it, and she thinks I should snap out of it. This is how we judge each other. Despite my apologies, she is in the wrong.

I try to remember if I had misjudged her, if she'd shown any earlier penchant for enthusiasms. I can't think of any. Her whole attitude is a turning away. How can she hope to maintain a critical distance on the world's enthusiasms if she goes and gets enthusiastic herself? Ahead of us lie thirteen hundred kilometres in which to photograph gum trees. Apparently there are hundreds of species. I hope not all are photogenic. It's only a pity her old news project is over. If she were still restricted to photographing places the day after events, we'd be safe from the tyranny of the camera. West of Penrith, nothing ever happens. But these days she'll photograph anything that appeals: traffic jams, flesh, little flecks of burning bark caught in cliff-side updrafts. Her current Big Project is war memorials. We will pause along the way so she can record their meaningful architectures, their lists of names, their settings amidst arrangements of petunia-filled tubs. At each stop, she will close down all relationships but that between herself and her vocation.

Maria: she who brings about loneliness.

*

I try to remember if I have known any of Maria's previous boyfriends — whether she had a pattern of dumping us, whether each boyfriend was also an enthusiasm unreservedly embraced for a time, then no longer relevant — but I cannot recall Maria's men before me. I know nothing of them, not even whether they existed. She kept our relationship separate, not part of a continuum. I know only that a replacement exists.

'What does he do?' I blurt out.

'Who?' she says, a rapid exhalation which makes even this single syllable sound shorter than it ought to.

'The nameless and undescribed but still somehow attractive boy.'

She screws up her face and doesn't answer.

She who brings about loneliness carries the equipment back to the car. She's no longer happy. When she's unhappy she gets what she wants and I let her. Believe me, there's good reason to be afraid of the consequences of doing otherwise. (See mentions of silence, above and below. Maria: eradicator of words.)

She lays the gear across the back seat, over my jacket. She gets in the driver's side. 'I'm driving,' she says.

I get in the passenger seat and do up my seatbelt. Deli-man taps at the window and Maria lets him in.

'Thought you were going to abandon me there,' he says, attempting humour. Maria doesn't respond.

'She's not that bad,' I say. 'Sometimes.'

I open my window and Maria opens hers too, but without reference to my action. We have independently opened our windows. I stare straight ahead. She starts the car and drives across the gravel parking area, stares briefly to the right and pulls onto the road without having come to a complete halt. This is Maria's version of angry driving. A constant speed, not fast, not slow, but hardly braking, constant speed no matter what the road does. I hold on to my seat involuntarily as we swing around the curves for a few more miles, north to the highway, then west. Our co-traveller says nothing, attuned to his status.

*

The road straightens after a while. There's the moon in front — a headlight in the smoky sky — as we bump west. The windows are open; there's the smoke, the three headlights, our smoke-induced tears. I tell her all this. She's always liked my poetic turn of phrase, and in this manner I am temporarily reprieved. Maria smiles at me once or twice. Anyway, she smiles in the period immediately following. It's possible she is smiling at something else, a memory or the accumulation of ash in arcs beyond the reach of the windscreen wipers. But the atmosphere in the car changes. The trip might become almost bearable, might sustain Maria's initial lightness for another one thousand three hundred kilometres.

I resolve to speak nothing but gossip and travel stories. Has she been to any parties recently? I haven't seen her, but I've been a bit of a serial party-goer — a bit lost, she wouldn't mind me saying — and know all the news.

'Tell me about it,' she says. This is Maria the Regal, Queen Maria. She asks for information and it comes out sounding like, 'Amuse me!'

'Well,' I begin (Jester to Queen), 'The scene: Jamie's lounge room. Night, lit with three darkroom globes in a plastic chandelier. I am slightly inebriated, but not more than anyone else. I'm wearing a shiny party hat.'

'Beautiful.'

'Thank you.'

'I think I was there,' says Passenger, then sighs deeply. 'With Walter.'

'I don't think I saw you. About forty, forty-five people in the house and not a thief among them until Robert A arrives much later on. James M was there, descendant of a Famous Australian Landscape Painter, and saying as always, "A nice guy, my great-grandfather, but I don't think much of his painting" and hoping he could convince someone — anyone — to go upstairs. He was going on about how much some big shot in News Limited had offered him for a fuck. Alison kept saying, "Ooh I don't care if he's gay, he's just so gorgeous." '

'He's hideous,' says Maria, supportively.

'I know. Andrew, Nicole, Theresa and Paul (who should form a faction called Yuppies in the Kitchen) spent the night being serious about the Greens on council, saying the usual "how could Patrick support Claudia's amendment?" and "thank God Greg cast his Chair's vote against them". I didn't hang around there for long.

'Then Bill M goes into the bathroom with Anna-Marie and ooh how romantic except that they went in there to shoot up: Anna-Marie dropped the spoon into the sink afterwards. James W picked up the guitar because he plays keyboards for In Storage and thinks bad music improves his attractiveness. Jaki (J-A-K-I) beat out the rhythm on the floor. She is about fifteen though doing a PhD in psychology and a really understanding person according to Sandra who thinks everyone is.'

Maria laughs. This is when she remembers my few likeable characteristics: loyalty to friends, charm, capacity for serious analysis of contemporary urban culture. Is she thinking back to our easy attraction for each other, how we found ourselves together as though it were the most natural, most right outcome? I wonder if she has this concept 'outcome' in her mind, if she is struck by our position now (smoked?) and its wrongness, its movement beyond 'outcome' and into a grey, nothing zone not properly infiltrated by language.

But I am making myself despondent again, which is not a helpful attitude, not the attitude to speed the journey. It's the wrong kind of hopelessness. The kind of hopelessness I must project is one made out of charming impracticality rather than despair. Let despondency confine itself to the back seat.

I make a positive effort to portray more gatherings, more people bumbling their way through them.

'Okay. Another week, another party. I'm skunked to the gills. It's a small gathering, Julie's birthday in the back room of the Rose. There are two guitarists performing songs of heartbreak, really dirty sound; in the foreground, an improvised smoke machine: a toaster burning white bread. This is Australian improvisation, the whining lead breaks and the smoking black toast.

'Nice, huh?'

'Lovely. I love carbon,' Maria agrees, gesturing to the glowing forests.

'It was a triumph. We wiped the pool table with our opponents. They sank exactly zippo. My partner was on a roll. He was invincible: he potted the black between two of their balls on an impossible rebound. "Yes," he said, as the black ball trickled into the centre pocket, and he punched the air.

'Our opponents said little for fear that we would invoke the "drop your dacks" rule for players beaten so comprehensively. This would have been unfair of us, especially as we were playing against the birthday girl. It might even have been poor etiquette on our part, not to wait until they had sunk at least one. But I couldn't help gloating a little, despite only sinking one while my partner, who incidentally had been the singer in the duo, sank seven. Maria, it was a triumph.'

This, I know, is the correct attitude. Ex-lovers must always speak of how well their lives are proceeding.

Maria's driving has improved, and she tells me a story in return.

'I don't think you know my old friend Diana?'

I shake my head.

'She was in this really unlikely relationship. When it finished, well. . .

'I last saw her ex-lover about five years ago, not long before the last time Diana saw him. I can't actually remember if we spoke. We probably didn't: at most, he may have grunted hello. He was a bit of a grunter, pretty hopeless at non-intense personal relations. He probably tried not to notice me and I would've tried to make him. That's the way he rubbed me up, and most other people, from what I know.

'After they split, Di kept nothing of his, not even a souvenir like an old jumper. I have the only thing he left in our house, a book which I recently tried to read. He may have lent it to me or he left it around and I took it. It's not important. He did respect me more than most of Di's other friends, possibly because I liked talking about art but didn't insult him by trying to make any. That was about the only allowance he made for anyone else's artistic sensibilities. He didn't think much of the painters we shared a house with. He thought they were a bunch of derivative hacks, and didn't mind them knowing it. You can imagine how that went down. His idea of himself was incredible, completely caught up in seeing himself as gifted and insightful beyond comparison. You know the kind of person?'

I nod that I do. I can't think of anyone in particular though, so let it pass without contributing a list of supplementary names.

'The guy just didn't think these painters had earned the right to their tormented brushstrokes. He hardly ever spoke about himself, but it was obvious he saw himself as uniquely troubled and torn, his experience of the world's pain heightened by a delicate sensitivity. He expected others to respect that in him, though he refused to see it in anyone else.'

'Nice bloke.'

She pauses for a moment. 'Yes, this makes him sound fairly unlikeable.'

'He doesn't sound much fun to sit down to a meal with,' I say.

'Which is true enough. He wasn't. But anyway, likeable and attractive are different things, and he, though not particularly good-looking either, was attractive. He was kind of charismatic. Enigmatic in a romantic way, I'm sure Diana thought. She was completely besotted with him. Hopeless really. She saw all his flaws — arrogance, snobbery and the rest — as proofs of a strong personality.'

'Great,' I say. 'She's good on character, is she?'

Maria laughs for a moment, then looks serious again. Switch, switch goes her face. 'It's not very good, the book he lent me: one of those books in the voice of an alien. The front cover's missing, so I don't know the title or author. It's about the failure of human civilisation, told by a member of the next civilisation. I didn't enjoy it very much and didn't finish it. Too much space is spent on really obvious ironies. You know: commercial culture mistaken for religion so that the narrator thinks people worship money — get it? — and there are paper-recycling plants taken as archives and that kind of thing. Perhaps Diana's guy got more out of it than I did. Some people are good at finding depths in science fiction.'

'I think I know that book,' pipes up our passenger. 'From the sixties, yeah?'

'I don't know,' says Maria. 'Could have been the fifties even. Did you like it?'

'Think so.'

'Probably was a different book then. But anyway, for a while Di thought her man was more sensitive than the rest of us, then she didn't and then she did again. That's how she seemed to me at the time, on and off, up and down depending on how she thought it was going with him. He upset her.

'We didn't think he was sensitive — he was such a prick to most of us, in his indirect way — and we laughed at him behind his back.

'I guess it's possible our attitude covered up how insecure he made us feel: we took his pose as criticism of our relative lack of spirituality or something. These painters smeared their own blood around the paintings, and thought that was pretty good. I agreed with them. Not sure I still would.'

'Pretty bloodless, your photos,' I say, supportively.

'Thanks for that. In his favour, he had at least read a few books and seen some good movies and looked at a few paintings, which was more than we'd done. I'm not saying I'm better now, either, just that Di's bloke had his faults and we had some too.'

'Yes,' I say, and nothing else. Let her admit it for once.

'We'd find a favourite artist or writer and think we'd invented them. I guess what we did wasn't so terrible, lacking insight while thinking we had it. But he actually did have some sense of history.

'He was a pretty sullen guy, but somehow he stayed together with her for months. I don't know how it ended or who stopped it. Frankly I can't imagine how he began a relationship with anyone. It just doesn't seem possible that anyone else could consent to something so one-sided. Di must have poured out admiration and support and received such short replies. This is how I picture them, anyway.'

Backseat clears his throat to say something, but thinks better of it.

There's a short pause, then Maria continues: 'He was so assured that no one laughed at him to his face or teased him for all his world-weariness. In our group, everyone else copped silly temporary nicknames. He only did when he wasn't there.

'Poor Di only heard six months after it happened that he was dead. I was with her and she burst into tears. I was shocked too, it felt so impossible. My friend Robert had mentioned it in passing. He thought Di would've known. He said, "There was all that really strong heroin around then, and a lot of people died."

'Diana was saying, "It had to be an accident. He was always careful with quantities. He was always certain about his sources."

'But I don't know if she was right there. What about the Dransfield poems and admiration for Burroughs? She was ignoring the open notebooks left on the kitchen table which were no doubt supposed to show his self-critical openness. I read them and everyone else did too. Di was saying, "No one could have saved him. He was happy living like he did. I know he was."

'She was saying, "I knew him. I really knew him."

'And then she was shaking her head about how she should've kept in touch with him, could have done all these things for him. And I was there saying, "Oh, you know, what could you have done, you know? What could you have done?" and feeling completely useless.'

Maria falls silent.

'Shit,' I say, sympathetically.

'That is just so sad,' says the man in the back, 'but your girlfriend was right. People act so badly sometimes. They really do.'

It occurs to me that Maria chose to describe a relationship that, first, ended worse than ours and, second, avoids all mention of her lascivious new boyfriend, nameless and undescribed but still somehow attractive. Maria the diplomat.

The sun has set. In the west, there's a strip of pale daylight on the horizon. For Chrissake, it's night-time, I feel like telling the blackening sky. Get dark, you light, stop hanging around. The full moon's on our right, a different, less complicated story than Maria's and mine: the moon is red and blurry through smoke from the bushfires. The night is too warm, somehow heavy.

*

Throughout our time together, right up until the moment of Grand Vision and her setting up of the failure of our relationship, Maria always told me how environmentally determined my big mouth was, how predictable I am in my inability to keep silent. I was sure she was joking. I joked back at her: recited the regulations on the reverse of train tickets, sang through shopping lists, read aloud classified advertisements feigning distress that anyone would be forced to part with furniture, wondering at the quantity of unopened gifts and 'unwanted prizes'. I babbled at her, made up crude riddles about recently dead rich people, exaggerated the characteristics I thought she was only pretending to criticise.

'I can't help it,' I'd complain. 'If only I could stop, but I'm driven on and on. The words are always there, and so is the impetus, the reflex, to vocalise them.'

Or Maria would plead, 'Don't you have any hobbies? What can I do to keep you quiet for a little while?'

I might propose sex: 'That sometimes works.'

We got on well, most of the time. The jokes were all on me though.

'You can dish it out, but you can't take it,' I'd tell her.

'Most of the time, you don't even remember what you say to me,' she'd respond. 'You wouldn't have a clue how well I cop your insults, or even how much you abuse me. There's too much of it. It's endless. And this is only a tiny proportion of what you say.'

Maria blamed my parents, my teachers, my peers. They had encouraged me, she said. She claimed they must have asked me questions and listened to my views, that they didn't always ridicule me and everything I said — whereas, of course, they should have done. Perhaps, she said, they'd thought I was a good arguer, a potential leader. They may have respected me for an image I'd deceitfully conjured in their minds. They may have mistaken my verbosity for knowledge. She was wrong in her assumptions: I recall no encouragement from family or friends, only indifferent attention from peers and pedagogues.

According to Maria, they may have expected me to talk, and so — suggestible me — I did.

Later I could see the problem more clearly: it was all her fault. I'm sure I was happier before, even though I was lonely and had nothing to do and no one to do it with. I did nothing with strangers I met in local pubs. I sat on the beach by myself. I read the newspapers thoroughly and kept up with the daytime soap operas. I saw many contemporary films, read books I'd borrowed from friends, lent my books to other friends, so that we all had these patchwork book collections. I travelled a bit, which meant I went to Melbourne and really liked the atmosphere, the pubs there, the people I met who hassled me about coming from Sydney while I made out that I had somehow been forced to travel south.

I was flexible, could decide what to say and who to be on a whim. With Maria, suddenly I had to be constant. I had to recognise that, irrespective of my silence or volubility, my character on its own meant nothing. Even when I was on my own, my acquaintances' first questions were always about Maria's well-being. I was constantly readjusting myself, as she might also claim of herself.

'You're not the only one who's had to compromise,' she said. 'That's the idea: if we want to be together, we have to make space to do it.'

'I'm here all the time,' I said.

'Don't be so literal.'

'Don't throw so many meaningless abstractions at me then.'

But we didn't argue much. Or even complain at each other. What is a relationship but an extended exercise in self-censorship?

'For fuck's sake!' I exclaim out loud, almost without realising.

Maria jumps and the car gives a little swerve towards the road's soft shoulder. 'Jesus! What, Jack?'

'Just sitting here, regretting...' I say. 'Didn't mean to startle you.'

'Shit.' (Back seat.)

Maria frowns and decides against pressing me for details. Then her face relaxes. She can do that, allow things to pass, but this too is unpredictable and therefore a failing.

We drive on — she drives on. She's in an okay mood. She cannot read my thoughts. This personal illiteracy is one thing which will hold her mood until the next time I'm exposed as thinking, the next time I speak. It's one thing in her favour, looking at her from here. Also, her chin looks good. She looks good. She's a good-looking driver. She's attractive when she gets behind the wheel.

Radio on.

A deep and serious voice informs us that the fires have cut all train services.

'You know, it's really good of you to take me this far,' says our spare man. 'Otherwise I don't think I ever would have escaped from Sydney.'

'That's okay,' I tell him. Mr Sincerity is me.

'I needed something to break the pattern,' he continues, 'and your trip was the perfect coincidence.'

'It's fine, you're welcome,' says Maria. 'Broke what could have been a pattern for us too.'

'Hardly a coincidence,' I say. 'Thousands drive the same road every day.'

'Yes,' he defends, 'but not many sympathetic listeners drop by the shop to stock up for westward journeys coinciding with particularly low points in my day.'

'Don't tell me,' exclaims Maria, 'someone to out-pedant Jack.'

'I didn't mean to be pedantic,' says the passenger.

'I'm not pedantic that often,' I claim.

'Sure,' she says. 'Sure, sure.'

The car is full of darkness. When other cars pass in the opposite direction, I watch Maria's eyes. The pupils contract, then the car passes and I can no longer see her, and when the next car approaches, her pupils have enlarged again. Maria is dynamic. I think about the other changes she's undergoing from minute to minute. Her skin slowly shedding, ageing too, even more slowly. Saliva building up in her mouth, a swallow, and the cycle begins again. Blink, drying of eyes, blink. Minor adjustments to her heart rate as other cars approach and pass. Her other needs steadily increasing. Her bladder fills. She becomes hungrier. She moves further from her last and closer to her next sleep, her next fuck.

I can accept that most of the above is also true for me. Somehow, that's okay. I can cope with my own organic being. I don't necessarily enjoy it, not as much as looking at Maria, but it will do. It has to.

Maria's face shows the image of steely determination. She's like a movie star off set, unable to throw her character. She continues to drive with great concentration. She seldom turns from the road or towards me, only rarely checks in the direction of her hitchhiker. Her manner accords with the occasional roadside banners placed by the Department of Roads which exhort her to 'stay alert and stay alive'. I have no idea what she's thinking, not even about these government-sponsored death threats. I try to remember what I think about when I drive. I know there are journeys during which kilometres do not register, at the end of which nonetheless I arrive somewhere. But even then I cannot bring back the daydreams which replaced consciousness of the road. Her face darkens, is lit, darkens; the features resume with little change every few seconds or minute or two minutes, the frequency seemingly random, the space between approaching cars unknowable. She's so familiar that I'm thrown by our changed circumstances, her clearly stated inaccessibility. Maria's mouth, slightly thrust forward as she follows the headlights with her eyes; her steady, reliable nose shows fewest changes; eyebrows exhibit minor shifts in level; her eyes are light-affected, vulnerable.

If we were together still, the presence of the passenger would mean nothing. Now, the sense of him accentuates all that is unreachable about Maria.

I think: her lips could do with pressing my lips. Just this once, just to see, just to remember what we had. An experimental kiss, or conventional but with an experimental bent. A kiss because we know how to kiss each other, and used to like it, want to make sure we still do. A kiss because the opportunity exists, here, which is nowhere, which is not part of our lives. A kiss to see if kissing is the thing to do, and once we kiss it will be, because it will be what we are doing. Or a kiss with purpose, a pragmatic kiss, a kiss of need, of lust, a kiss of transposed desire, each of us a proxy kisser for an absent love or (as she would be for me) a potential and future absent love.

A kiss for the drama of it, or a kiss which begins quietly and is overridden by drama. Kiss of longing, of urgency, of departure. Yes, a kiss of farewell. I think of all the farewell kisses I've ever seen or read, those that are fleeting, those that last for minutes or chapters, and I think: I want one of those, a passionate farewell. We would know each other so well that the speeches would be dispensed with. One look from each and we'd understand that this was the last time. We'd be reluctant to begin, because we'd know we were beginning an end, and we'd hover with our lips not yet touching. She'd be trembling. I'd be certain. I'd tremble. She'd fix her eyes. Our lips would be neither dry nor moist, but just so.

I'd feel her arms hook around behind my neck. I'd grasp her to me, Maria, who once kissed me before I understood what we were doing, who is sitting beside me in a small car on a long drive. We'd have a farewell kiss and then we'd say goodbye, and we'd understand that each would turn and walk sadly away. Instead, against the proper way to behave, I'd turn to see her turning and though we have said farewell, we must need a further farewell from farewell.

I cannot think how to start this ... process. Once a letter might have done it.

*

*Dear Maria,*
*I found this for you, headed 'Internal Memoranda'.*
*To:    Heart          Date:  16th April*
*From: Brain          Time:  1:34:32 pm*
*Message:  I think of you always.*

To:    *Brain*            Date:   *16th April*
From: *Heart*            Time:   *1:34:33 pm*

*Message: Oh I beat for you and I pound for you. I throb for you and you alone. If it were you were not around, I'd set to ice, I'd freeze to stone.*

To:    *Heart*           Date:   *16th April*
From: *Brain*            Time:   *1:34:34 pm*

*Message: Every second I realise I am still alive and every second I know we live for each other. Our tragedy is that we may never merge, nor meet, nor — even — come any closer. But we have our correspondence and through it may we sustain our love.*

To:    *Brain*            Date:   *16th April*
From: *Heart*            Time:   *1:34:35 pm*

*Message: So clear are your ideas, at times by comparison I feel myself a mere functionary. Only the poetry of my rhythm justifies your love for me.*

To:    *Heart*           Date:   *16th April*
From: *Brain*            Time:   *1.34:36 pm*

*Message: Each time you send me a heady blood rush, I know you are always four parts poet, never functionary.*

\*

'Do you think we met too soon?' I ask. 'We should have waited until we were in our mid-forties, then moved out together with our nothing careers, a child from my second marriage, your two horrible teenagers, into a house we'd fill with dusty mementoes piled up in milk crates, and there overcome your alcoholism, my gambling problem, with a quiet, tender sort of love.'

'Jesus Christ.'

I think back, put it all together. Over the months I watched her change shape, slowly waxing, slowly waning; but I only made a memory note every few weeks — a mental film-frame — and in recalling these notes now, the changes in her are fast and smooth. Inside my head, I chuckle. Outside, I am silent for a few seconds. As if regretful again. In the sky, through brown smoke, the moon has turned a sickly yellow.

We sit in this car, approaching the crest of the mountain range. Beyond these mountains lie the great pastoral plains of New South Wales, where dynasties last exactly ninety-nine years. Four generations of farmer, and the great-grandchildren find themselves landless, dispossessed. The dynasty evaporates into bitterness and demands for renewed rights, for the option to buy land with peppercorns. Ninety-nine years was the length of pastoral lease generally allocated by the self-proclaimed landowner, Her Majesty. The Crown — that shiny hat which is also known as New South Wales. I imagine the representatives of the Crown stuck in their corporeal counting, the mathematics of the hands, trying to think of the biggest number possible. They could have said anything: they had said numbers with no reference to anything real in the past, declaring the land unpeopled, unpeopling the land with a few words and closed eyes, saying the number zero. But this number, ninety-nine, why that? The Australian trees burn, but they'll grow back in the foreseeable future. One hundred years is the limit of the imperial imagination.

Maria drives and I am a passenger. Sometimes, as set down earlier, we alternate these roles. The roles, though, are fixed, without fluidity. Each seat is a body-contoured, personal paddock as we drive between immense, eucalypt-dotted enclosures. The brake handle and gear stick fence us apart, or are the road between us, a little road racing over the great curving bitumen artery. Ahead, for the length of our journey and beyond, are inorganic capillaries, pasted superficially over the country, signs of the ninety-nine-year imagination.

But this car, with the fires everywhere but here, seems hermetic. We are sealed together, despite our separation. I could tell Maria that we belong together, except this would be asking for misinterpretation.

In the past, Maria and I behaved like lovers, went among other people as all lovers go. The lightness of the social can be so aerated that it seems outside touch; it seemed that we moved through it but that the real existed only when the two of us were together. We were in love.

No doubt we followed the model recorded by a postgraduate disciple anxious to broaden the application of particular theories of some famous psychologist-mentor. We were, I have no doubt, ideal: greeting people in the predicted order, smiling, conversing for predictable numbers of exchanges, quantities which tallied with like couples in like social situations throughout the western, researchable world. As with all lovers misplaced among other humans, all the while each of us connected only with one other in the room — she with me, I with her — and this produced in each of us a serenity, a distance from other smiles, other conversations; we were charming and polite, gifted with these attributes by our self-containment.

This social distance allowed me to charm strangers in a way I cannot be charming for Maria — she knows me too well, she knows me as a lover, as someone intimate beyond manners — in the same way she couldn't charm me with a smile or an elegant comment.

But, hang on. Speculation has suddenly exceeded evidence. Could Maria charm me?

What if, for example, Maria were to say, 'Jack, I have revised my opinion of you. You do, after all, have value'? If she were to say this or something similar, some exclamation of affection, and smile and allow my reply rather than beat it down with her wordlessly eloquent sourness, would I be charmed? I think I might. I suspect I'd allow Maria to charm me in an instant, to seduce me in any way she chose. I believe Maria could easily charm me if she were so inclined, but that may be only because I can fairly estimate the chances of Maria attempting to charm me. What's red and green and goes round and round at two hundred miles an hour? Frog in a blender. I can't remember when she last made an attempt. Our relationship was full of deferral.

Maria changed shape and I lost value. Maria gained the capacity to criticise; I became more familiar, became susceptible to criticism. I remained susceptible to charm; Maria became impermeable. Maria became nasty, but remained attractive; I remained equable, increased in repulsiveness.

This is how I interpret Maria's view. Even so, when Maria tells me not to be upset, to calm down, not to take something or other so hard, I can excuse her. She had a vision of the person I could become. I am not a valuable person, but I had potential when we met.

And although I wouldn't dream of imposing these perceptions on her, I have the right to perceive my mental states in the way which suits me best, to allow Maria's statements and actions to impinge on my emotional well-being as I choose. I can be natural, just as the magazines suggest. Magazines which could be found to embody Maria's attitudes to love.

'Close your window?' requests Maria, closing hers. I close my window. I lose what I was thinking, as if it were attached by a fragile thread to something inhuman and volatile outside the car. Neatly, mockingly empathetic, the smoke sinks down around our knees. Both the loss of thought and the descent of smoke are probably for the best.

A column of flashing lights passes in the opposite direction. No sirens.

'Red on black. Safelights. Your colours,' I say.

'Pleeease, stop. Stop speaking.'

'Aw, come on.'

'Really. I'm getting exhausted, and we've got so much further to go.'

I run out of things to say. (It happens.) Smoke clouds flick past the moon.

She stops the car.

Our passenger groans, whether in response to our irritated conversational interchanges, to Maria's exasperation or to yet another pause in our journey I cannot be sure.

'You drive,' commands Maria.

The moon is white. A cloud moves in front, glows white. Brown smoke drifts across, freezing the scene sepia. Maria does not think to take a photograph here. Perhaps she misses it, perhaps I have a better eye for the opportunity than she does. I resist pointing it out.

I drive, she fiddles with the radio, which has come on again at the end of a dance tape. The singer is lonely, the song subject will be sorry, though sorrow may be some time in arriving.

We drive. The earth shimmers red all around us, as though we tracked across the surface of an expiring star.

We pass the old, famous hotel at Medlow Bath, follow the rail line west: forest on the right, glowing; grass between road and rail to our left, flaming high. There's a break in the fire as we creep through the next town, Blackheath, but the smoke picks up again as we curve left and right out of

Blackheath and we soon reach Mount Victoria, our speed getting up towards thirty kilometres per hour.

'Good going!' I say, indicating the speed on the dashboard.

Coming around a bend, there's a cleared flat area on our left. A stooped, silhouetted figure waves his thumb at us.

'Jack, hitcher. Stop,' telegraphs Maria. 'The fires.'

'Two lunatics in the car is enough,' I say, not explaining which of us.

'You two are fine,' half-laughs Backseat. He has steadily gained confidence.

'Hmmm. I don't like the look of him,' I say, but I stop anyway.

I have often picked up hitchhikers since I bought this car. I am defined as a person who picks up hitchhikers. I used to hitchhike before I owned this car and it had often been difficult to find a lift. This is my rationalisation. I also feel a nervous thrill as I pull over: stories of violence and distrust are lodged in me.

The old hitchhiker climbs into the back of the car, resting his stuffed-full airline bag on his knees. He smells of cigarettes and aftershave, neither of which I use.

'Bathurst?' he asks, and I tell him, 'No, only as far as Lithgow.' He looks puzzled. I explain it isn't very far and he seems annoyed. I am satisfied to have told him Lithgow rather than agreeing that we would pass through his final destination. First impression: unpleasant.

After the old hitchhiker makes his bad impression on me, I wonder for a moment whether he has any weapons in his airline bag. He begins talking in a too loud yet inexplicably hard-to-follow monotone.

'The truck blew' [or 'threw'?] 'a valve on the hill out of Penrith,' he says. He'd been towed into Blaxland where the prime mover went to Grandpa Tom's repair shop and the trailer somewhere else, or the trailer to Grandpa Tom's — in which case Grandpa Tom's was his load's destination — and the prime mover somewhere else. This is the order in which he recounts his story to us.

'In Blaxland,' he says, 'I heard my parents had been killed on Thursday night.'

I assume without evidence he means they'd been killed in a car accident or else by a burglar. The hitchhiker doesn't clarify, and I don't ask. No one else asks him anything either.

'So that's how it is. I turned around and the prime mover's got to be towed, then the next thing is I turned around and my parents are dead. So now I'm going to Orange.'

Is Orange his home town? I can only guess that the funeral will take place there. If there is a funeral. As he tells us this story, I half believe him and half disbelieve him. I am disturbed by the equivalence he gives the story of the truck and the story of the deaths of his mother and father, who he only ever refers to as 'my parents', unindividuated. Despite my doubts, after he tells me his parents have been killed, I decide to take him to Bathurst even if the drive should turn out to be harrowing and/or uninteresting. I do not tell him of my decision in case I decide to reverse it once more.

'So I heard there's a welfare in Blaxland and I went in there for some help. They offered to pay for a rail ticket to Orange, and I said fine, and then they attempted to book the first train to Bathurst and a connecting train from Bathurst to Orange. That was fine, I said, but then they turned around and said to me the next available train didn't leave until the next morning, and I turned around to them and said that I had to get to Orange. I asked them if I might make a telephone call and they said I could. I rang a bus company and discovered they had a number of buses, all with available seats, leaving that night. I turned around and said this to them and I said to them the bus fare was twelve dollars and they turned around and said to me they could arrange to put me up overnight in a hostel in Penrith and I turned around and said to them I didn't want to sleep in Penrith. They turned around and said to me they were only able to pay rail tickets because of how the voucher system reimbursed them for expenses from the government department.'

He doesn't specify whether the agency was governmental or privately run.

We have dropped down the Victoria Pass and entered the orchard district when he announces, 'It might sound callous, but I feel like going back there and wringing their scrawny necks.'

No one else comments, though 'callous' seems to me an unusual word choice. Also, the permanent plurality of welfare officers strikes me. Maria says nothing, gives me an alarmed glance. I sense the poor guy from the delicatessen's shift towards the door behind me.

The hitchhiker complains it took him from six in the evening to travel from Medlow Bath to Blaxland. To reassure him, I say that hitchhiking is generally much slower than driving, and that his time was 'not too bad' for hitchhiking that distance at night. I explain that I have done a lot of hitchhiking. I'd inferred from his hurry that he hoped to continue hitchhiking to Orange that night. I begin to advise him that there is no point in trying to hitch out of Bathurst late at night. He is better off going to a truckstop and making a placard.

He immediately becomes irate. He raises his voice in pitch and volume and shouts, 'I have been a truckdriver all my life and I don't need you to tell me where to hitchhike from.'

I try to apologise. He continues to speak angrily, refusing to be pacified. 'Have you done Melbourne to Brisbane ten times in a week? You haven't, have you? How many times have you even driven through floodwaters? Not once, I'd guess.'

'Okay. Okay. I was only trying to help,' I say.

The hitchhiker becomes quiet. 'You shouldn't say things you don't know.'

He says, 'And this on top of the death of my parents.'

He folds his arms and says no more. A few minutes later, we reach Lithgow. Instead of city gates, neon-lit truckstops stand either side of the road. Huge bright signs above the service areas clarify the branding strategies of the two petrol companies, announcing their different proprietary claims to environmental credibility through fuel-filtration systems or vaguely pronounced high ideals. For immediacy, rather than a choice between these paradigms of corporate citizenship, I pull off the road into the left-side service station, the car's swerve reflecting the suddenness of my decision, and say, 'This is Lithgow.'

The last passenger accepts that this is the end of his ride. He steps quickly from the car, still complaining to himself, or perhaps to me, about my rudeness. I drive away. No one waves. We will never discover where his conversation might have led, and my feeling of relief for this, even abstract gratitude, is audibly shared by our shop assistant and Maria, who only says, 'Thank God!'

'Jesus,' breathes the back seat, reduced once more to one. 'What a monster.'

He adds, 'That is, if he wasn't telling the truth. Or even if he was. But weird.'

He adds, 'Not that I thought he was.'

He adds, 'So I think turfing him was the right thing to do.'

He adds, 'Hence my first comment.'

'Yes,' I say, 'I don't think I'm ready to speculate on that just yet.'

We drive through this petroleum-architecture roadscape into the main town of Lithgow.

'Sorry about this, but I really want to stop here for a few minutes to take some shots,' says Maria.

'Here? You want to wait around to photograph that weird guy?'

'In Lithgow, not right here. The memorial. Hope that's okay.' She addresses our passenger (statement, not question).

'Sure. I could do with a few minutes,' I say. 'That was really bad. Horrible.'

'In his head he really seemed to believe everything he said, but none of it quite went together. No idea about him apart from that.'

'Poor guy,' I say. I mean it, but am also thinking: perhaps a psychopath. 'I think he discovered the barrier marking the end of my sympathy and personal capacity for involvement.'

'He needs a professional,' says Backseat, with certainty.

I notice that the car still smells very strongly of the hitchhiker's aftershave. Despite the smoke-filled air and open windows, his pungency remains as we cruise the empty streets of Lithgow.

*

The evening feels like a childhood memory: waking in the car at night and feeling the silence around, parents in the front in motel-search mode, always having driven a little longer than intended, a little tired, but with that many miles under our belts.

We've driven only ten per cent of our journey and already have reached this point.

'Do you know where this landmark of yours is?'

'Sort of,' says Maria, flipping through a notebook.

We find it, and Maria determines to photograph it using the natural floodlights rather than a flash. I'm feeling edgy and glance around from time to time, expecting to see the man with the airline bag, expecting more chastisement.

'Done,' says Maria. 'Let's go.'

'What are you going to do with these?'

'Not exactly sure till I've developed them. Something about the architecture of memory.'

The guy from Leichhardt suddenly looks depressed again, his foremost memories mapped in two simple, practical aisles and along a glass-fronted counter.

'Sounds grand,' I say quietly to myself, then louder, 'I want to grab some truckstop food on the way out of town. And a drink wouldn't go astray either.'

'You want to stop again?' asks our back-seat moper.

'It's okay. We can get takeaways.'

We drive slowly through after-hours Lithgow. I try to think some more, but about quiet, calming things. About being a tourist, about the processes of laying highways across countries. I think about travelling short distances with Maria, seeing things. Travelling with Maria along roads. Hmmm. Maria is on my mind, it seems.

A red-brick hotel promises a Bottle Department, so we pull over. If hotels were the world, I guess there'd be a

Bottle Minister, and the person in charge of cans would be untitled.

We enter through the door marked Bottle Department. I look through the glass door of the beer fridge, deciding whether our journey warrants special beer or whether a couple of longnecks will do. Our passenger is hanging back, not looking at anything lest it commit him to contribute towards our drinking. After all, he'll only be with us for another hour or so. Wouldn't want too much involvement.

Maria, meanwhile, is at the border between red and white wine. Towns west of Lithgow surely keep yuppie beers and wine in bottles, but my unreliable friends claim you need a codeword to gain access to them, that they're secreted behind the counter and handed over in plain brown wrapping.

Although the sign above the door claims that this area is a dedicated bottle shop, its counter stretches through to the main body of the pub. A glass door and a couple of metal strips form the divider. There's a man at the bar who looks slightly familiar, and when he waves to me, I raise a hand in non-committal greeting. He gestures for me to come through. I shrug. He makes the come-here sign more emphatically and I begin to think I do know him: an old schoolfriend, someone who worked near me when I was a shish kebab salesman at fairs and showgrounds. Or a ticket seller, librarian, postal worker, newsagent or any one of hundreds of other people with whom I've had momentary relationships. Maybe there's something he does need to tell me, something I should know, a disaster befallen another colleague in one of the above categories, or an opportunity he's heard about which would suit someone in my line of work. He gestures 'come on' with both hands. I nod, hold a palm towards him meaning 'in a second'.

Maria has a bottle of white in one hand and a bottle of red in the other. She holds them towards me, sommelier-like. I indicate with the back of my hand that she should decide, then point next door and hold up a finger to mean one minute. She raises an eyebrow, and we both smile at our fluency.

I go through the door.

'Mate,' says the man, with a nod. 'How are you?'

'Okay. Do I know you from somewhere?' I ask. 'I really can't place you.'

'I'm a very common facial type,' he says. 'The name's John, so I'm a very common nominal type too. Are you already drinking, mate, or are you about to start? Get me one, will you?'

'Sorry. I'm just on my way out.'

'Mine's a schooner. Is that your woman?' He points back through to the bottle shop.

'No.'

'Not yet, eh?' he laughs. 'Got to steal her from your best mate yet? That feller there who hangs around in doorways.'

'I've really got to get going. Thanks anyway. See you later.'

Why I'm thanking him, I have no idea. I begin to turn.

'She'll wait for you, mate. I know these things. If she wasn't thinking about it, you wouldn't be a threesome.

Believe me. At some point, the two of you will leave him behind. I know these things. I'm a man of experience. Listen...' he begins.

*

You get to drinking and you want a girl. Happens to everyone. I down one or two and immediately I want Bermuda Parker. That one over there, she is. Every time I drink, it's her, I tell you. She's got to be my personal goddess of imbibement. I'll be Lord Ethanol and she'll be the Lady of Misrule. Mate, she's Bacchus with breasts, but this life of mine has got plenty of points both ways. One side of it, it's this woman I'm telling you about. Other side, well, every day minor deities stamp their ways through my besotted skull. I soak up some bourbon, I squeeze some back into the air through my over-stuffed pores, and I want Bermuda Parker so much I'm going to cry or split my dacks thinking about it.

*

'Sorry, mate. I'm going,' I tell him again. 'Bye.'

He stands up, taller than I'd expected, and places his hand firmly on my shoulder. Without acknowledging my farewell, he continues.

*

There she is beside me, a slab of beer balanced between her feminine hip and her magnificently tapered arm. I am going to have her this evening, and I'm going to drink a fucking lot of beer. I can taste what it will taste like. It will be the sort of beer you can feel flowing through every capillary, which will fill you to your fingertips.

I say, 'Here. Give it to me, love, I'll carry it.'

But this Bermuda isn't going to let me act smooth.

'What're you going to do, balance it on your cock?' she snaps.

I laughed at that! Me with that beerbox — nine teetering litres waiting to be sucked! Unbearable!

I jog up to the car and open the back door, and I close it again after Bermuda tosses the slab on the back seat. I'm hoping I have no bloody friends to join us, no soon-to-be exes like you're lumbered with. The beloved fucking neighbours always ring the doorbell when we're about to do the old two-headed spider.

'At home?' they grunt, and I say, 'Nah, we're just going down the coast. Back next week.'

'Who's the chick?'

'It's Bermuda, you idiot.'

'Ha-ha, didn't recognise her under all that booze.'

And then they piss off. Or else we tank up with them, and every drink's a chaser for the last and a big bloody promise for the next. We drive around under the six-cylinder roar and the neighbours bray. I hunch over the wheel refusing to smile as I skid along the nature strip. I throw the neighbours out of the car at their house.

'Thank God for the ends of journeys, thank St Bloody Christopher and his medal,' I exclaim, my skull deities conspiring, forcing me to speak through the ethyl vapours condensing on the car's vinyl ceiling. I tell her I'm aching for her, that my erection is killing me, beerbox or no beerbox.

'Piss-fat, is it? Too much liquid for your hardworking bladder?'

'No, baby,' I tell her in the special half-whisper. 'It's all pure lust for your nubile bod.'

She looks down, reaches out to grab a feel. Sometimes it seems that all the world is staring at your groin, can't hide that bulge anywhere, even if you wanted to. Five minutes later I'm watching her retrieve a condom from the bedside drawer. She undoes my trousers and rolls the prophylactic on in one easy, non-skin-catching movement. So organised, so very organised. No fumbling about in the dark for condoms with her. No preliminary 'where did you put the thing?' nor any suggestion of 'it will never roll out that way, no matter how many hairs you try to untangle from it'.

Fucking follows me everywhere. I'm not a bloke to complain, believe me.

'I wonder if I could accommodate a really big one,' says the waitress to her colleague, as Bermuda and I sit in a bistro. It's Friday, and everyone's eating and watching the races. The pub is like a massive self-sexual organism. I'm also immediately interested in the waitress, who sounds experimental, though not as cute as Bermuda. I go to buy more beer and the Tim Bleary leaning on the bar confides in me, 'She's practically a club: the doorman stops you and asks, "Are you a member?" '

Hahahahahahahahaha. I tell this to Bermuda who does not laugh. I tell her I said to the Bleary, 'Aw good on you, old feller.' I'm on a fucking roll with this one. Hilarious it is, and Bermuda has to laugh pretty soon. There were two young men called dick and rod and dick offered rod a prod oh yeah.

I mean you drink five maybe six beers and all of a sudden there's:

> *this little dickie went to market*
> *and this little dickie stayed at home*
> *this little dickie arises and browses*
> *and this little dickie stays in the trousers.*

At the next table, they're advising each other, 'And that's what I mean by life, son. Someone beats you down and you beat someone else down, or else someone beats you off, gives you a bit of a tug, which is far better.'

Every journey to the bar for more drinks gives inspiration. 'Hello waitress, what's your name? I ask because are you a friend of Jim's?' She tells me, but doesn't write anything down. Whisky always comes first, you can see it on the radio any day. How was I? Did you like that or can I belt you again? Makes me feel young, how love and frustration are exactly the same thing.

So, Tim Bleary: do you stand for the queen? Hahahaha-hahahahaha. Goodonyer, cyclops. I mean, imagine if you never lost your erection. Imagine that!

You get to drinking and the whole thing starts again. You just can't say a thing to bitches. She says I know how you think and I say how do you know that, are you my fucking alter ego or something and she says well actually I am and I say and she says and I say and she says, you know?

Ten beers later and why did you write 'penis' in the space marked distinguishing features? Snort! How could you do that? Yeah, well, I'm a man. That's what I say to Bermuda.

Bermuda says, 'Snap out of it. Stop staring at the barchick.'

I try to think of something else to say about my penis, but I just can't slip it into the conversation and the night's getting later and later and a barman's going from table to table with a huge stack of schooner glasses balanced along his left arm while dozens of people at different tables tell him, 'You wouldn't want to trip there, would you?'

And other people respond, 'At least they're the empties, eh.'

Two in the morning and this is Lustralia, the land of ache. The jukebox is screaming 'I want you, I want you now, I want you bad', and everyone believes it, yes, they want to believe it with the throb of the bass and of pulses in necks. There's been only six hours of drinking and already this is final, this is the last move and the last chance. The woman at the next table is choosing carefully, choosing her words to elicit the most telling replies, choosing between the two men, youth and age, energy and experience, practised ease and ingenuousness. The men are doing their best, trying to fix rules, trying to maintain a drunken camaraderie, trying to be easy and to appear used to it.

'They all believe the others know what they're doing,' I comment to Bermuda.

She doesn't know what I'm talking about, thinks that I don't know what I'm talking about.

'Them, them.' I'm trying to point with my chin, but my neck movements repeatedly coincide with the beat of the music. Bermuda rolls her eyes and glugs at the drink, whatever it is. I've switched to red wine, a carafe balanced dangerously at the table's edge. I go to the Gents where my piss is as clear as French bloody *aqua mineraley* or however you say it. I notice in the stainless steel sheet which passes for a mirror that the colour of the wine has remained inside me; it has become me. You can see it in my eyes, irises bobbing across the redness.

'Let me take you home,' I shout-whisper over the noise at Bermuda, who is deciding between me and some vodka concoction. 'Everything here is shitting me, you know? Let's just go.'

Chin-point at next table, where the three of them look so stiff in their fake relaxedness that they might shatter at any moment. Bermuda still doesn't seem to understand and I'm jabbing towards them with my elbow now. I'm subtle as an icepick in Mexico but still polite.

'Come on. Let's go, sweetheart. Let's go now.' I'm trying to convince her through repetition but it's not working. 'You want me to do all that stuff over there?' Point with little finger. 'Fine. It's like this, isn't it: Put on a record, will you love? One of those jazz records of yours. That's it, smile. Ooh, she's smiling. Her and her fucking anarchist badge and her up themselves friends and their friends and Jeremy's car. That's what they're doing over there. How fucking seductive. You want to do that scene? You don't really. I mean, you get to drinking. That's what I do, anyway. So let's go.'

I wake up the next morning not remembering how I got home. This woman is beside me, this woman who attracted me the previous night and all other times, bloody often, truth be told. Tell you something, Bermuda's grey in the mornings. No surprise to me. Mucus has petrified into little granules around my nostril rims. I run a bath then shake Bermuda awake. I'm in no hurry to do anything, but I'm awake, aren't I? She says 'oh' a few times, or 'aw'. Her nightshirt's falling off her and as she sits up her right tit comes out from behind the bedclothes like it's sunrise. We get in the bath, which feels really unusual. It takes a while to recognise the liquidity. Some barrier caused by who knows what covering the surface of the skin. We kind of stare at each other. I'm going to say, come on, let's do it now, in the bath, and am waiting for her to give me a sign like I'm waiting for a fucking printed invitation or something.

'Two hundred black coffees and I'll be ready to do it all again, whatever it was,' she says, which is completely the wrong thing.

We towel ourselves dry, watching all the little droplets spraying onto my cement bathroom floor.

Anyway she stays, and every Tuesday we change, so it's one week white wines and one week reds and in this manner. What kind of a thing to do is that? I could list the rest of the drinks, I really could, but the sun would set twice before I got halfway, and this little cute bar-chick over here would think I was giving a mighty order like I'd just won the fucking lottery, and I haven't even got a ticket. We think we're heroes, absorbent as anything, but those little mini-gods continue to dance and dance in my head. I feel the footsteps. The first time we woke up, she's holding the pen and paper for my phone number and I say, 'I'll write that for you' and she says, 'What're you going to do, dip your dick in the inkwell?' Oh, hahahahahahahahaha. How do you respond? That's 7351–1327. Again? 7351–1377. Huh?

Just keep dialling, keep dialling. And Christ, I love you.

\*

He waves to Bermuda, who gives an extremely perfunctory flip of the hand in reply. He laughs again. 'She's hell, mate. She really can be. Hope yours is quicker and a lot more friendly.'

He curls his forefinger and thumb together inside his lips and actually whistles for the bar attendant. She folds her arms and glares at him.

'Anyway, mate,' he continues, 'I will have that schooner after all. Good to talk to you too.'

I give him a two-dollar coin.

'Another of these'd be good,' he says by way of gratitude.

I say, 'Er, can't do that today,' and escape back into the bottle shop.

I hear him call, 'A middy, mine'll be.'

'What was all that about?' Maria asks as I join her in the queue, an edge of impatience in her usual serenity.

'I have no idea,' I reply. 'He wanted to tell me about his girlfriend.'

'Do you know him from school or something? He looks like a piss-head.'

'No, but I gave him two dollars.'

'He is a piss-head.'

'Yes.'

'He told you how often he has sex.'

'He did.'

'Good story?'

'For a piss-head story, it was right on the mark.'

'Took his time. I thought you'd decided to stay here all night.'

'He looked like he would physically prevent me from leaving.'

'Aw, you poor man. I should have rescued you.'

'Actually, I think he would have taken that as evidence that we blokes had even more in common than our mutual maleness.'

Maria has opted for the red. I'm not feeling upmarket after the piss-head's story, so I grab two longnecks, take them to the counter.

'All together?' asks the cashier, waving at the three bottles.

'Sure,' says Maria, pulling a bill from her pocket.

'Bit of a contrast, eh?' she winks to Maria. 'I had a boyfriend once, and we'd never drink the same things, but he was a good bloke anyway. We still get on, though we don't see each other that often. We were pretty much the reverse of you two, I suppose, he'd be making like a wine reviewer, going on about palates and noses and length. I'd be saying, "This beer really hits the spot." '

She directs all this to Maria, but sees my disbelieving face and goes on, 'Of course, I don't mean to put the mozz on you. Granted it's different for everyone.'

'We've got to go,' I tell Maria, pointedly not addressing the cashier.

'We get on just fine,' says Maria. 'He'll drink anything.'

'Very funny,' I say, as the cashier puts the three bottles in an unbranded white plastic bag and pushes it across the counter. I don't trust the handles, so hold the bottles to my chest all the way back to the car.

'There are plenty of things I won't drink,' I say, eventually. 'Remember?'

Maria shakes her head. She remembers nothing.

'Would have been faster to drink it there maybe,' complains the extra passenger.

'It wouldn't,' I tell him. 'Believe me.'

I start the car. The bottles remain in their bag. Ideas arrive, ideas about Maria, and I've got a bad feeling about expressing them. Slowly, slowly, alternative scenarios come to me, everything which could have kept us together.

We could have saved our relationship. I like the language: 'saving' relationships. Rescue and investment, combined in undying love.

We could have changed our location: moved house, moved cities, moved countries. We could have replanted ourselves, found climates more suited to sustaining us, sprouted anew, grown in different directions, rerouted and rerooted. We could have settled in Lithgow and thus have already been some distance towards Adelaide by the beginning of the journey: a head start.

We could have gone into business or given up all work. Timetabled ourselves. Coordinated, synchronised and, ultimately, matched. Become partners in the sense set out in the Corporations Law.

We could have changed our diets or appearances, taken up meditation or hobbies, got fit or eschewed physical activity, spent more or less time together. Run a set distance together each day, and our times would have improved as we did, our time together reduced towards the parameter at the height of human endeavour, towards world records.

Our lives could have begun or continued differently. We could regret the circumstances of our births, relive our schooldays to make them the best days of our lives. We could have been reborn in wealth or squalor, in Lima, Goa or Oslo. We could have met in a bar, at school, in the street, been introduced by relatives rather than friends, met by way of a newspaper advertisement or on a train. Any beginning could have determined, made certain, salvaged our continuation as a couple.

Anything could have happened. We could have continued until another kind of ending, been fairy princes and princesses for each other, people who never have to deal with mundanities, temporalities and ephemera. We could have lived focused lives. Like photographers.

At the next truckstop, this one marking the town exit, we pull in for a hamburger. Bushfire brigade trucks are parked everywhere. There are seemingly hundreds of firefighters in yellow canvas overalls. They queue to pay for chocolate bars and pornographic magazines.

My hamburger is delicious, the shredded lettuce hinting at crispness and the egg yolk runny. Plenty of tinned beetroot. Maria and I nod approvingly at each other about hamburgers. We consider chips. We reject pineapple fritters. Maria takes photographs of a brigade in front of their fire truck. With flash. Without flash. They smile. Click. They pull faces. Click. They fold their arms, football team style. One or two horse around, overacting, hanging by their legs from protruding bits of fire truck. Maria gives no instructions, but somehow they understand exactly what she requires.

One asks, 'Hey, you work for a newspaper?'

'Mm,' Maria tells them, truthlessly. 'I do.'

'You too?' he asks me.

'Oh no,' I proclaim, honest if only by comparison. 'I work for her.'

Some of the firefighters laugh. Maria gives me her half-a-smile, this time meaning 'get fucked'.

Whoo-hoo, I've done it again. I feel sheepish and rebellious at the same time, if that's possible. For her sake, at least I've diverted the otherwise inevitable and unanswerable follow-up question: which newspaper does she claim employs her? We take our soft drinks back to the car. She drives. The wheels protest slightly over the service station's cement forecourt. Then we're back on the road.

Every now and again is a town, lights, a neon sign. There's a motel.

'There's a motel,' I point out. 'There.'

'Um, you stop when you have to,' says the passenger anxiously.

'We don't have to stop,' says Maria. 'You'll get to Bathurst.'

What did we imagine we would speak about for one thousand four hundred kilometres? What did she imagine? The radio crackles out the same advertisements as in Sydney, but the reception's worse. The songs are the ones on the stations we don't listen to. Forest alternates with towns, fire with protected civil spaces.

My underscored joke changes Maria's face, but why should she be angry? I have told her she attracts me. Why should my attraction diminish simply because she no longer likes me like 'that'? Imagine all our characters as completely fixed, I want to say. You decide on your feelings for me completely independently of mine for you. And vice versa. I am holding myself back.

What did I think we would say to each other from city to city? Things could yet turn out better, could turn out like my daydreams. We rekindle our love for each other. Maria says she cannot imagine what drove her from me, but she knows beyond anything else that she wants me now. I say, yes, yes, we are made for each other.

Or: Maria is in love with me, but I no longer want her. (In my daydream, this is not a shallow inversion but a genuine sign of my strength.)

Maria is quietly angry. She does not want me to attempt jokey seductions less than two hundred kilometres from home, to suggest that she could change her decision within the space of two flashes from my car's left indicator light. Perhaps she does not even want me to desire her. That, I would not be able to understand. She does not want me to propose sex without clarifying its implications, and I am absolutely sure she does not want me to discuss the implications or potential implications of us pulling to the side of the road, checking in to a motel, undressing, going to bed together. She would feel unhappy were I to go into detail about the likely texture and temperature of the motel sheets. I predict all these responses from the change in facial expression my indication of a passing motel brought about. I will never know, because these are not scenes it is proper to undertake.

Already the most absurd penitence is necessary. Silence. It is not one I am capable of making.

Maria appears angry, or perhaps she is thinking about my suggestion, allowing herself daydreams with me as a hero, as a villain, as a person who may one day acquire value, as a mistake which went on for too long. I cannot criticise Maria's thoughts, particularly as they are only my projections of them, but I am not in favour of her anger. On that, I know I am in the right. Without also imagining fantasy alternative versions of this trip (at least to the degree where we allow ourselves to relate now without every comment carrying the full weight of our failures, allow ourselves to communicate now without setting aside a potential for being together in some way in the future), we cannot talk about the hurtful past, the empty future, my resentments, Maria's plans. We can only discuss how far we have come and how far we have to go.

'Sixty kilometres to Bathurst,' I say, cheerily. 'That means only twelve hundred and sixty to Adelaide.'

'No counting,' she warns. 'Anything but that.'

'I don't mind,' says the spare passenger. 'Sixty is good.'

A car passes, heading towards Sydney. As its headlights strike us, I see Maria remodelling herself, determinedly becoming friendlier.

We drive. Perhaps this time her pupils contract and do not open out again. It's getting later every hour. I feel as though I am working hard, but cannot discern towards what.

There are no streetlights, even among small clusters of houses. Fire must have eaten through the power grid. I try to find a better radio station, but there's only sixties light pop or white noise. I leave it untuned, hissing and gargling.

'Very cool,' says Maria satirically.

'I know. Like, imagine I'm this artist,' I tell her. 'I turn my life into art. That kind of figure. It's my role. I transform the mundane into performance. Example: I project my voice towards tourists' video cameras and purr "I love you", so that on dozens of screens in dozens of countries, friends and relatives of tourists hear me proclaiming love.'

'Sorry, I can't picture you as that kind of artist, Jack. Anyhow, that sounds too purposeful to be art.'

'I guess you'd know about the purposelessness of art. You're not exactly Robert Capa yourself. Instead, I stand in the centre of the city. I ask lots of people for directions to the same place and write down their answers. Or I enlist co-travellers. I go for long drives and find the purpose along the way.'

'Yeah, you enlisted me.'

'Me too,' pipes up our passenger. 'Are we on a "journey"?'

'And do you mean "find" or "seek"?' asks Maria.

'You tell me.'

'If I'm supposed to know the answer, it'll only be "seek".'

'I'll probably have to reconfigure the quest then.'

'Attaboy.'

This is typical. Maria is skilled at being careful, reinforcing parameters, clarifying situations, and I've noticed that she's very, very encouraging of anything I suggest which resembles a goal. Now she leans down and switches off the radio, which had begun to represent my general lack of focus. I'm secretly glad she did, because it had accidentally become a point I was making and was probably irritating me more than it irritated Maria. Her annoyance had been more broadly based.

'That's one fewer thing to talk about,' I say, trying to sound satisfied.

'You had nothing to say about it anyway.'

'That kind of noise is something I usually don't notice.'

It would have to be drawn attention to. I should have taken a photo of it, for the future historic diary of our journey, called it *Radio with Bad Reception*, installed it in a gallery surrounded by Maria's photographs of gum trees and fire and with a multi-track recording of silence in the background.

If one reason to travel is to accumulate memories, either purely mental or else assisted by *aides-mémoire* such as photographs, postcards, receipts, scars, this trip will be unique. Most people who travel together travel to know each other better, even if it's not the sole purpose of their trip. They get to know each other better along the way. We're unique, Maria and I. We're travelling to know each other less well. We're journeying to unknow each other, to undo our relationship. We will finish the trip with fewer memories than when we started.

As our relationship came apart, Maria saw my resistance to her projects as pessimism.

'Jack, you're so pessimistic,' she'd say, if I expressed the possibility that remaking myself as a goal-oriented person might not be completely successful.

'Yes, I've nothing to say, am overcome with negativity,' I comment, now. 'Silenced by superior logic.'

She rejoins with a lighter response. 'What happened to your quest of a mere two minutes ago?'

'We're driving along. We're in a car. There are a limited number of stories in which we could be implicated. The quest is impossible, as you so thoroughly demonstrated. We have no shared aims. We are not configured for questing. We can only exist in other, less noble genres.'

'We're common?' demands Maria.

The road is straight. Everything pauses but our journey, our movement away from one city, towards another. A lull, you could call it, this silent duration, but this would imply I do not control its length. Better put it this way: there is silence while I refrain from speaking. I am a passenger, resenting the difficulty of putting speech into the cabin. Still, I have the capacity to set the length of the silence. Maria, on the other hand, governs its character. The silence has a lot in common with the weather this time of year, I think but do not say.

The distance markers reduce by five every few minutes. Each post, we draw closer to being alone, to a new commencement. This new beginning will produce new connections between the two of us, I feel sure, new understandings. Our passenger makes occasional exhausted, grateful noises. No doubt he is thankful we have provided him with a bridge across which to escape thinking about his personal rejection. Then we're following the road through Bathurst, its great turns right and left to discourage speeding motorists.

'Just here,' he says, parallel to the town centre. 'I'm just going across there.'

'It's okay. So are we,' says Maria. 'I'll drop you at the memorial.'

She hangs on to him for an extra minute, delays our time. I insist on staying in the car while she photographs. I say goodbye to our passenger, who says, 'By the way, my name's Patrick.'

Maria and I pointlessly introduce ourselves.

'See you around in Sydney, no doubt.'

'One day.'

He walks off, bag over his shoulder in the approved walking-off style.

I stay put, tracing my finger in the remnant ashes on the dashboard. Maria goes off to photograph the historical concretions.

She returns. She drives. We leave Bathurst. We have set out at last.

'Welcome to Australia,' I say.

'I have always thought, Jack, that you have too much regard for talking.'

'Eloquence is next to joy,' I say into the darkness. 'There's one for the desk diary.'

'Not my brand of desk diary,' says Maria.

Immediately, I have greater understanding of the failure of our relationship. There are never limits to my behaviour:

time, place, never appropriate. Sometimes I have to speak. This is at the heart of my character. I remember clearly, can almost feel the fingers: a muscular friend at school gripped me around both biceps and said, 'You're a fucking smartarse, Jack, and no one likes a smartarse. One day, your tongue's going to make you serious trouble.'

I can't remember if I had the courage to meet his gaze at that moment, but I have always known his description was correct — unlike, so far at least, his ominous prediction. My big mouth didn't seem to worry Maria. She simply mocked me for talking so much, saying so many idiotic things and going on at length about things she thought I knew nothing about. She accused me (only half-jokingly) of hypocrisy if I criticised a 'commentator' for 'commenting', though I in the same tone defended my right to unmocked private and unsolidified remarks on any subject, compared to the roped-in, wheeled-out bovines on TV. I explained the abuse of the Hindi word 'pundit', supposed to refer to people of knowledge. I defended what I saw as my unique attitude to points of view: that I wanted to hold weak opinions, to represent those who had not yet made up their minds, to articulate in favour of the uncertain, to fill this niche which The Media (from time to time I might have got carried away, I freely admit it) had for too long neglected.

It was a game between us. She'd pretend to pretend to scoff, and I'd pretend that I thought she was genuinely scoffing and pretend to pretend to stand up for myself.

Somehow, though, the game became incorporated into Maria's general dissatisfaction and, once Maria began to develop her hideously overblown Goals and Aims, the joke she had sustained throughout our good times became a deep criticism of all that had formed me. Where Maria had spread blame with a laugh, a joke about oh-so-serious holders of views on whether Inheritance or Environment was the Primary Cause in producing the Person, she now seemed to believe in what she had previously mocked.

How could I possibly respond in other than an apologetic manner? I apologised both for my genetics and my upbringing. I should have been taller and I should have had better posture. I apologised for places I'd visited by chance, and those I'd set out to see. I apologised for people I had intentionally or unintentionally conversed with. I expressed regret for previous friendships, those I maintained which made me worse and those which would have improved me had I not failed to maintain them. As with every other thing I said or did during the months of our love's decline, these words were misconstrued as not serious enough a response.

Maria's frowning, or so I imagine as we drive along the lightless highway approaching midnight. She says nothing.

Still, in my current mood, when ideas happen in my head I have to say them. I have to. I become afraid that otherwise they'll be lost. Perhaps. I have concluded that, were I to remain silent, I would unfairly deprive those in my company of the opportunity to share my ideas, to appreciate them. I honestly believe people like to hear me speak.

As soon as we are alone, I start to get these thoughts which must be spoken. Perhaps I should apologise again. To her, I mean. How is it possible not to speak?

Gambit: this car is not mine.

'This car is not mine,' I tell Maria. 'It is much larger and faster than mine and it has bench seats. Picture it, will you? It's a very spacious American family car. Plush, real leather upholstery. The brochure's in the glovebox, if you'd care to look. Note the happy couple, all smiles, so happy to have such a roomy vehicle.'

I believe I have maintained a lightness in my tone, contrasting with the external heaviness, the weight of the smoke in the air. Maria, not unusually, interprets otherwise.

'Forget it, Jack,' Maria says. 'I'm not fucking in a Volkswagen. And I'm not fucking you.'

'It's not a Volkswagen,' I insist. 'It's a Renault. It is at least a medium-sized vehicle.'

'Whatever.'

It is, I suppose, fortunate that even as I began to speak I felt ambivalent towards this unnoteworthy attempt at seduction. Otherwise, Maria's dismissive attitude might have hurt my feelings. Also, I recognise that I'm not much of a gambit man: none of mine has ever been successful. I'm no good at planning relationships, no matter how short-term. I've heard of others who can carry off the most unlikely allures with simple repeated statements: 'I can't help myself; I just really love women.' Perhaps it's all in the delivery? How else can you account for the interminable successes of hairless-chested TV stars who cannot get her out of their minds, God knows they've tried ... how they've tried. And the charismatic men in movies who utter captivating lines with such naturalness you hardly notice the cinematography: 'How beautiful you are in this light; I was forgetting how impossible it should be between us. I've forgotten all about impossibility.'

Promises alone fill cinemas with nodding people who can only look forward, never remember, paying amnesiacs who have learnt to foretell love from the superimposition of two portraits on the one poster. If anything, unlikelihood is a predictor. Should I hold off for a while and then say to Maria, 'How inconceivable that we should find ourselves together like this, how unlikely that of all the couples in the world, we should have this chance!'

What would Maria say to this? Odds on she'd remind me that impossibility is unlimited in its pervasiveness. And once again I'd be making debating points: come on, Maria, what about the suspension of disbelief by cooperative co-travellers, the reaching of situational understandings? How is it we might set out to be in a no-place, a utopia where we might live the unimaginable?

Of course, I've already imagined this scene, with its atmosphere of temporary desperation, desperate temporariness. It lies somewhere ahead, this side of Adelaide. The question is in the car now. I have caused awareness, and

Maria only has to speak one word to produce the scene. Not even a word. The merest gesture of agreement.

But not even I believe that we could ever resemble the happy couple in the brochures. Maria's agreement, she lets me know by breathing, is not foreseeable.

She sighs irritably and the car is silent as before. When it comes to ideas, probably I should spend a little more time on the development phase. Not much more time, just long enough to consider possible reactions, to protect myself, to shore up the plan, to cover against rejection. In accordance with Maria's advice, I do my best to forget it, however temporarily.

There are plenty of other things to think about. New South Wales is on fire. The nation is burning, as though to assist me over Maria's rebuff; Australia conflagrates to my short-term benefit. Maria's annoyance also helps. I mean, if she's not going to bother pretending my suggestion was a joke, how can I remain hurt? How can I regret doing or saying anything to annoy Maria if she actually does get annoyed with me?

Even so, there is no clarity. I can't explain my ambivalence. I can't explain why Maria's calm — her exterior certainty — solves nothing in my head. Indignation never touches a lover's good manners and the converse too is true, that her amity cannot soothe my own foul demeanour. So when she is annoyed, when I do challenge her lightness, even if I feel as out of control as when I was an adolescent in producing her response, I

119

cannot regret it. I only regret my poor planning, poor idea development, try to premeditate with a wider view to consequences, phrase later attempts better.

Still, I thought this idea was sweet, nostalgic even.

I'm so bloody glad that human thought is impervious, is what I'm thinking, with a little smile to myself. All those hundreds of miles ahead and I'm already beyond the pale.

'We're the buddies in an appalling buddy movie,' I say. 'We're hopelessly mismatched. We're thrown together by circumstance in a small car driving through a disaster zone. At the end we'll have learnt something about people and will stop to make love.'

She glances at me with what could be a sneer — a very faint, curling smile. It's an expression I remember without sickly sentiment, like coming home to all the bad things.

She could be retrained, I think, to avoid pulling faces like that. Politicians and sportspeople are coached to maintain agreeable visages, not to respond to external influences such as criticisms or difficult questions, let alone mere hypothetical film scenarios. And that was a reasonably cute one, harmless and cute. I could have cast her as vampire or machine, as something both less and more than mortal. I could have imagined all the human qualities onto myself, the capacities to laugh and persist, to strategise and adapt.

Maria says: 'When we decided to do this drive, I thought it was going to be only you and me, two people. But now we're driving along with all this baggage, the ashes of our affair...'

I must look especially hurt at this, for she adds: '...or, if you must, relationship — the battle between your ego and your libido over how to be with an ex-girlfriend.

'Now you've even got me talking about myself like I'm this objective person surrounded by your various madnesses, patiently allowing you to do whatever you need to do while I deal with it with sympathy and responsibility. You're so sensitive to the roles supposedly allocated to you, the way you're structured into your ways of living, but what about the role I'm supposed to have around all your self-analysis? I'm to be the listener, am I?

'It reminds me of this friend who'd always invite difficult people to her house in the hope of engineering conflict. She no doubt thought of herself as a student of human nature. Fucked if I'm going to sit in this car and learn about difficult relationships.'

Maria really ought to learn more self-control, Maria who believes herself to be so good at organising and at planning her life. Maria of the Projects has become Readable Maria. She can't help but communicate. She's Maria Who Confesses. Maria who'd be a crappy politician or sportsperson, who, despite her characterisation of me as negative, has negativity engraved from chin to forehead.

Maria who'd be the 'before' photo in advertisements about how certain breakfast cereals or sweet biscuits can make one happy. She'd effortlessly earn captions like 'Sour? Sweeten up with Brand Y!' or 'Brand Z could plant a smile even here ... well, maybe not here...' Formerly lovable Maria who values steadiness and steadfastness, reliability and progress, yet who has altered as tangentially and chaotically as anyone.

I form some other words in my head, then I speak again.

'For a month, every hour I imagined you with him, this new boy. I let myself think about it,' I say. 'Walking hand in hand, laughing, at ease, talking, fucking. This was my picture of the two of you, a laughing couple in the distance whose words cannot affect the depth of their happiness. In my mind, I saw you and him in many settings: cities, along the beach, at airports, in restaurants, hotel lobbies, shopping centres, in dim private rooms or intense Australian sunshine.'

Maria's driving, facing forward. I'm looking at her, turning to the road, turning back to her.

'Don't tell me this,' she says. 'There's no need. I don't want to know this much about you any more.'

'I've never seen him, he's completely faceless for me,' I continue, 'yet he didn't need an individual identity to stand in the centre of my mind. He changed from moment to moment, as if to fit the mood. I saw your face, Maria, and someone else with you. I watched quiet images in which you leaned towards each other and whispered inaudible insights, where you flung your arms around each other, where you seemed almost absurdly natural together. Although I knew it shouldn't trouble me, to be a person not in the picture, I let myself follow these thoughts for as long as they occupied me. I suppose I decided to let them go on, to see where they led, but they rarely finished. I'd see the two of you, you and this anonymous man, from morning to night.

'This failed completely as a jealousy control strategy.'

Maria laughs.

'It doesn't sound strategic at all,' she says. 'Jack, you've got to leave yourself alone, you've got to give yourself a chance. And don't put all this on me. It's not that easy for me either.'

'You did everything wrong,' I say. She can be malicious. Believe me. I could list examples like this for hours. My openness, her judgment. Almost simultaneously we wind down the windows. This has little effect. It is so hot; even with the windows open the night air is still.

Maria sighs. 'I can't say anything to that,' she concurs.

We are silent again. I have temporarily expelled this lascivious new boyfriend, nameless and undescribed but still somehow attractive, apprehensive as they grow to know each other.

Thin clouds hover like a portico in front of the moon.

'Look,' I say, changing the subject. 'Cheap, tacked on, inappropriate, façadist.'

'Look, Jack,' she says, dragging me backwards with point-scoring tenderness. 'You fall in love at the drop of a hat. Your normal state is heartbroken.'

'You can put anything into words except your own life,' I say, crossly. 'Terrific.'

For some reason, she gives a single laugh: 'Ha!'

I wait for elucidation, but she gives me nothing further to react to. This is the problem with conversation ... with

Maria. Still cross, I lean back, pull Maria's camera from the back seat and photograph her.

'This is Maria driving.'

Click, wind.

'Here she steers slightly to the left, following a slight curve.'

Click, wind, click, wind. The whirr of the film advance mechanism after each shutter depression represents her camera's mild assent to my belligerence. Maria makes no comment. Very restrained, I think, circumstances or no circumstances.

'I only want to remember the bad times,' I claim. 'It'll make me feel better about the future.'

She still makes no comment. Fair enough. I take two or three more shots, but we both know I cannot continue without her reaction. These photographs will be grey, I believe, but they may show a dark, ghosted Maria, glaring, pouting, or the whizz of long-exposure car headlights provoking a hint of eucalypts behind a shadow which is Maria's lightless absence. She may see her doubled or tripled profile, blurred in oncoming lights, staring ahead towards Adelaide.

'Don't forget to send copies,' I say, my voice snapping out more intensely than I intend. I am unable to break my mood.

'Include a stamped addressed envelope, sweetheart,' she mutters.

We pass through another smouldering forest. The whole state must be burning. Our headlights catch a mob of kangaroos. For a moment the road becomes an outlandish theatre production: roos in the spotlight, the moon backlighting bare forest. The animals freeze like a coat of arms, stare along the road towards us. The danger of our approaching car, now braking rapidly, must be processed at a certain instant, and they race into the trees all at once, compressing and uncoiling. As they leap off amongst the trees, the moon and our car's progress contribute to a strobe effect. The encounter finishes, the last beast bouncing out of sight. The beauty of the image changes our moods in an instant — how could it not? — but neither of us speaks.

Ashes blow along the now bare stage in front of the car. Approaching headlights reflect in a mirage. The road curves; when we straighten, the mirage is gone. We continue to drive in silence through the forest. Here and there a tree stump continues to burn. Every sound seems related to the fire, becomes interpretable as the explosion of branches; sudden emissions of steam as sap or gum impede the fire for mere milliseconds. Ash adheres to our foreheads. We're both perspiring. Maria arches her back to stop the shirt sticking to it, to stop her shoulders sticking to the vinyl seat.

My cotton shirt is soaked through too. I think about removing it, holding it out the window to dry or cool it a little, but no longer know whether it is acceptable to strip down in front of my ex-girlfriend, or how she may misinterpret this. Or, it occurs to me also, I am being careful not to appear too desperate to return Maria's thoughts to our discussion of carnality, to the surviving possibilities of reunion.

There is, it seems, enough time to think through every potential variant, and I'm not convinced this is to the good.

I open a bottle of lemonade. It hisses violently and fizzes over my hand, trickling along my wrist. I hold it out the window for a moment. Maria looks across with a brief frown, then back to the road. When the lemonade settles, I offer it to her, and she takes a mouthful and passes it back. My hand dries fast and remains sticky. Black storm clouds move across the sky. The moon disappears behind them.

'Good idea, this trip,' I say. 'It's not often we get an opportunity to spend time.'

I smile benignly, so that when Maria looks across again she cannot tell if I'm serious or sarcastic. I'm not sure I know myself.

It begins to rain big heavy drops, black with soot. All around, the hissing coals burst into flame. Why is this? The windscreen wipers flick back and forth like maddened nightbirds. Maria stares through them, straight ahead.

The moon follows like a fool as we race along.

*

Eventually, we're both too tired to drive further. There are town lights ahead.

'Cowra,' she explains. A town famed for its war memorials. 'We can stop there and I'll take photographs in the morning.'

'It is the morning, just.'

'The real morning.'

We drive into the centre of town and once more I recall the feeling of late-night arrival during childhood holidays: long drives through darkness which emphasise the brightness of country or beachside towns, blinking awake to emerge from a car into the humid or suddenly cool or salty air.

Entering Cowra we pass a range of similar-looking motels, some set above the road, some abutting it, some sunk into hollows. They promise telephones and air conditioning and television, exotic or home-cooked food. It is said that there is something distinctive or at least interesting in Australian motel architecture, those that boast of luxury and amenity, those that promise homeliness, those drawing historical association from the soil on or near which they stand. I don't know about distinctiveness, but this categorisation reflects the choice of three types we face on Cowra's broad main street. Luxury, indicated by tubes of coloured light and an elevated setting, costs thirty dollars more than history with its incandescently spotlit motel names and bronze-look statues. In the end, conscious to decide before running out the other side of town, we opt for domestic simplicity, fluorescently lit except for a black square on the vacancy sign which must cover the word 'NO'.

We ring a bell at the office entrance. After a couple of minutes, a squinting man opens the door. He is tying his dressing gown as we enter.

'Lucky to wake me,' he grumbles, 'I'm a pretty deep sleeper.'

'Sorry about that,' I say.

'But of course you're welcome, and I hope you enjoy your stay. Just the one night is it? No forms to fill in here. That's a matter of principle.'

Maria requests a twin room. We receive a key to a room in the middle of the row, and I park the car diagonally at the front door.

*

Television sound comes at us through the walls. We are lying on the unbreached single beds in our clothes, with the width of the room between us. A television is set on the opposite wall, midway between the beds.

She switches it on and there's a momentarily blare of music until she mutes it, then she channel surfs past several unwatchable sports: ice hockey, motorcycle racing, truck colliding. No channel has clear reception. There's a drama.

'I'm going to get ready for bed,' I say.

It's not the sort of motel that has white towelling bathrobes, with or without logos, so after I brush my teeth, I strip to my underwear and climb into bed. Maria goes and returns from the bathroom in a long T-shirt. I'm trying not to look at her. She's too attractive. We settle into the beds, our propped heads facing the TV. It's hot, so we're each under sheets and have thrown the quilted-look bedspreads onto the floor. There's a movie about a couple who start out as friends, are determined to remain friends, but inevitably fall in love. Maria, with the remote control, clicks the sound back on.

'Corn,' she says, 'yet somehow engaging.'

I say: 'Says the woman in the motel in Cowra at one in the morning.'

We watch the movie, despite the occasional fall-offs in picture quality. As it approaches its finale, we hear people arriving in a neighbouring room: even later than us. Before long (even before the kissing scene), raised voices come at us through the motel wall. Too clear, as though we are within the same house.

'It's so fucking hot!'

'Will you shut up, you imbecile.'

'Leave the fucking fridge open, I said.'

'Look, turd, it's not going to cool the fucking room. It just shits me.'

'It fucking will. It stands to reason. It's got cold fucking air in it and the room's hot. It's going to fucking cool it down.'

'You're stupid. I wish you'd stayed home. Or I wish I had, and you'd visited your idiot brother on your own. Close the fucking fridge. Close it!'

I hear a struggle. I don't know the outcome, but after a while there is a crash, then the sound of two people giggling, then silence. I sit up and Maria announces, 'Our glorious neighbours.'

'If this goes on, I'll bang on the wall,' I say. This would at least alert them to the motel's excellence in sound transmission.

The front door slams, a car door opens and slams shut, the motel room door slams again. Thoughtful people. I'm imagining them in my head.

*

Sam tosses his hat across the room and it lands on the collapsed stack of pirated cassette tapes near the small portable stereo.

'I'm home!' he announces, mock-joyous, although he has merely been out to the car to collect his guitar and cigarettes. He steps and gestures, uncoiling his left hand towards her. He is both the Kelly boys, Gene and Ned. Luisa says nothing to him. She smirks at Sam's dance, but she refrains from telling him out loud how lacking in grace he is. She could have said something, but his moves weren't that bad. She would have been lying. Instead, she talks to someone else. She picks up the telephone receiver and presses some buttons on the handset without looking. Someone answers. She hits the speaker button.

'Hello?'

Sam hears a middle-aged man's voice crackling through the speaker phone.

'Is Jim there?'

'No one here called Jim. What number did you want?'

'Sorry.' Hanging up, she quarter-smiles across the room at Sam.

'Minimal nuisance calls,' she says.

Her upper lip twitches. She's hopeful always, but Sam never has acknowledged her tactical wins and he doesn't now. Instead, he grunts. He walks across the room to the TV and switches it on. He is agitated. He brushes a pile of tourist brochures onto the floor and, as he suspects, the remote is underneath. Luisa sits on the sofa. She folds her arms and waits for the television to clarify, sound then picture. Sam picks up the remote and holds down the 'Channel Up' button. Each show appears momentarily and is gone. He can't find anything to watch. He presses other buttons. He switches rapidly from channel to channel trying to find something, flicking between three then two programs, an elimination process without rules, pausing for thirty seconds at one point to watch a car advertisement featuring an Australian actor.

'You fucking imbecile,' he says to the ad. 'Isn't he a fucking imbecile?'

He switches back and forth between his two remaining options a few more times without waiting for Luisa's response, which, in any case, she doesn't give.

Eventually he settles and they watch a 1960s American situation comedy. At a background table, six tuxedoed extras pretend not to react as the anti-hero stumbles over a chairleg and falls on his face. The laugh-track is not so restrained. Luisa has become overly conscious of the laugh-track and tenses every time it activates. Her lips are sometimes pursed and sometimes pouting, but Sam is intent on the TV and never looks at her. At the first ad break, he takes a softpack of tailor-mades from his shirt pocket, pulls a cigarette free with his lips and lights it. There are two male characters in American comedy: one who says, 'Ladies, I have the world's largest penis, ladies' and one who says, 'I just can't get it up.' This program's anti-hero is of the second type, and it doesn't matter that the beautiful woman with her hair set like cedar veneer has failed to notice his attraction for her as she purrs through her naive-suggestive one-liners. Neither Sam nor Luisa laughs at any of the jokes. There is a second advertisement break as Sam lights the second cigarette from the butt of the first, and another as the fourth consecutive cigarette burns towards his fingers.

While Sam smokes, while the anti-hero's expressions of love are misinterpreted as clumsy gestures of helpfulness, Luisa is very slowly losing colour, her red fixity bleaching out as she tenses, the capillaries withdrawing from the surface of her skin. Changes in the editing rhythm mark out one advertisement from the next. The laugh-track sounds from time to time, occasionally accentuated by a rich resonant male laugh louder than the others, sometimes by a half-stifled female giggle as someone purportedly gets the joke too stupidly late. Luisa reaches to her right across to the telephone table, pulls the flaccid carnation from its vase of putrid water beside the telephone and swings it by its limp stem into Sam's forehead. Sepia petals fall over his shoulders, settle down the back of his collar. An alga-rich droplet slides down the ridge of his nose. Sam does nothing, just keeps staring at the TV. He hadn't even tensed for the moment of contact. Luisa lets the stem fall onto the two-tone brown carpet. She stretches her feet out and pulls Sam's guitar towards her with them. She finds a pair of scissors in her make-up bag and, with a brief glance at Sam, snips through one of the strings of his guitar. He reacts this time. He leans across Luisa and snatches at the guitar without bothering to get up, fisting it across the floor until it is in front of him. Then he stamps his foot through it. The noise is terrific, but unrepeatable.

Luisa, who had almost jumped as the wood splintered, tells him, 'Why don't you just leave? I don't want you here. You're pissing me off, too. I'll go back on the train tomorrow.'

She is exasperated and her voice cracks to a higher pitch on the word 'want'. Sam gets up and goes into the bathroom. The front door is the other way. Luisa hears the ring-pull tear, the fizz of beer, the splash of overflowing beer on the tiles. He comes out, switches on the radio and turns off the TV. He sits on the sofa, staring at the green-black television screen. His neck thickens and diminishes as he gulps at the beer. Luisa knows that the beer is slightly too warm. The esky has never worked as promised. Sam is sweating, his biceps glistening and his shirt covered in dark blue sweaty patches. He finishes the beer and throws the empty can under the TV. He gets up again, goes into the bathroom, takes another beer from the esky and returns to switch off the radio. He then starts playing with the air conditioner. Luisa cannot stand the pace at which he moves around the motel room, the scuffling strides and the too-long pauses while he selects which beer can might be the coldest, which radio station best reflects his agitation, or which setting on the air-conditioner will complement his beer. The Roman numerals around the air conditioner dial correspond to nothing measurable. He turns it on full so it pumps freezing cold air around the room.

'It's not that hot,' Luisa tells him, her stretched-thin lips extruding the words like machine-generated pasta.

He sits down and pulls at his bootlaces with his left hand. He is not watching because he is pouring beer down his throat and his eyes are closed. The beer is not as refreshing as in the ad, and the trails down his chin quickly take on a crustiness he has never seen on TV. The right bootlace is knotted. He tugs at it distractedly. Luisa hugs her upper arms to her chest. Her skin has textured into tiny lumps. Although she can see a cardigan across the room she does not get up. Sam's bootlace snaps. He pushes each boot off with the instep of the other. The boots hit the ground with two loud bangs.

Luisa says, 'You're pissing me off, Sam. Your feet stink.'

Sam takes his socks off and hangs them from a tatty piece of rope strung across the front of the air conditioner. When his back is turned to Luisa, he hunches the base of his skull towards his shoulders, as if Luisa might try to spear him in the neck. He throws his boots under the TV.

Luisa gets up, walks past him and opens the window beside the air conditioner. She straightaway receives a powerful whiff of diesel and a blast of truck noise, so closes it again. In the moment the window was open, the room temperature rose marginally, but she is still cold. She takes the cardigan and puts it on. She sits down in the armchair opposite Sam and lights a cigarette. She is staring at his ear. He doesn't say anything. She quickly finishes the cigarette, dropping the butt with its long, still-glowing ash cone into a chipped glass ashtray. She goes into the bathroom and opens a can of creamed sweetcorn from the esky. She stands in the doorway between the two rooms eating out of the can with a fork. She eats quickly, taking small mouthfuls in rapid succession, hardly stopping to chew.

Sam says, 'Shit, Luisa', lies down and pulls a pillow over his head. She takes another couple of mouthfuls standing there. Then she switches off the air conditioner, sits where he had been and switches on the TV with the remote, muting the sound. She finishes the corn and watches the silent TV. It is the second half of a half-hour news broadcast: a foreign air crash with maps of the region and a dotted line leading to the red and yellow point of impact, stock footage of soldiers running and an internment camp full of grim-faced South Asians, some advertisements for cars, a succession of golf-swings and victory air-punches, a list of names of swimmers, soft-drink commercials, twin tottering giraffe calves. She cannot concentrate. She knows Sam is waiting for her in the bed. Perhaps she will go to him and perhaps she will not. This is what Sam is thinking, she believes, although she has gone to him every previous time. She traces the fork around the bottom of the can, gathering the remains into a small, liftable ridge of yellow cream and forks it into her mouth. Finally she walks around to Sam's side of the bed, still carrying the empty can with the fork in it.

He's lying face down. Luisa puts the can down in the doorway and sits beside him on the bed, her knees drawn together.

'I'm sorry, baby,' she says. Sam doesn't say anything, but she sees the tension in the stringy muscles across his back.

She reaches forward and touches him on the shoulder. She can feel he wants to loosen; she leaves her hand resting hesitantly, a little too lightly, on his shoulder blade. Sam remains face down with his head covered by the white-cased pillow. He pulls his left arm from under his chest and straightens it back towards her. Then he lifts his hand over and grips Luisa's thigh.

*

It is not possible to predict where love will appear, though why these neighbours should have it in larger measure than Maria and me is beyond my comprehension. In our twin beds, we are subjected to the noise of their lovemaking. Maria is pretending to be asleep. I know she is not asleep because she is breathing rhythmically whereas she breathes more erratically when she really is asleep. At first, this alarmed me. Now, it is a special knowledge, perhaps one which her new boyfriend has yet to gain — nameless and undescribed but still somehow attractive as he is, apprehensive while they get to know each other, grandiosely thoughtful. Despite his superiority to me in all other facets, I know more about Maria than he does. I will not ask Maria to confirm this, will allow her to believe that I believe in her false slumber.

The neighbours are finally quiet. I soon sleep too. As for Maria, when I wake next morning, she is rasping and uneven in her breathing.

I suppose that most relationships must be ordinary, because that is what extraordinariness is defined against. People must be satisfied with ordinariness, not that this is such a bad thing: an ordinary human relationship does contain a high level of communication, due to the complexity of human language, and desire is another fundamental of human existence, existing everywhere, the question concentrated in every relationship.

Is this what Maria and I had? Ordinariness? Is this what Maria rejected by sending me packing, thus reflecting her lack of understanding of the human? Has she taken this drive to confirm the rightness of her decision? Is her art practice somehow related to her problem with ordinariness, her seeking after the repetition of the art of memory? Or is her photo project a quest for the meaning of memorability, of what she values in relationships? Is Maria chasing not extraordinariness in itself but merely sacrifice, extraordinary or even ordinary?

Hmm, this could be a worthwhile revision. Have I made a lucky escape? Why then am I lying beside her now, intending to spend another day sitting with her, beside her, engaged in complex verbal and non-verbal human language, in a car awash with the question of desire?

Our correspondence reappears in my head, these letters which might have promised ordinariness in all its perfection.

*

*Dear Maria,*

*On a recycled brown-paper bag I found this quote from Coleridge: 'Friendship is a sheltering tree'. So, then, on we go. Enmity is a pine in an Australian hailstorm. Relief is a pecan in autumn. Avarice is a valley line of willows. Enigma is a field of chrysanthemums. Lust is a one-tree plain.*

*Dear Maria,*

*This year I am weakening. I've already changed my drink from scotch to scotch and dry. Then I joined the Labor Party. Now, I admit I love you.*

*Dear Jack,*

*When I open the window, the breeze enters the room.*

*Immediately below, an aluminium can rolls over and over, denting itself (I imagine — I can hear it but I can't see it) against the kerb.*

*Over the other side of the street a dog barks, and someone calls out, 'Hey!' Perhaps the person is talking to the dog and perhaps to another person.*

*Beyond the sound, I can see a room flickering red and blue and green behind translucent curtains. Television land. An aerial gives the game away.*

*Still further, the wind continues to blow. It tears off pieces of conversation and motorcycle noise, wrenches them into the air, hurls them through the window and bounces them around the room.*

*The scene so far is set against, and delimited by, a huge concrete cube. Nothing escapes from this, not a single photon, not a renegade soundwave. The cube is grey and marked with black rectangles.*

*Behind this cube (a building six or seven storeys high), a hill stretches up to the horizon. On the hill, and immediately behind the cube so that it appears to surmount it, is a small, white, flat-based isosceles triangle hooded in red. When a tungsten-yellow rectangle glows just below the triangle's apex, I know you are sitting in your room. I'm glad we can keep an eye on each other.*

*Dear Maria,*

*Disappearing already, huh? (I conclude this after one unanswered telephone call, which rang itself out.) I know about disappearances. Missed news broadcasts, meals down the hatch; ourselves swallowed, engulfed, subsumed into clubs, workplaces, vocations, psychoanalysis, fads, responsibilities, embraces, kisses, orgasms, intellectual disputation, large shirts and the music. Reappear!*

*Dear Jack,*

*If the universe is a kaleidoscope, we are one instantaneous phase, shifting grains of light which might overlap for an immeasurably small time or else miss each other completely. Everything is luck, and why not?*

# DAY TWO

W<small>E LIE IN</small> our beds as the day once more overheats. Maria wakes soon. I go into our motel bathroom to urinate. On the wall high above the cistern someone has scratched a limerick, still visible despite a weak attempt at over-painting:

> *There was a Greek woman whose clitoris*
> *was exactly the flavour of licorice.*
> *Her sexual need*
> *was pure aniseed.*
> *She would've melted the wings off of Icarus.*

I finish, and call Maria to show her the rhyme.

She reads it. 'Ah, where are all the great women poets?'

'America?' I suggest. 'Victoria? New Zealand? Paraguay, awaiting translation?'

'I was being rhetorical,' she says, and leaves me to wash my hands with the sickly pink, floral-scented motel mini-soap.

We eat fruit for breakfast, and Turkish bread. I make bad instant coffee with the kettle which ends up sliding in a small pool of water. I mop the water with a hand towel. I am making the best use of resources.

\*

On this journey so far, Maria has sat in the car beside me. In her bag, she carries certain 'papers' (I employ quote marks because some of these, perhaps all, are not of paper but are actually documents composed from various plastics), which I have not seen but which I know to be there. In my right arse pocket, I have similar documentation. At certain moments, members of the New South Wales police service (now renamed police 'force', due to governmental reclamation of duress) bounce radar beams off our car. They do not record the results. We are unaware of these events. From time to time on our journey we transact business. A cash machine prints a receipt. Information about these transactions will be presented in accurate or distorted form to the Australian Taxation Office. Our names will or will not be recorded. At times, I will transact by presenting one of my papers, a rectangle which identifies me as a person worthy of credit. Further information will be generated and will pass through a machine which notes only that these transactions are not noteworthy.

There is perhaps nothing insidious about any of this, or nothing more insidious than all the other habits and arrangements of western civilisation.

I'm expounding on all this (except the lack of insidiousness, which would detract from the drama of it all) to the motel manager as I pay our bill. He has struck me as a person who would appreciate such conversation. Maria is picking up and replacing pamphlets setting out the area's attractions. She walked away from the counter the minute I started engaging the manager. He is listening to me, but also going through the routine.

'Did you make any phone calls?'

'No, but didn't you already know that? Can't you tell that somehow?'

'Of course I can, but it's easier just to ask you. You looked too exhausted when you came in to try any scams.'

'I'm not much of one for con-jobs.'

'I don't believe you,' he says.

I try to look insulted, but he laughs. I sense Maria grinning. I'm not going to turn around. This would be a victory for her.

'I'm pretty good at judging character. I used to be a student of literature,' he begins. 'I was at Melbourne University, which in those days was the place to study. Probably still is. I dropped out though. I read too much Kafka for my own good. It got to the point where I'd only answer to "Franz". This really bugged my mother, who'd fought with Dad for a month over what name to call me.

No matter, I thought. That's your problem, not mine. Since then we've largely reconciled, and she and Dad occasionally come to stay here in the low season. This Kafka thing was the turning point of my life, and I was too young really for such a major digression. The effects continue, though in much muted fashion. Sometimes even now I imagine that I am living in Franz Kafka's head, that I am a young fucked-up student all over again. You know about his diaries?'

'I've heard of them,' I say. I probably had; they sounded as though they ought to exist.

'Well, let me tell you about them, because they're marvellous. Flawed, but marvellous. The flaw comes from the love with which they were assembled, from too much respect. This is the kind of flaw you can forgive, but it still affects you. In the early 1960s, Kafka's good friend Max Brod edited an edition of the writer's diaries. He was careful, a good reader, a fine editor, but his edition left out anything likely to cause embarrassment or offence to anyone still living. I remember how Brod put it. I must have looked at these sentences a hundred times: "In several (rare) cases, I omitted things that were too intimate, as well as scathing criticism of people Kafka certainly never intended for the public. Living persons are usually identified by an initial or initials."

'Reading the diary back then, I had no idea how frequent these omissions were — you can't tell how much absence there is, how much has been left out; you can only read what remains in good faith, but Brod's disclaimer had taken my faith away. Its honesty shook the entire grand project. The reader no longer knew how reliable or creditable the editor's word was, only that he'd intervened. The alternative would have been to expose the living and the dead to all varieties of shame, for the reader to cringe on behalf of the living and to wish that Kafka had had the benefit of a sensitive editor. Obviously this is an insoluble conundrum for all editors.

'Although some sense of Kafka's waiting and unexpressed disappointment remained, I imagined the diaries to have been big enough for ten volumes instead of two. I read the two volumes and tried to picture in my head the hundreds of pages chopped out, kept from me, all Kafka's lustful thoughts and sensual acts. Can you imagine that? All this lust, just waiting for expression.

'I run a motel, so I don't jump to conclusions about people's relationships — ha! that's something you really can't afford to do, not if you want repeat custom — but you and your woman friend seem okay. I'm a good judge of character, as I said, I just don't exercise judgment too much. I mean, maybe your relationship is lousy; if so, don't tell me, don't disillusion me, I don't need to know that.'

He pauses, but neither Maria nor I confirms or denies. He continues, 'I dropped out of university to become the lustful Kafka. It took me ages to get over it. Now, I try not to think about storage systems for credit card records more than bureaucratically necessary.

'Your credit card is fine, by the way. It's not on my list.'

'I'm pleased to hear it,' I tell him. I've got my pen ready to sign the print-out, which he is now holding in his left hand but does not relinquish.

'Can you imagine what it was like for me then? Think about it in this way: Kafka's entire entry for a day, for 6 November 1917, was "Sheer impotence". He was having difficulty with his writing, couldn't make a sentence. I'd have liked to see his manuscripts. I imagine him writing and rewriting the same sentence over and over, crossing it out, writing it with the words slightly reordered, his page looking like a ploughed field. In my mind, though, the writing difficulty only reflected his unpublished thoughts, writing pressed hard into the notebook so that in places it would have ripped, blotched ink all over, regrets a centimetre thick for each week. Love can be very damaging, in my experience.'

'That's really sad,' says Maria, who for once hasn't left me alone to receive the lesson and has come over to the counter. 'You poor man.'

He adds, to reassure us, 'Thank you. Doesn't have to be though; I'm sure it isn't for quite a few people.

'Anyway, I couldn't stop thinking about this, Kafka's damage, stringing out the stories of his heartbreak, his love which travelled out into the streets and returned home empty. His love for these women denoted by initials. A lonely person amasses philosophy, can hold numerous parallel theories for personal phenomena. In those days I was not so self-aware, wouldn't even have called myself lonely, although clearly there is no other word for it. For myself, I foresaw marvellous relationships with the women in my classes, none of which ever occurred. Instead, all my ideas about relationships which failed to occur, all my bottled-up frustration, went into Franz. It went into me being Franz. What can I say? Pain supports itself.

'I kept a diary, added to each day, and began to consider myself a writer. Of course, I'd written nothing but a couple of very short stories and the diary. The stories seemed full of power to me at the time, and I remember the surge of adrenaline as I wrote this scene or that. I now know no one but me could draw their meanings from them. I admit readily that mine were poor imitations of Kafka's own writings. My stories portrayed the agony in full, but were short on character and setting. Thus wrote a sympathetic lecturer in the English department. When these hesitant attempts at creativity led to nothing, I imagined that I suffered an additional pain, of writer's block. I continued to attend to the business of being an up-and-coming young scholar, socialised with the appropriate senior academics, attended the appropriate conferences, sometimes gave gently challenging readings of small extracts from this or that modernist novel.

'The writer's block was something else, I now conclude, a different order of damage. At the university, I tried to live through Kafka's undescribed or unconsummated loves, and fully believed I imagined relationships as he imagined them.'

He's waving our unpaid motel account for emphasis. I notice that I have been unconsciously following it left and right with tiny movements of the pen, as though I could sign

147

it in the air. Maria's leaning over the counter towards him, and she is moved. This also makes me angry, or jealous.

'In my versions, though, disturbed by Brod's diary deletions, skin was everywhere, always touching or near enough to touch. This, I think, was what finished me off.'

He reaches under the counter and withdraws an old exercise book, a kitsch photograph of a lake and mountains scene on the cover. He passes it to Maria.

'Have a look, if you like.'

She opens it and we begin to read. The first page is headed 'Kafka's Diary: Complete'. The motel manager, meanwhile, has pressed the credit card bill onto the desk, awaiting my signature.

*

The glimpse of a woman's flesh is like a story that has to be told. The pale, blue tinge of wrist, the venous neck which hints at the depth of collarbone, the firm calf seen for an instant as a gust tugs at her dress seam, all these promise an unfolding. From a piece of skin the size of a small visiting card, one tricks out the entire body, allowing for the darkened and lightened areas, those covered or part-covered in hair, the folds and tightenings, indentations and extrusions, the muscled and fleshy expanses. When I see my darling M, she inspires me in this manner. Each exposure stimulates the imagination, and if only this impetus produced literature we would all be upraised.

Not so recently I gave up writing. I am just now attempting a few words of a new beginning. 'Gave up' is not the correct phrase, but 'was unable to continue' is not right either. Shall I say, 'Writing was withdrawn from my list of possible activities'? But then, this is as though I have a list wherein each entry has like value, whereas writing outstrips any activity I could imagine. For the sake of brevity, let us agree I wrote nothing, and no writing was produced by me.

If she arrives from the west, she is having an affair. If she arrives from the west by carriage, her love is for a military man; if she arrives on foot, he is a civilian. If she arrives from the east, M wants only me.

Cause and effect, cause and effect, as the scientists say. The effect is the stillness of my pen. The cause, well, I have had a most disturbing experience. A visitation.

If she arrives from the east, she loves me and will seduce me today. She will remove her coat and greet me with a kiss on the cheek, as is our custom, but at the same time she will drop her hands to my belt buckle and pull my belt from my trousers with a single action. This is not her customary behaviour. Her lips move, lift and relax in an instant, as though of their own volition deciding against a smile. I will inhale suddenly. My trousers will fall to my ankles. It is not a film with faulty focus and slowed-down action. My trousers will fall heavily.

I was once a soldier, my comrades shot to pieces around me. Still I could write, avoiding their last thoughts... Now

I can justify nothing, not a word worthy of publication. I am ashamed to expose my vulnerable thoughts.

If she arrives from the west, she will stay only briefly, and I will not encourage her to stay longer. I will not offer tea. I will avoid her question on the progress of my novel. I will not ask after her ailing father. If she arrives on foot, I shall act stiffly; if by carriage, I will be dismissive. I do not like the military, and I do not regard her affairs with the military as deserving my patience.

There is a story from India of a man who, to prove his devotion to a particular god, slices his head off at the shrine. The man's best friend following him into the shrine is so shocked that he too cuts off his own head. The first man's wife enters the shrine to search for her husband, finds two bodies and two heads. Distraught, she appeals to the deity for help. The god reassures her that if she places each head on its body, he will heal the two men; the god hasn't wished for this sort of sacrifice. Sure enough, as the woman places each head on a body, the men are reanimated. In her grief, though, she has mixed the heads around. Which one is now her husband? Do not agonise on it for even one hundred pages. I wanted her to know I was hers. Now I must tell her another story.

From the east, and her cold hands move straight up under my shirt, beneath my undershirt, sliding through my chest hair, sparse though it is.

'Warm,' she will say, and I will begin to unbutton her blouse.

I will whisper, 'I've been waiting so long' or a similarly inadequate tenderness. Her skin will never have seen the sun and will be so pale. There will be blemishes, little pink pinchmarks from the drawstrings in her underclothing.

'Mm,' she will mumble, leaning towards me, arching her breasts towards my long-willing hands. 'You are so warm, so nice.'

Recently I attended a symposium characterised by a proliferation of slips of the tongue. These slips followed a particular pattern: missaid word, 'er', correct word. For example: 'I walked along the hairway, er, hallway.' Most delegates placed no additional stress on the correction. That is, it would be inaccurate to write the sentence thus: 'I walked along the hairway, er, *hall*way.'

What is a hairway? Does this male delegate's neologism refer to female genitalia, for instance? Surely! It is ironic that such a slip occurred in the reading of a paper concerning psychoanalysis, that new science which delights in discovering meaning in such moments. Ironic is not the word. Perfect is the word.

Somewhere, in another account, I will write: 'A slip of the tongue means smooch.' (Regrettable, regrettable, despite my enjoyment of 'French' kissing.)

My subsequent behaviour has been, I confess, at least a temporary appeasement of this ego-denying aspect of my character. To fail to write, in these circumstances, has been absurd but also (and moreover) a kind of tragic absurdity in which I cast myself as the puppet of technological determinism.

From the west, if she arrives, I will walk with her along R Avenue and feel as ill at ease with her as I do for the moment with my work. It is obvious that although I feel a warmth, an attraction, it is not love.

I will utter a condescending nonsense, as, 'You are too young to know what I need from a friendship, too inexperienced to provide it. Do not feel rejected, for I feel an affection for you, but please visit me no more than weekly for the time being.'

I will not mention her unfaithfulness, for she would deny it.

In a limited way, my interests in slips of the tongue and in kissing make me, by way of category, an oral person. Some oral activities I do not find appealing. For example, holding the trapeze in my teeth while a buxom woman in glittering pink sequins and black ostrich feathers leaps from a high platform and catches my legs. I do not enjoy gargling vinegar, but I do not find it more repulsive than someone who enjoys kissing less than I do and pulls back before I am ready.

To be honest, I only heard three slips of the tongue during the symposium. I had been alone, and had taken absinthe and unknown medicines, suspecting them to be deadly. For comfort, I read Browning in translation:

*Rafael thought up a century of English poems,*
*Thought them up and wrote them down in one*
  *book...*

*Did the recipient appreciate this gift till she died?*
*Did she collapse, his English poem woman?*
*Dead, and with his edition beside her cushion,*
*Instead of his spent manhood...?*

Yes, yes, all write for love, though sceptics and disloyal biographers rename it 'seduction'. As for me, I cannot write, therefore I doubt love. So you see, Browning empathises with me. That's why I'm quoting him. He would empathise more if only he would lose his voice. I blame strange encounters and women approaching from all directions.

At the symposium, a second speaker told of lives 'hounded or, rather, bounded by religious routine'.

At the time no one laughed. I felt as though I were listening to a different language, hearing words with meanings not shared by the rest of the audience. The Spanish word for 'oven' (*horno*) means 'erection' in Italian slang, and at this symposium I bit my lip till later, then laughed hard, feeling like an Italian. The religious routine is not the one that has hounded and bounded and pounded me. It's the emotional routine of waiting for her next letter, her next note, her next visiting card, her next absence. Over two years will she dissolve or become more material?

She arrives from the east; we embrace, breasts to chest. One of my hands allows her to lean from me, so I can lean to her, and my other hand supports her middle back, so she cannot move too far. She links her hands behind my neck, and her naked wrists rest against each side of my throat. She moves forward and opens her mouth about my Adam's apple. I slide my hands down and press her buttocks towards me. We are kissing, open-mouthed and uncontrolled.

No military men here, no regimentation, no hierarchy, no rules. This is the power of the imagination. In the collapse of my love for M and of her love for me, and of her parents' regard for her and of their regard for me and mine for them and M's for them, all of this might have been planned by a strategist. All of this might have been plotted out by some hack playwright with no understanding of the muscles of the tongue and no understanding of heartbreak. In other words, a professional writer. In still more words, a writer whose slips are corrected by gangs of editors with their eyes to the public sensibility.

Another symposium delegate mentioned 'a vegetarian, er, veterinarian from Switzerland'.

This was a correction that needed to be made, surely. A Swiss vegetarian! Horror! This is a character who would earn universal opprobrium for his treachery — on what was Switzerland built if not the economies of flesh? — whereas healers of all species are welcome in zoos, circuses and civil life. If slips are confessions of desire (no, damn it, of lust), why had this colleague removed the meat from his delivery? Academic propriety? No such animal, not in my experience.

Yes, love is funny and it's also the disaster of my life. When I am not falling apart, I laugh. When I see myself from even a narrow handspan away, I think, well, with perspective, considering the length of human survival and human procreation, I shall keep a hold on hope. I amuse myself, and I amuse myself in that I see how others may find my situations comical: the woman approaching, the man uncertain; the man uncertain, the woman receding. In myself, without distance, I weep like an adolescent.

In my imagination, I hear Tragedy and Comedy conducting this endless conversation:

‖: Tragedy: We humans, we are all heading
    towards death.
    Comedy: Ah, conceded, but we're alive now! :‖

So what says she to that (and to me)? Am I comforted by it? Is she?

At dinner time in the back room of the local inn, two musicians fiddle songs of heartbreak. On the servery bench sits a loaf of fresh-baked bread. I am eating a stew of meat or meats unknown. ('It's kosher, so don't worry,' says the innkeeper. I've heard that one before.) I pick out the carrots and then the potatoes and swallow them. The meat I save till last. Goodbye, M, if only we had not changed our minds so many times.

Wednesday night, eight o'clock. Meal one, me alone.

*

We stand up from the book.

'Oh dear,' says Maria. 'But look now, you're going okay. You're going well.'

'This is a motel in Cowra,' he says. 'It's okay though.'

'Very homely,' I say, and while I have his attention, 'I should sign. The account.'

He nods. I sign. He doesn't check the signature against the card.

'Good luck,' I tell him.

'It's past the point of luck,' he says. 'I'm up to fate now. I'm entirely fatalistic.'

'Good fate then,' smiles Maria.

We hardly speak as we go out into the late morning sun. I start the car. Cowra is meant to be Maria's prime photographic location, with its prisoner-of-war camp and peace gardens and war memorials. She takes her photographs, but not so many.

She's interested in the Japanese gardens, which commemorate the Cowra break-out, when Japanese soldiers escaped the POW camp. About two hundred and fifty Japanese died, and four Australians. The gardens are rumoured to be a tranquil place to contemplate the horrors of war.

'I really don't get why you're taking all these memorial photos. Why not buy a book?'

'I'm interested in this move from commemoration to nostalgia.'

'Which means?'

'All these lists of men, lists of the dead, lists of soldiers who served. When these lists were made, the men were all around. They were the main people in these towns, the generation working, meeting in the pubs. They were the politicians and the business people. Now the war memorials are something different. They're like a recitation of history, don't have the same connection to the everyday existence of these places.'

'And what will photographing them do?' I try not to be impatient about the photography. Maria's photographs are okay. It's all the baggage she's built around it which is the problem. Maria's photography cannot be unlinked from Maria's unlinking from me.

'I don't know yet. Maybe I'll photograph kids playing around them or something. People with shopping bags. Monuments are strange, impractical things. Everything else has a tightly controlled purpose. I guess war memorials become focal on Anzac Day, practical, like a podium, but then the next day. . .'

'Sounds the same as your other lot, the day-after photos.'

'I guess it's related, but this is about something different, about the displacement of memory onto stone. They may stop people from having to be nostalgic so much.'

'You reckon your photographs won't be sentimental?'

'For fuck's sake, Jack, I haven't taken many of them yet, haven't processed them, haven't decided if I'll process them straight or not, haven't thought about framing or display. I don't reckon anything. I'm just saying I want to take a few pictures.'

'Okay, okay. I was only trying to save you from getting precious about it.'

'You can be a turd when you want to.'

'When I think of the architecture of war memorials, I think of 1950s' politics, that they're instruments for the suppression of difference.'

'Easy to say now.'

'Yes, it's easy. Agreed. I'm saying what my impression is, what my brain does when the subject of war memorials comes up.'

I leave her alone on the subject. Even in this heat, the gardens are pleasant to walk around. She takes her pictures. I meander around, not helping.

'What about that motel guy?' I ask, when she indicates she's done.

All she can say is, 'That poor fellow. Exhausted so young.'

I'm thinking, as we leave Cowra, continue west, my ex-girlfriend sticking to the seat beside me, love takes strange forms.

*

From a perfectly clear morning, there are now a few clouds ahead of us. They look as though they are streaming towards a point on the horizon. A plughole sky. I can picture the result with a semi-fisheye lens and polarising filter: curved horizon, impossibly deep blue sky, red soil, single black or silhouetted bird. I don't suggest it to Maria. Instead, aware of how close she must be to recognising the opportunity herself, I try to put her off.

'That cloud, it's saying something to me,' I announce. I press my palms against the windshield for emphasis.

Maria turns briefly, raises her eyebrows, turns back, makes a minor adjustment in one direction and a minor correction the other way.

'It says,' I say, ' "I meander across the sky and gather up with a whole lot of other clouds until we become the sky. Then we rain for a while. When the others leave I become a boat then a ducky. Later, I obscure the top of a tall building. I wish I were more than an obstruction." '

'That's kind of sad,' comments Maria.

'I think so. You like it?'

'Doesn't look much like your cloud'll realise that rain ambition.'

'Not with any degree of precipitousness.'

Maria groans. I ignore her and change the topic, just as we pass through a small settlement of a few houses and a roadside stall.

'I think I'd like to live in one of these weird little towns that have no reason to continue existing,' I announce. 'Hang in one of the pubs, get to know the shopkeepers, make a few friends who grew up around here. There'd have to be some okay people, wouldn't you reckon?'

'No idea at all,' says Maria. 'Do you think you would?'

'People from Sydney would come and stay. I'd like one of those places with a big verandah all the way round and lots of rooms. It'd be cheap as anything out here. I could live off roadkill and sheep rustling.'

We pull off the road to examine produce at the stall. At that moment a poodle clipped in the lion fashion leaps from behind the stand and begins to bark at us with high-pitched aggression.

'Brooky!' calls a voice, and the dog retreats. A young man peers around a tree. I'm wondering what else is lying in ambush here. 'Don't worry about him. He couldn't muster mosquitoes.' And referring to the produce, a few zucchini and several crates of jam: 'You right there?'

'Fine thanks. Just looking,' I say, as though in a Sydney clothing store.

'Anyhow, take what you like and leave the ready in that tin,' he says. The tin is marked 'Pay here' so I had kind of assumed its purpose. He disappears, to re-emerge with fencing wire, do a lap of the tree, and then, when he's out of sight for a third time, we hear hammering.

Maria says, 'Yeah, sure you'll sustain yourself on flat wombats, Jack. Just like everyone else. But have you noticed that there are butcher's shops in all these places?'

'My optimism would outlast a butcher.'

'No one else's has. They're all resigned to buying things from time to time.'

'You've got no evidence for that at all. Up the north coast, all the hippies are into self-sufficiency and they're not even competent.'

'That's very rich coming from you!'

'Well, that's judgmental of you, and extremely highly moral.'

'I'm not going to let you put shit on me, nor tell me what I think about you. Why should I? You want to check out some real-estate agencies?'

'Yeah, why not? Get a sense of it. You don't mind a quick double-back?'

'It's okay. Your reputation in Sydney would be recast, you know. You'd be Jack who lives out in the middle of nowhere, and people would come and bum off you for months at a time.'

'I'd put them to work mowing the big brown lawns and building little holiday bungalows out of chunks of sandstone.'

I'm claiming the surrounding hills with my hands. We return to the car, without zucchinis, and head back to Cowra. I do park the car outside an estate agency and Maria comes with me to read cards in the window extolling the exceptional micro-climatic fertile perfection of various brown rounded hills. I stare at the photographs and descriptions for a while, but don't feel the capacity to commit myself to this or that property. What would I do? We could ask to see a place to rent, spend the rest of the day getting there, and then? 'Okay, this will do me. I'll stay. You take the car, Maria, and drop it back whenever you're next passing through.'

Despite my inability to commit to ruralism at this time, I'm not sorry to have confessed my momentary dream of country life to Maria. Although I'm fairly certain she'll use it to embarrass me in a minor way at an unexpected moment in the future, I'll be ready and have daydreamed a series of witty recovery responses to show me as charming and sensitive.

At least in expressing interest in moving to the country I must have communicated to Maria that I've got other things to do with my life than mope around after her. I am capable still of astounding her with my ambitions. At such moments I have a sense of my semi-opacity, my personal complexity. I cannot be reduced to a set of met expectations, not even here, gazing into a real-estate agency's soap-streaked window.

But just as I'm in the midst of this particularly warming self-congratulatory moment, I am surprised by a large and hideous man with a three-day growth and a great red weal across his neck.

'Welcome! Bloody welcome!' he growls.

'Thank you,' says Maria. Never assume irony.

He heckles us: 'You looking for your hearts, are you? Think you'll find them in some lovely unspoilt country town?'

For a moment I feel as though my thoughts have become transparent, even this fleeting wish to move house, it being the kind of thought, like murder, that most people never carry out.

'You Sydney folk never got issued with them, so you may as well give up and go home. No one wants you out here. You may as well head straight home now. I was in Sydney, and I'm on the bus to Narrabri tomorrow, and then the day after I'll be home with people who know how to treat people.'

'Sounds like you had a bad time,' says Maria, silent when she should speak and speaking when it can only make trouble.

'At least our people are straightforward in their bad behaviour. You beat up your friend and then you have a laugh. None of this malicious snickering. In Sydney, cops are rotten, general people won't stop to talk for two minutes, and even the bloody barbers, who cost a tenner and ought to be good for an opinion or two, well they're the most vicious of all. And people are so thick. Bloody Neanderthals, the shape of their heads.

'I was in Sydney four hours, intending to stay a good week — why not? it's a famous place — walked here and there, stared in a few shop windows, went to sit for a quarter-hour and get a haircut, and after that I was on the first train out again, one of those express trains with the pointy nose to make them go faster. I wasn't waiting to see what the next day would bring me over there. I value my life too much for that place. Cut-throats, the whole lot of them.

'That express train happened to bring me here. I'm wounded but at least I haven't spent good money in your city. I've been to Melbourne before and it wasn't anywhere near as bad. Maybe I'll even stay here in this town another day or two. At least you get conversation out here.'

'I've actually had several conversations at home in Sydney,' I say, 'and very few since leaving. Only one in fact, and that's with her.'

I indicate Maria with my elbow.

I say, 'I don't buy it that Sydney and the bush are opposite places. And frankly, I'm sick of hearing about it all the time, how things are so hard in the country, or so friendly, or so big, or so real and direct. I just don't think those distinctions exist any more. Anyone, vicious or not, can live anywhere. Everyone in the city and the country watches the same things on the TV, listens to whatever music appeals, chooses friends or who to dislike. The only difference is the coffee, as far as I can tell.'

'Come on, Jack, what about the way country people relate to the land?' puts in Maria. 'Don't you think that difference goes a little deeper?'

'And the distances are greater,' I concede. 'But these things are learnt from experience.'

'You know bloody nothing,' says the man, rubbing at his wealed neck. 'I've half a mind to teach you a lesson with my bare hands, just because you're from Sydney. I'd do it too, but from what I've seen you're probably armed with a fancy weapon, nunchakus or some nasty little handgun, or a cut-throat razor like that murderous barber who took a slice from me.'

'He didn't mean anything offensive,' says Maria.

'He tried to cut my blooming throat!' shouts the man.

'No,' said Maria, pointing at me. 'Him. Him!'

'And I didn't think your injury was so recent,' I say. On reflection, this was not so exculpatory.

'You didn't think at all, is the trouble. But I've had enough now. I don't need any more Sydney lectures. I'm going home to sit down, do nothing but grow a beard.'

He gives a final glare and stalks away.

We get in the car without having entered the real-estate agency. I sense that Maria is disappointed, perhaps with her failure to provide a life for me without her, or, otherwise put, to pack me off. As we wind out of Cowra, Maria does not mention the photography of clouds, despite their continuing beauty.

*

We stop in Grenfell for something to drink. We've now finished most of our Sydney purchases, passing pieces of fruit back and forth in the car between gear changes. I'm very thirsty already. Maria has the camera around her neck, looking more the tourist than a photographer. Too hot, I guess, for all that posing.

We stand at the door of a milkbar, considering whether to sit at one of the two of three remaining formica tables (the third table is occupied by four uniformed police), or to take drinks back to the car. We decide to go in.

'It might be cool in there, you never know,' Maria argues.

I'm easily convinced. Another unnecessary break in the drive; no doubt it will provide another bad cup of coffee.

It is very cool inside, almost chilly by comparison to the instant-perspiration weather outside. We sit down, Maria facing the door, me towards the brown-tiled sandwich counter at the rear.

'If we were athletes, we'd put our tracksuits on now,' I whisper. Maria screws up her forehead in reply. Not sure why I'm whispering, though the policemen are ribbing each other loudly and happily about something or other.

The elaborate brown-bound menus offer the usual egg and chips, sausage and chips, steak and chips choices as well as various Chinese foods: chicken and cashew nuts, fried rice. I consider ordering a malted milkshake, this being a traditional milkbar in the midst of old Australia. I go for lemonade instead. I'm thinking that I should eat something. I say I'm not hungry, but tell Maria I'll have another stale white-bread sandwich anyway. Maria ponders the menu and opts for a faux-sophisticated, pre-packaged Italian ice cream and an iced tea.

'You know what you want?' asks the milkbar person.

'Sure do,' says Maria, Americanesque, obviously affected by this tourist way of wearing her camera.

At that moment, oblivious of us, one of the police stands up and begins to sing operatically.

'We don't need the fucking requiem,' shouts his colleague. 'Just get on with what you're saying.'

'Amen,' says another.

'Amen to you too, you unappreciative buggers. I was merely trying to illustrate a sense of the solemnity of his crime and to prefigure his tragic end. But if your foreshortened attention spans will only bear the abridged version, that's what I'll give you,' says the singer. 'Okay then, there's wool and blood all over the fucking camp. His trousers are red from the thighs down. He's red-handed too, you could say. And his rucksack's practically still trembling with the poor creature's rigor mortis. The grazier's tut-tutting from his horse. Robbie and Tom — know them? — are no doubt gearing up to give him a bit of a hiding on the way back to the station, and I'm the one who sticks to the rigmarole.'

'Constable Fucking Procedure,' mutters the shouter.

'You got me right. So I tell him, "We're going to arrest you for the sheep, you silly coot." He stands up and he's looking like he's going to come quietly. I'm thinking, there's a first time for bloody everything. Nice and easy, hands forward ready for the cuffs. World needs more criminals like that, if you ask me, head bowed, fully cognisant of the crime and his likely incarceration.'

'Dead set, mate,' says the amen-er. 'Next thing you'll be inviting him to the Christmas barbecue.'

'A feller like that, and he admitted anything at all,' agrees the first opera-hater. 'Miracles in our lifetime.'

'Ha! Not fucking likely. No cooperation actually happened. Instead he says, "Okay then, haul me in from here, bloody coppers," and he jumps into the bog. No help from us, I swear, much trouble as that stupid bugger has been over the years.'

The fourth begins to laugh. 'That what you told the coroner, is it?'

Maria raises her eyebrows. I reply with a short nod, agreeing to silence.

'What do you think, John? "Yes, Your Worship, whilst we had no part in the unfortunate man's actions, and had indeed taken all care to prevent self-harm on his part, we had previously consulted on optimum launch angles and velocities." Wouldn't have minded too much, but of course I wouldn't do it. All my friends'd agree to that about me. In fact, many have in earlier circumstances. Besides, as you know from your own extensive training, such courses of action are against the rules. I don't have a rule-breaking bone in my body.'

'The gentleman doth protest too much, methinks,' says John to the other two, who laugh briefly.

'Well,' admits the storyteller, 'we might not have stood by in entire and unreserved idleness.'

More laughter. Maria mouths 'Fuck!' Our food arrives and is not a departure from expectations.

'And the stains on his trousers did require immediate rinsing. But let's agree he pretty much propelled himself. Say seventy per cent self-propulsion. Or at least sixty. Anyway, I genuinely liked him, despite his deep-seated recidivist criminality.'

'Yeah right,' says John.

'John, I was a broken man afterwards. I wept for weeks. I loved him like a brother. You ask anyone. Ask his bloody mother.'

'Right,' says John, smirking. 'I might do that.'

'Sure you will. Dig her up and ask her. And while you're spading away, I'll visit that other accident-prone feller's widow out by the dam, see how well she remembers you. Very nice that one, in all her mourning.'

John adds a syllable to his previous utterance: 'Right-o,' and continues, 'Got me there.'

'Thought I did. But listen to this: the old bugger's hardly in the swim for one second and he straight up disappears. Never refloated. No bubbles, not a single fart.'

'Aw,' says one of the others. 'That's very sad.'

'Crying shame, isn't it?' continues the first. 'Grazier, name of Marston, Mr Marston to you, turns around and trots off without a word. Remaining three of us, grade-A coppers all, staring like frillnecks at the flat brown surface. Nothing there, and Tom's panicking straightaway. He's shaking like a baby and he says, "Jeez fellers, what'll we do about this?" Then Robbie — you blokes know him?'

John assents, but the others shake their heads.

'Big, slow fellow, but smart and about as level-headed as a school boater, decides, "No *corpus delicti*. Looks to me a lot like nothing's happened here." He says, "Hang on" and puts his ear near the ground. "Nope. Nothing. No cavalry." Tom gets excited about this method, squeaks out, "No *corpus*, no forms!" and Robbie says, "Amen. *Requiescat in pace*," and I'm saying, "Anyhow, *homo ovi* fucking *lupus*." Three of us never breathed a word to anyone and no one ever asked. Probably no one missed him.'

'Straight in, no splash?' asks the fourth cop.

'Straight in. What a fucking hero. Makes me want to weep.'

John interjects, 'Weeping's orright. Just don't fucking start singing again. Nellie bloody Melba.'

All laugh.

'We've got to do something about this,' whispers Maria.

'Who'd believe us?' I whisper back.

'I don't know,' she says.

The four policemen wave at the proprietor, who gives a friendly dismissal, and begin to leave noisily and without paying.

Maria jumps up suddenly: 'Excuse me?'

'What can I do you for, darling?' asks John, with a repellent wink.

'Can I take your photos in front of the milkbar? I'm a photographer, very interested in country towns.'

'Heap big photographer for Life magazine, are you? What do you reckon, fellers?'

'I forgot my comb,' says Number Three.

'You look fine,' says Maria, prompting a couple of elbows among the police.

She leads them out and I follow.

They line up in front of the shop window. Maria gets them to fold arms, as she had the firefighters earlier: is this a style developing? The police shift about with masculine unease.

'I like your natural swagger,' Maria announces. 'You guys ought to do a calendar.'

This induces protruded chests and sucked-in stomachs.

'Great!' says Maria. 'Perfect! Hold it right there.'

I'll say this for her: she knows how to get the best out of the men of Australia.

After three or four shots, she says, 'Thank you. I'll send you copies.'

Number One writes the police station address onto a sheet of police notepaper.

'This kind of thing happens to us pretty much every day,' says John.

'Sure it does,' says Maria.

We go back inside for more bad instant coffee, no doubt cut with barley.

The last thing we hear through the open door is: 'And Robbie — you fellers meet him? — he's been posted to Melbourne. He's a fucking detective now. A big metropolitan cheese.'

'Jesus,' says Maria.

'Almost seems like I'm not so bad,' I say. 'All things being relative.'

'Yes, Jack. You'd make a top cop,' she says.

'You going to report this?'

'I guess so. I don't know what else to do.'

'Caption the photos, maybe.'

'Yeah, if I can get them published somewhere.'

'Mm,' I say, trying not to respond to her conditional.

But we have no time to discuss police violence. The door swings open and we get a blast of hot air as someone else comes in.

A voice says, 'Maria? What the hell are you doing here?'

'Peter!' she exclaims.

I turn and see it's one of her rotten friends, one of the less unbearable ones, it must be said. He even remembers my name.

'Jack, how are you?'

'Not as hot as I was.'

This was the worst thing about Maria's friends, always interpreting others' gestures and, worse, purposefully making gestures in order to be interpreted. Before projects, Maria's friends were the worst thing about Maria. My friends are predictably unpunctual, solid, well-suited to a game of pool at any pub in the inner city. They're good too, said the right sorts of things when Maria and I split, took me out to drink and listen to music. Put it this way, my friends are a bunch of good-for-nothings and I love them. Maria's friends: I guess their mothers must like them, but probably wish they'd had more children to dilute the amount of interaction.

'We're just passing through,' Maria says, 'on our way to Adelaide.'

'What's in Adelaide at this time of the year?'

'Just stuff,' says Maria. I add it to my mental characteristics list of the boyfriend — her knowledgeable boyfriend, nameless and undescribed yet still attractive, apprehensive, thoughtful, who can himself be thought of as just stuff.

'I'm doing research into Lambing Flats,' explains Peter, unasked. 'The anti-Chinese riots on the goldfields south of here. Led to the beginning of the White Australia policy, but you probably knew that.'

'Sort of,' I reply. Maria smiles in a way which means she intends to indicate she does know her history of Australian racism.

'It's my dissertation subject. There are some local historians who know heaps, have been very helpful and hospitable. There are some evil bastards too, lend truth to the "a little knowledge is a dangerous thing" saying. I've seen some gruesome souvenirs.

'But I'd actually planned to come up here when the weather was a bit kinder and I'd spent the summer holidays surfing, walking around Sydney late at night, drinking beer in Sydney pubs, going to the cricket, staying well away from the university and from anything resembling hard work, unless you call sunburn hard work. I intended to spend a couple of months doing all the good things. Life intervened, I'm afraid.'

He explains, for my benefit, 'My scholarship runs for another year, so I'm making the most of it by abusing all my privileges.'

'Did you bring Louise up here?' Maria asks. 'I heard you two had got together.'

'Here's my confession, Maria. I'm up here at the moment to escape very recent heartbreak.'

'Oh, you poor thing,' says Maria, who can switch voices when she's with her friends — has the capacity to become all girly, as I'm immediately reminded. 'What happened?'

I'm resenting Maria for putting me through this. She could have offered general expressions of regret. Instead, she shifts across and pats the vinyl seat. There are only three people in the entire place, and us all sitting in the same booth unbalances it completely. And I don't think he would have stayed if Maria hadn't invited him. I think he was going to buy some takeaway.

'Yes, we got together at my birthday dinner party. There were several pairings that night: us, horrible Thomas and Theresa. A couple of others too. But Louise only gave me a fortnight. Then the big stop signal: two flat palms, whoa, whoa, all that stuff. I pleaded with her, I completely humiliated and degraded myself before her. She didn't want it at all, not a moment of mortification of my soul. She wanted a dignified stepping back. Can you picture me? That's not my style at all.'

'Oh dear,' says Maria.

'I sent her flowers, first pink roses and then, when she didn't telephone to thank me, white lilies. I telephoned her, left message after message, recited gorgeous, overblown poems to her answering machine; I wrote her desperate one-liners and ten-page outlines of my case. I bribed her friends with meals and bottles of wine to genuflect on my behalf. They returned with her business-like replies: cooling-off periods, time to reflect. I sent her sarcastic notes, which I don't regret at all. I'm not a used car, am I?

'A fortnight! It's completely out of proportion. I wanted her for five years. She acted as if nothing real had existed between us. She thought we hadn't even started. I didn't cope at all. She was so cold about the whole thing, that's what was strange. I liked her warmth. She's beautiful, she melts a room, I've seen her walk into a room and suddenly everyone's a bit nicer. She's like that.'

'I don't know what to say,' I say.

'Sometimes that kind of beginning-of-relationship intensity's scary,' Maria advises. 'She might realise in time what she's missing.'

'Oh, and Thomas and Teresa are thinking of living together, acting completely married,' he continues, making a vomit signal by pointing into his mouth with an index finger. 'I mean, no offence to you two. Your relationship's different.'

I clear my throat to set him right on that one. Maria looks at me alarmed, gives a little shake of her head. I'm thinking, why shouldn't I? Why should I set aside my personal history for this friend of Maria's, when suppressing it won't in any way alter Maria's behaviour?

'Peter, she's dumped me,' I say. Peter looks disbelieving. 'She has. She's given me the flick. I'm only here because I'm weak and desperate.'

'You bastard,' he says. 'That's a really bad joke.'

'Tell him,' I order Maria.

'It's true,' she says, as sincerely and gently as she can.

Peter looks from Maria to me, a little wildly.

'I'm sorry I confided in you, Maria. You are a pair of fuckwits. I'm sorry I came here to this cruel place, where people think stolen pigtails are antiquities. I wish I'd listened to my friends in Sydney, stayed with them as they suggested,' he says.

Maria's saying, 'No, no, you've got to listen.'

He stands and leaves, tries to slam the door but is prevented by the hydraulic door governor. Maria immediately gets up and runs after him. I hear her in the street calling, 'Wait, wait! Peter!'

I sit there trying to feel slightly self-righteous through the guilt. At this I'm reasonably successful: why would we need his Sydney story disturbing our trip? Why should he have to drag us through the small agonies of his tiny two-week relationship just because he bumps into us by chance? I finish my lemonade and read the menu again.

Before I can ask for anything with black bean sauce, the milkbar person calls, 'The kitchen's closed.'

'It's okay. I'm not hungry any more,' I say.

I order a second lemonade and a packet of corn chips. I am slightly hungry. I let the chips lie there unopened, am suddenly aware of a different kind of sound around me now that I am alone, the car engine is silent, I am not in the city. A woman gasps, delighted; there are unidentifiable birds, and I wonder without reason if they could be budgerigars; the traffic cruises slowly down the main street, and once or twice a semi-trailer rattles the glass; from behind the dining area one or two pieces of cutlery drop to the floor, the word 'shit' is spoken with an over-emphasis on the final expectorated 't'. I hear the door open and turn, expecting to see Maria. Instead, a very pregnant young woman enters and stares at the ice-cream poster for a while, orders something, then addresses me: 'Is that your car just outside there?'

'Yes. Is it in the way?' There could be no other reason she would want to know.

'No, the opposite. It's great where it is. Thing is, this little kid in here could decide the time's right any second, and you seem a nice, calm sort. Mind if I sit here?'

'It's fine.'

'Yeah, the kid's a couple of days overdue, so I'm constantly preparing. It's driving me wild, to tell the truth. And it's so bloody hot. I wish the little bugger would get on with it.'

I nod. The ice cream arrives, not one from the poster but a large sundae covered in green topping and cream, with a couple of wafers set in like angel's wings. She eats with great relish, biting and chewing.

'I'm famished,' she explains. 'You wouldn't believe how hungry I am at the moment. Funny at this stage, or so my sister reckons. But I've been like this for months. I'm not usually a lime sundae kind of girl.'

I open my packet of chips, take a couple, offer them to her. She takes one, out of politeness I think, then resumes her ice cream.

'Thanks a lot for the security,' she says when she's finished.

'You're welcome,' I manage.

She leaves with a light wave of her fingers. I feel an odd sort of loss, almost like desire; it's as if I've fallen in love with her in those few minutes. I'm picturing her and me settled in to farm life. I try to stop myself because it's too absurd. I take a third lemonade from the soft-drinks fridge and ask for another packet of corn chips.

'The kitchen will reopen in two hours, if you're still here,' says the milkbar person. I ask to use the toilet.

Maria returns half an hour later.

'I know why you did that, why you had to say that to Peter, and it's all right. I've explained everything now.'

'So he knows you ruined my life?' I smile slightly, to take the edge off.

'Well, that's not how I put it, but yes. He knows. He sent his apologies to you. He said his grief has turned him inwards and that he should have listened to you. We had a good talk. The poor guy. The two of them made it so much worse for each other than it had to be. If only he'd slowed down a little.'

'Or she'd sped up, I guess. While you were out, someone came in, sat here with me and told me I had an aura of calm.'

'You? You must have been asleep.'

'Thanks, but I was awake.'

'It must have been a mistake. Who was it?'

'No mistake. Just someone who walked in off the street. Admired my car. Should I understand from your tone that you're in a better frame of mind than a little while ago? Or have you used up all your pleasantness on your acquaintance?'

'I'm fine. Thanks for asking. Pleasant as ever.'

'We should get going then. If we're still here in an hour they'll open the kitchen and we'll have to eat something from this menu.'

'Instead of more corn chips.'

'Yes.'

We leave the milkbar. I'm still feeling a little bit of the risen hackles. Peter storms off and Maria chases him, acting as if it's all my fault, despite me being completely in the right.

I say, 'I guess I could have been nicer to your friend. Sorry for that.'

Maria is just about to accept or reject my apology when a man dragging a shopping trolley passes.

'Were you apologising to your girlfriend, did I overhear?' he asks. 'I could tell you a thing or two about apologies.'

Maria suppresses a giggle: he's dressed very strangely, in a floral shirt and golfer-length knickerbockers, and wearing totally opaque sunglasses.

'It was nothing major,' Maria assures him, still smirking. 'He's done much worse, and often.'

'Thanks,' I say. It is hard to worry about guarding private matters in front of this clown-like person. I'm trying to work out if he takes himself seriously or knows he looks ridiculous.

'My approach now is to admit nothing, but if you want to confess, it's best to speak openly and freely. Try not to omit anything.'

'I'd go on for weeks,' I tell him. 'I have enough trouble keeping my speech under control as it is.'

'That's a good start,' he assents. 'An understanding of scale. How about you, young lady?'

'I'm fairly choosy about my confessors,' refuses Maria, though in a friendly enough way.

'Think of it as a load-lightening exercise.'

'I'd imagine it would have the opposite effect,' says Maria.

'You do sound choosy,' says the man, meaning that Maria has never apologised in her life.

I nod. My turn to smile.

'It's like this,' says the man. 'Get yourself in a confessional frame of mind, and let it all flow. You know exactly what I mean, don't you, young man?'

'Oh I do,' I say, raising my eyebrows at Maria.

'Try this,' he says, 'as a warm-up.

'Yes, I confess to some confusion. I believed that fear and malice were compatible. I made promises without substance. I failed to locate the missing ingredients. I bled on the carpet. I allowed a vast weaving together to occur and did nothing to hinder its tendency to entrap. I was one of those spared. I engaged in conversation with the enemies of my friends. I used my friends as a barrier against personal change. I built barriers around myself in order to negotiate social engagements. I changed my expression to pacify those whose values I held in contempt. I valued short-term material rewards. I rewarded employees according to the depth of their bows. I sought entry into the United Kingdom. I let my elbows rest on the table. I painted colours I knew would cause discomfort. I danced without thought for those around me. I avoided criticism by pretending absence or illness. I went on my way as I'd intended. I stated the obvious.

'You with me?' he asks, looking to each of us.

'Mm. Mm,' we say, trapped in the rhythms of his admissions.

'Good. Then I shall continue.

'Oh, and I confess to some certainty. I was one of those implicated. I actively participated in the construction of conflicting reports. I signed contracts while still under the age of consent. I made little effort to follow the blueprints. I claimed certain documents were illegible even though they were clear and precise. I left the premises noisily. I failed to control my needs. I believed that time and practice were unnecessary. I took the words of my teachers at face value. I pleaded innocence when I knew blame would be attributed to another. I blamed the situation of others when the fault lay with my own situation. I heeded the warnings of those with vested interests. I used contrived and simplistic language. I travelled without a ticket. I failed to back up my hard drive. I smoked in the corridor. I allowed the window to slam repeatedly. I showed the soles of my feet. I switched on the light although I knew you were sleeping. I left blank the space in which to list previous insurance claims. I neglected the house plants. I jumped below my best. I embraced the comments of those whose patronage I sought. I forgot the tune.'

He bows, straightens, then jumps into the air.

'That's it. I feel so much lighter.' He laughs and adds, with exaggerated enunciation, 'I'm so very sorry. I've done all I can.'

He turns to Maria, says, 'You see, you needn't hold anything back.'

To me: 'You know it, don't you?'

'I sure do,' I say.

He laughs again and walks off, pushing the trolley, still laughing.

'He picked you a mile off,' I add, a little cruelly.

'What's that supposed to mean?'

'I don't know, but it's good there are people around who value a decent apology.'

'I'm glad you're selective in whose views you choose as support, and note they're not necessarily the most likely candidates for the description "credible".'

It was obvious he'd got to her, that she recognised herself as the person worthy of criticism. If I were admirable, I would have let it rest there, been happy enough with my knowledge. But I remember that I am not a valuable person. How could I not carry on, with such an opportunity?

'It goes back to what I was saying before we broke up. If only you'd listened to me. If only we'd talked when I suggested we needed to.'

'You arsehole!' But then she laughs. Something has shifted in her, so that she can now speak lightly. The past has receded a little, and our relationship as it was, as it ended, has attached itself to the past.

For her, that is. For myself, I cannot be sure. For this reason, I let the conversation finish there.

Maria drives. We stop in the middle of nowhere. We swap. I drive. Australia slips beneath us.

I'm thinking back to the coast, our mistake in having left it, my error in having failed to explain to Maria how we were bound to the city on the coast.

*

*Dear Maria,*

*I chase the setting sun as it angles up the headland but never catch it; it has passed the tops of the apartment blocks. Across the harbour, there remains a rich yellow glow behind the hotels. Earlier, driving through the storm, the sun came out then two rainbows — one going through the spectrum twice, a double rainbow, which I'd never before seen. I chased the sun up the headland, never catching it, past all the buildings marked 'For Sale' or 'Auction', thinking these are the bad times and even the rich are selling up. There is a sign in the gardens: 'No Dogs'. Malnourished cats are everywhere: with every step a stain-nosed kitten runs from me. Along the low sandstone wall at the water's edge sits a line of gulls. Now and then one whistles quietly. I am blurry-eyed and the harbour is grey-green. In focus, the colour breaks into grey-blue troughs and yellow-orange crests. In the distance, ferries pass and there are a number of small yachts. The red clouds and the grey clouds seem immiscible. A cormorant glides easily above the water. Walking back with the water on my left, I try to work out how I feel. I try to think. I try to encapsulate my feelings for you in words. I find none and know that I am using the wrong tools. I stand still and stare across towards the bridge. I try to think whether I believe in omens. Two boys in a clearing are throwing a frisbee back and forth, delighted that it spins, that they can catch it, that sometimes they miss, that the outcome is not determined. It occurs to me to join them, but I decide against asking their permission for fear of disturbing their game's symmetry and for the effort of speaking. How do I know if I still love you or what was that vastly deep thrill washing over me when we met once more after two weeks without seeing one another, after we were no longer together? Ripples stretch across the bay, slide landward, curl themselves up against the foaming shore. I can't make myself think forward. I remember that I am only guilty if I know I am. And at this idea I am a little ashamed, or perhaps self-pitying, that all I can take comfort from is a saying; I throw it off: I know guilt so I must have guilt. Instead, I picture you with me: you, very near, where all I can see is your face, and we stare at each other, touch each other, and I touch your face and watch you squint as your cheeks move up towards your eyes, you press your lips together and you twist out a smile and your eyes glisten and you stroke my arm and I must have a big stupid grin the whole time so that you can tell I do not believe any of this stuff could be possible. Your arms are around my neck and I stretch mine as far as they will go around you, which is three or maybe four times, and we fit together so well and you have to keep saying just that, and so do I, surprising as it is. I keep these pictures. The colours of sunset fill up the sky. The streetlights illuminate nothing but themselves against the red. When it's dark and I've walked inland, through the commercial district to another park, someone on the point sets off fireworks. I don't know what there is to celebrate. The day means nothing. Fireworks fill the sky. Time, you know, time; I think what it would be to regain touch.*

\*

As we drive I'm glancing across to Maria, this flat land behind her. I suddenly feel myself blush, as though my thoughts are available. But they're not, and she's fiddling with her camera. She lifts it and photographs me as I'm looking at her. I wonder if the red hue of my face will show up in the prints, whether my embarrassment will appear as a reflection of the land around.

'That was good, Jack,' she says. 'You're a natural.'

'Yes, a natural driver.'

\*

In West Wyalong, we cruise slowly up the main street. I'm kind of hungry, in the way you are if you eat corn chips and drink soft drinks for breakfast and/or lunch. A sign outside a pub offers counter meals all day. An early dinner would not necessarily rule out another stop later at another pub for a drink or two.

'This'll do,' says Maria.

'I'd rather eat a meal than a countermeal,' I quip.

'I'm sure it's famous for its country-length sausages. Or steaks that overflow the china. Counter refers to size, I think.'

'Avoid ocean fish is what I've heard.'

'Oh, no! Those would be the least bug-ridden. Freezing kills many bacteria.'

'Though rethawing promotes bacterial growth.'

'Shall we risk it?'

'Only live once, so may as well cark it in a pub in West Wyalong as anywhere.'

'I'm feeling really positive about this too.'

We park outside the pub. There aren't too many other vehicles, but perhaps it's too early or too late for people to eat round here. Hard to predict what's considered a decent lunch hour away from one's own warm and understanding peer group.

The pub looks okay, a little quiet perhaps. There are only three or four men inside, and they appear to have been here for some considerable time: one wears a nylon jacket the same colour as the bar, and the join between his elbow and the bar surface is no longer clear.

Another looks up as we walk in.

'Sydney people,' he announces.

I nod in a way that's meant to be non-aggressive and yet still avoids friendly conversation.

'I used to live in Sydney,' he continues.

'Yeah, we know. We know,' one of his mates says. And to us, 'A word of advice: don't get him started.'

'They might be interested, Phil,' the first one protests, then turns to Maria and me, 'Do you take drugs?'

Maria appears not to have heard him as we try to make our discreet way around the bar.

Ever the diplomat, I say, 'No, mate. We don't.'

The publican is not helping us. He's stacking peanuts and has his back turned. Polite, we refrain from calling out.

'It's just that I once had a barbiturate problem,' says the man.

'That's too bad,' says Maria, as we continue to edge past.

'Aah, there's the menu,' I say, pointing to the far end of the bar. We have turned away from him as much as possible and face a blackboard that says: 'Sausages. T-bone. Half Chicken. Fish of the Week. All with chips, peas and gravy. Sauce on request.'

'I wasn't taking them, oh no, but I still had a problem with them,' says the man.

'Mm, tempting,' says Maria. 'It's so hard to decide.'

'Between having a meal or a packet of barbecue-flavour chips?'

'I ended up in court nonetheless.'

'Leave them alone, Max,' says the second man. The other two are watching greyhounds on a screen above the bar.

'Phil, they'll be interested. Sydney people have catholic interests.'

'It's fine,' Maria dismisses him, waving her hand.

Max misinterprets.

'Picture me in the courtroom,' he says.

Maria and I are trying to get the publican's attention, but he's a skilled waiter in the Sartrean sense and avoids all eye contact.

'This university type takes a girl upstairs, like he's some Viking or caveman.'

'EXCUSE ME!' calls out Maria.

'Be right with you,' says the publican, not turning around.

'I'm the only witness anyone could find. The only respectable man in Glebe.' He adds, for Phil's benefit, 'That's a suburb of Sydney.'

'Fuck,' says Phil. 'I've heard this story two hundred bloody times.'

'You should've seen me in the courtroom,' says Max. 'I was fucking wonderful.

'You're not here under any kind of duress?' he asks Maria. She takes a step back. I judge it involuntary. Max turns to me: 'What about you, mate?'

I don't answer. He laughs.

*

'I don't know. Something about shoulders,' Max begins, and we know he's begun his story because he changes his voice, loses his bantering manner and also his intimacy. And his eyes change too, as though he is staring right through us. Staring through me, really. He fixes on me.

'Fuck,' says Phil. 'Fuck it. This is fucked.'

'No. I don't remember,' Max continues, looking at my eyes in this disturbing unfocused way. 'Something about shoulders to shoulders and hotels. That's all. He reached across. He might have touched her. Touched her. He might have. Perhaps her shoulder. He touched her dress. She wore black — we all wore black really. I don't think I'm guessing. So if she'd been wearing something else, I would have remembered that. So what? So I'll stick to saying "black". That's all. Look, there's no point in asking me about this, as I told you before. Right, I'm at the hotel. The hotel. So I was there. She's just standing there. How should I know what she's doing? Sure I was near them. Okay, so she must be doing something. That's what you say, at $1200 a bloody day.'

He spins around and glares at the publican, who hasn't said a word, who has in fact climbed a stepladder and commenced dusting bottles of spirits. 'That's my answer. I'm responding to what he says. Why shouldn't I say that answer? Sorry, so I won't place his questions in context any more. I'll answer them to the best of my ability and fully and frankly. As I've done so far.'

He returns to me: 'Ah, she's telling a story. She's talking to the man. His name's Bob, as you know.'

And back to the publican: 'Fine. I won't tell him what he knows, only what I know. As I've said right from the start, I don't know. I know what he knows as well as I know what happened at the hotel.'

'Fuck, Max,' says Phil again. 'I'm trying to hear the television.'

Max ignores him, looks at me yet again. He continues in this way throughout his anecdote, transforming me into the lawyer, the publican into a judge, and Phil, like a victim in the Mad Hatter's tea party, is pointed into character as the loathsome, heartless Bob. Maria, for him, appears to become the woman in the story.

'So he touches her dress. The man touches her. Well, I don't see why I should have to make things easier for all of us. It doesn't make things easier for me to be here. Making things easier for all of us would be to say, "Thanks for coming in. Off you go." So it's you who has this power of simplification, with all due respect. Yes, I'd agree they're conversing. It's not like he's come into the bar and touched her without at least greeting her. Bob. I said "Bob" before. I don't know what they're saying. "Hello. What a nice black dress." Mate, if you already know, why ask me? So maybe they do talk about particular subjects, greetings and dresses aside. You've already formed your view of what was said. Okay, I'll state your view in my own words. I'll state my view in my own words. They keep quoting amazing things to each other. Oh, like "The cock cops coops" or something. That sounds particular enough to me. How much more particular do you want? I can't give you a verbatim rendition of the evening's intercourse. I apologise again. It's not a joking matter. I agree with you. I'm agreeing. That wasn't meant to be a joke. Yes, it was an unfortunate turn of phrase. I'm not supposed to be sensitive. I'm supposed to use my own words. That's what he said. It's what you said. My words are cheaper, believe me, but if you want cheap words I've got plenty.'

'No one's arguing with you,' says Phil. 'But shut the fuck up.'

Max ignores him and carries on: 'The hotel. I'm near the bar. Bob, or whatever his name is, with his back to me. I know his name's Bob. How should I know what he wants to do? They're his motivations, nothing to do with me. I'm not his confidant. I'm the bloke standing nearby in the hotel.'

'You're too bloody near to me,' says Phil, this time more quietly, as though finally resigning himself to Max's full rendition. The publican climbs back to ground level and goes through a door behind the bar marked 'Private'.

Maria shouts, 'No! Wait!' but he doesn't wait.

Max turns to me. 'You with me? Okay, I'll think of something to say about his thoughts. This is ridiculous. I shouldn't make value judgments. At least I wasn't contextualising. I'm learning from you guys, and I'm sure it'll make me a better person. His thoughts, as I sensed them through the back of his head. He's thinking about all those who had fucked her. There. Look, they're his thoughts, not my fault about the language. It's not a contemptuous way of putting it. So exclude it or expunge it or whatever you can do to my inexpensive words. I don't care. Haven't you been to a hotel?'

He winks. 'I'm doing okay, aren't I?'

I try to lower my gaze, but he waits for me as if he's wrestling eye contact, and there's nothing I can do.

'I couldn't hear exactly what he was saying. He wasn't saying anything to me, because it's obvious that if he was talking to a woman, he wasn't talking to men. Well, it seems obvious to me, but I forgot you haven't been in a hotel. You tell me what I should assume about your level of knowledge and we'll start from there. It's just that some people's "beginnings" are further advanced than others. Yes, I'd seen Bob around for a long time. I cannot quantify. Years. Or weeks, I agree, it could be. Of course I recognise him. I'd say hi to him, but he isn't talking to me on account of you are.

'I gave them heaps, Phil,' he says, aside, and continues as before. 'Yes, I'd met him before today. I'd met him before the alleged event, whatever that means. I know what it means. I'd met him several times. Not only drinking. Not only inebriated if that's the expensive word you want me to use. I wouldn't say I'd known him sober. I did see him not drinking, but that's not the same. I can say what I like? I don't think I ought to. I might get into trouble. You seem pretty strict, with all due respect. Him? He's a pussy. Oh, Bob. Nothing heavy. Nothing I know about. Maybe some marijuana, but that's no crime. Not for me to judge if that's a crime. Bob had habits. Sure he did. He thought it would be better if we had a joint each instead of just one for Chrissakes. Not for Chrissakes. A habit! You see how naive and innocent I am? Didn't even occur to me what you were implying, in that manner of yours. Look, I know nothing about pills. I'm completely down the line there.'

The publican walks back in, sees that Max is still going and leaves again.

'HANG ON!' shouts Maria.

'You'll be lucky,' says Max. 'He's got a brother in the law, so he takes all this personally. I truly gave them some that day.'

'Can't you summarise?' pleads Phil.

'It wouldn't give the total flavour, not like a full account. You listen, Phil. You know what I said to that bastard?' Max grins. 'So name some then. You're the guy with the research. Not that I'm implying anything, not on your salary. Yep. Yep. Yep. I recognise the names. We'd get mandies from our fourteen-year-old daughters. That's a joke. There is no "we". I don't even have a fourteen-year-old daughter. I'll answer about the pills. Mandrax. I already said that. Bennies. Nembutals for saying bye-byes. Not me, though. Just dope, me. I'm a lungs 'n' lines man, I am, not that I'd do anything illegal, nothing which might reflect on the value of my testimony, as you might say, given an extra half-day on the public purse.

'You should have seen his face at that one!' He's talking to Maria but pointing at me. Then he turns to the door through which the publican has disappeared.

'Yes, of course I'm sorry. It's just the way he looks at me gets me going. Yes, I don't know about Bob, but it doesn't surprise me if that's what you say. Not that anything surprises me. Attitude-wise, the guy was a bit out. It would be fair to go that far. A bit of the cult of self, it could be said. Yes. He argued with everybody too. Nearly everybody. Not me. I'm not an argumentative type. Bob was a cynical guy. He'd say anything and laugh. Had no respect for legal institutions, most probably. Yes, that is speculation. You seemed to ask me to speculate. He believed behaviour was God-given. His politics reeked. I'm not just saying it. I'm responding to your question. I mean what I said. I can't be more particular. I don't mean he was a Communist. Well, I'm sure that's what you think smelly politics is, but I didn't intend the expression in that way. I meant it about his way of being with other people. Yeah, I don't see why that's a contradiction of what I said before. So I've never seen him talk to a woman close-up. You're perverted, you are. Yes, I remember I'm under oath. Don't ask me about his endearments, I know nothing about it. I said I knew him. That's completely a different thing from eavesdropping on his lines. I don't know whether or not he had "lines". It's not out of keeping with his character, but it may not be how he operated. Overall, I'd say about his character: a real bastard. Why can't I say that? You're kidding. You're truly pulling my dick. My dick. Don't start on that again. Really, don't get threatening here. It's a common saying. It's common. Of course my contempt is directed towards Bob

194

rather than this court. Him. Bob. Look, you call him the defendant and I'll call him Bob. Tell the typists whatever you bloody want. Okay, sorry. No, I'm perfectly sober. What do you want me to say? Bob is not a good character. Are you happy now? Of good character then. Thank me? No, thank you. I mean it.'

\*

There's silence, then Phil claps twice.

'I was brilliant,' says Max. 'I showed those bastards they weren't so smart.'

If my facial expression resembles Maria's as much as I suspect it does, we must both look horrified.

'What's the matter?' inquires Max.

'That's enough now. You've said your bit. Leave them alone,' orders the publican, finally returning, and without apology for his absence. 'Steak for you and the chicken for your wife?'

'He's my ex-boyfriend,' says Maria, completely unnecessarily.

'Jesus. I'm sorry. I didn't even hear you split up,' says the publican. 'What with all that carry-on.'

All the men but Max laugh, overdoing it with a last few guffaws.

'Let's get out of here,' I whisper to Maria, who nods briefly. For once she is with me.

'Two packets of barbecue-flavoured chips,' says Maria, smiling serenely.

As we push through the doors, we hear Max's final pronouncement on us: 'Two bloody packets of chips! I told you they were from Sydney.'

'Barbecue,' agrees Phil.

*

We pass back into the dry late-afternoon heat. The difference in temperature between the pub and the road makes our journey of a single step into a border-crossing.

'Thanks for explaining our relationship to the madmen,' I complain.

'We'll never see them again,' she responds, dismissively.

'I actually hate barbecue chips,' I say.

'Me too.' She's holding the two packets between forefinger and thumb, letting them swing slightly, well away from herself as though they stink. We laugh together. There's another pub opposite, across the wide, flat country town main road. We are still hungry. Two kids of eleven or twelve ride past on mountain bikes.

'Hey!' calls Maria. 'You like barbecue-flavoured chips?'

'Oh yeah!' enthuses one. Maria tosses them each a packet.

'These haven't even been tampered with,' says the other, possibly with gratitude.

'And,' rejoins the first, examining the back of the pack, 'they're still within the use-by dates.'

'Cool.'

They open them and ride off, holding the open packs against the handlebars.

'Don't choke,' Maria calls after them, as they hadn't in the end thanked her.

As we head towards the other pub, we see someone leaving it, unsteadily. He wobbles towards us, but instead of passing in the middle of the road, he stops and turns to Maria.

'Milly? Is that you, Milly? I can't believe it! God's smiling on me at last.'

'Sorry, wrong person,' says Maria. We cross quickly.

Meanwhile he has turned and follows us, calling, 'Hang on, Milly. Just a mo'. It's been ten years, so you could spare me five minutes.'

'Oh great,' I say. 'Do you think we're meeting a fair cross-section of the local population?'

'I don't care about statistics,' she says. 'Let's get to the car and go somewhere else.'

We turn again to cross back, but there is now a steady stream of cars and vans creeping along behind a caravan. The man catches up to us, wheezing for a few seconds, hawking but not spitting out. Maria begins to back away, bumps into me as I'm watching for a break in the traffic.

'Milly, listen here.' The man addresses Maria in a serious voice, insistent and mournful. I don't think he sees me at all. Maria takes me by the bicep, but the man stays where he is.

'I'm not Milly,' she says. 'Sorry, but you're mistaken.'

'You're Milly, or else my memory's dunna runner,' he says.

'No.'

'You've come back and a feller's in luck.'

'No, she hasn't,' insists Maria.

'Milly, you're still sharp as Worcestershire sauce.' He takes a small step forward and stops again. 'And you can't half tell my Milly's still a peach. The years haven't touched you.'

'Please. You've got the wrong person.' She has tightened her grip on my arm. The man is freaking her out, and me too. The traffic in one direction has stopped, but now there's a hold-up the other way.

'I had the right girl, all right,' he says, 'but now she can't pick me from a street full of beery strangers. Struth, Milly, I've been good and stayed away from stoushes and cops. Don't break my heart now. Not now. In half an hour we'd know if we still could make each other melt. You know I wouldn't kid you, Milly.'

'And I wouldn't kid you. I'm not Milly.'

'She's Maria,' I say, as though believing a third voice could straighten him out.

'You don't be rude to me, you little beggar,' says the man, responding to me but still staring at Maria. 'Because I'll have you in two seconds flat. Milly, I just want to make you proud again, and see your eyes shining.'

'No,' says Maria.

'Let's go,' I say, as the road is at last clear and for a long way in both directions.

'I'm going now,' Maria tells him, slowly. 'I hope you sort yourself out.'

'Yes, I sorted myself out for you already. That's what's happened,' he agrees, adding, 'And I'm sorry about decking the American, Milly. But it's ten years and even a woman like you could forgive something that far back.'

'I do forgive you,' says Maria. 'But it's goodbye.'

'We're meant to be together, Milly. You once said it yourself.'

Maria opens her mouth, shuts it again.

'Come on,' I order.

'Goodbye,' Maria tells him again.

'I once requested a kiss from a girl,' he says, 'but now I ask for nothing.'

We cross the road, hurrying. I hear him either laughing or crying and look back to see him standing there, shaking his head. Maria's trail of abandoned men.

'You treat her right, you lucky, cheating coot!' he shouts across the road. 'I don't choose to say goodbye!'

We leave the town, still hungry. There is a small fire burning in the middle distance, a grass fire most probably, as trees are few out here.

\*

We drive west of the west, west of West Wyalong. Somewhere between Weethalle and Rankins Springs we enter the Fruit Fly Exclusion Zone. The terminology is the same as in international wars. The Fruit Fly Exclusion Zone is marked with a thick pink line on our map and it covers an area as great as a state. We know we've entered the zone because a sign warns us to eat or dispose of any fruit. We have no fruit in the car. We have several flies, but none seems to be a fruit fly. There is no marked human border here, nothing which makes sense as a boundary. I can see how a dingo fence works, how national borders do their thing. I've observed the occasional reports of the southern migration of cane toads from the cane fields of Queensland south through New South Wales, the 'vector' of the rabbit calicivirus from its supposedly isolated test site on Wardang Island off the South Australian coast to all parts of Australia — there were rumours of pastoralists paying for infected rabbit corpses. Our trip makes its way in the reverse direction of the flow of disease, up the virus river towards Adelaide. The earlier story was that calicivirus was spread by blowflies, that the insects broke boundaries. Either that or newspaper journalists.

'This is no dilemma for us,' I joke to Maria, 'because we haven't eaten healthy food for ten years.'

'Speak for yourself, matey,' she says. 'My diet is in accordance with several principles recommended in several books.'

'Sure,' I say, doubtfully. 'Are we moving from or to a higher concentration of agricultural spraying? Do you think we're safer breathing here, or less safe?'

She shakes her head. 'I read something about this. You don't want to know.'

'I guess it all depends on whether the fruit fly exclusion is enforced by pesticides, or whether pesticides are needed only in the areas where fruit flies are not excluded,' I say.

'There was a pesticide "incident" here a few years ago.'

'How do you know that?'

'Friends in the Department of Agriculture. They keep me pretty up to date with local environmental disasters or potential disasters. They like freaking me out.'

'These are friends I don't know?'

'They are old friends who I speak to from time to time without informing you.'

'Old friends. Like schoolfriends?'

'Old schoolfriends, no one new. I hear from them from time to time. Don't worry. If I'd known you were that interested in agricultural apocalypse, I would have forwarded the emails.'

'Don't bother.'

'Fine. Do you want to know the risks of the road ahead?'

'It depends.'

'From what I understand, it's safer to be human than fruit fly around here.'

'Okay, tell me.'

Ahead I can see what appears to be a murky dust storm and all of a sudden I'm confronted with the possibility that pesticide usage couldn't be too bad, because we've entered a locust swarm and the little bastards are smearing all over the windscreen. I hold down the spray button and put the windscreen wipers on maximum speed, trying to keep the view clear through the locusts. I can see the road, but the view is marked by arcs of locust remains.

'Wow, a locust conurbation,' I say. 'I guess the chemicals couldn't be worse here than in Sydney.'

'Put it this way, if you were a fruit fly, chances are you'd be useless as breeding material. There are zillions of irradiated males flying around. They've been zapped with radiation at the nuclear reactor at Lucas Heights, and released into the wild to shoot blanks. They're randy as anything, but completely sterile.'

'What about the females?'

'I don't know. I guess they can't tell a good man from a dud.'

'Ninety-nine per cent?'

'That's the ratio the department was aiming for.'

'Is that enough to make the population non-viable?'

'I have no idea.'

'You'd think the fruit flies would be blown to where there was fruit and then they'd thrive. One per cent should be enough to create a superfly. End of Darwinian story.'

'I never speculate,' says Maria.

This is true. I scan the horizon for crop-dusters, but can't see a single plane.

There's a car parked on the verge ahead. A woman in a uniform waves a fluorescent baton to indicate that we should stop. I stop. She comes around to the window and I get ready to enter cop routine.

'Hello. What seems to be the trouble?'

'Hello, this is a spot check for fruit. Do you realise you've entered a fruit fly exclusion zone?'

'Yes, we saw the signs.'

'You have any fruit on you?'

'No. None.'

'You sure? You wouldn't have any apple cores or anything like that?'

'We only eat fried food and soft drinks.'

No amusement displayed.

'Mind if I check the boot?'

'No worries.' I switch off the engine, hand her the keys and get out to follow her around to the back of the car. 'It's funny, we were just talking about you government people, about irradiated fruit flies and so on.'

'I'm just going to look in the boot, mate. I'm not going to pull out a gamma-ray gun.'

What should I say to this: fine, I was merely a little concerned regarding my sperm count? I change subjects. 'What about these locusts? Is that normal?'

'At this time, the locust population is rated as moderate, but this is an area of major infestation. All goes back to heavy autumn rains. Autumn rain therefore summer locusts. Glad you asked?'

'I like information. Thing is, see her?' I flick my eyes towards Maria. 'She has contacts in the Department of Agriculture, so knows about the fruit fly sterilisation program. She's using this borrowed erudition bit by bit, so whenever I try to discuss something, she comes out with some snippet to end the conversation. This is causing me some stress. So I'd like to know something which she doesn't. Could you perhaps share some knowledge?'

'It's like that, is it?' She looks along the road, but there's no other traffic. She's inserted the key in the lock but has yet to turn it. 'I've been in the department for twenty years, but yours is the first punter's inquiry with such a perpendicular purpose. What kind of information do you want?'

'I guess something about the survival instinct, these poor afflicted insects carrying on despite the odds.'

'Can't help you there, mate. They don't. It's entirely a departmental decision whether the resources required for eradication within a given region or area should be implemented, whether we intend to proceed to zero pest population within the specified boundaries. Best way to describe it is: pest persistence is at departmental whim. In this instance, the goal was ninety-nine per cent infertility among males. This has been met. My job is to ensure the ratio remains steady by targeting travellers like you lot. At another time, the goal could be 99.5 per cent. But if you do the mathematics, that'd cost twice as much, because we're not touching the number of fertile males already out there; that remains constant. Simple explanation. Say you have one fruit fly male in a given population. You need ninety-nine infertile ones to get to the first percentage, to make that one fruit fly only one per cent of the total. With me?'

I nod.

'Okay. But you need 199 to reach 99.5 per cent. That one has to be only one out of two hundred, not one out of one hundred. Is that clear enough? I mean, you're from Sydney, aren't you? So I assume you've never had to deal with real events like this.'

I confess, 'I was hoping you'd tell me something a little more romantic: fruit flies travelling hundreds of miles for one night of passion, then dying, sad but fulfilled. Locusts blown ten thousand miles off course, struggling back through cyclones to their lifelong partners. That sort of thing.'

'Jesus. Locust love, eh? The only romances I know have nothing to do with bugs.' She grins to herself and opens the boot, looks back at me.

'Mate, listen, I spend a lot of time driving around the state, not long enough in the one area, hardly ever. I've got family that I return to in holidays, mum, dad, a little brother, but the rest of the time I'm travelling. Know what I'm saying? If a relationship is to be memorable, it has to have legs out here. You don't want some cocky talking about flies and crickets all the time. It's irritating enough to have to think about them during the day.'

I realise the conversation has begun to head off course.

'It's actually the flies and crickets, as you put it, that I'm interested in learning about.'

'I know, mate, which — no offence — is why I'd never give you a second glance if I bumped into you in any Department of Ag regional office. I meet ten new people a week — that's to talk to, not just to check for fruit, which is a rarity for me — and most of these are handsome, well-muscled men, used to working outdoors, physically capable. I'm quite engaging, when I want to be, so some of these blokes get pretty engaged. These are beautiful men, but I'm picky. It takes a lot to catch my attention.'

'All respect, you're the one that asked me to attend to you,' I say, peeved.

'This is my job, mate. Open the bag, will you?'

I unzip the large sports bag which contains all my worldly clothes. She pulls the opening apart, but keeps her hands out.

'No fruit in there,' she says, which is obvious. She puts a hand on the boot, ready to slam it. 'I could tell you all about my love life. I don't know if you'd be shocked or turned on or indifferent. I'm very happy, put it that way. You seem to want to keep her happy, which is a good start. Only advice I can give you is to find things out for yourself, and don't bullshit. Insect romance stories don't help anyone. You know what I'm telling you?'

She closes the boot and tosses me back the keys, an easy parabola. 'I'd wish you luck, mate, but I reckon I'd rather wish luck to your girlfriend there. Bye-bye.'

*

A luminous sign gives distances. Adelaide is last of the towns listed. I add and subtract kilometres in my head. We have come a fair proportion of the total now: we're more than halfway there.

I say a soft joke: 'From now on, no matter how bad things may become, it's faster to continue than to turn back.'

Maria has the courtesy to laugh. 'As the Irishman said to whoever.'

I believe, I tell myself, that our journey from here will be much better, our time together will improve, and that after the same distance again, we will have succeeded. In what, I couldn't say.

I wish, though, that I found Maria less compelling. I would be happier if we could drive together and at the same time I could forget her, that she would blend into the background. I might like to undertake even a few kilometres of this journey as a tourist: opening the guidebook and following the suggested alternative routes, one labelled historic and one scenic, visiting the museum in each town with its Aboriginal skulls now replaced by replicas, debate continuing with local communities over the return of other skeletal remains. Panning for gold under supervision, and delighted with a few specks magnified in a glass vial filled with water. Tasting the local wines, deciding that they do compare with those available at the pub on the corner just up from Maria's place, but that I won't buy them anyway. Eating lunch in the RSL and losing five bucks on the pokies, all in the space of a middy.

But with Maria here, forget tourism. I'm spending this drive wishing for her, wondering about the meaning of every expression change, controlling all my responses in relation to her potential reactions. She shows no sign of shifting her attitude, but I am still entirely reactive. Do I see any sign of dependency in her? I look very hard. What is wrong with her, that she won't undertake anything to win my approval? Perhaps, after all, she is warming to me, to the image of the future in the past sitting beside her. I could easily allow myself to believe it.

*

The road ahead wavers with imaginary liquid. It reflects the rich, early evening blueness plus a gum tree or two, but without precision. Australia, purportedly famous for big skies, has captured the sky in an illusory puddle. We are somewhere famous, and I'm trying to place us, but the only image is of generic beer advertisements. Maria sings a couple of them, but in crooning, country music tones instead of the slick, city's-as-real-as-bush, Sydney voice of the campaigns. We've come through a test already, surely, succeeded in getting to here, more or less negotiated a way to travel. I'm beginning to relax, this far in, this far across the country. Despite Maria's attitude.

Maria sings on; she has a pleasant voice. The road curves gently through the repetitive landscape. We occasionally sight small birds of prey hovering near the road. I'm thinking that from here everything will be easy. Maria and I will like each other. Beyond that, what happens, happens. I'm not saying I completely like or accept the way things are between us, only that I'm more relaxed. I see that out here a less fierce and frenetic approach is the way of the future. From now on I will be indirect.

Too soon, this vision of quiet travel ends. Relaxation is not to be. My car, which earlier in the journey had failed so absolutely as a seduction lever, develops an additional shortcoming. Smoke or steam appears at the front, blowing rapidly over the bonnet. Maria eases the car to the side of the road. Neither of us had noticed the temperature needle moving up into the red zone. The car had been fine in the heat of the day, so why now? And why here?

'Fuck,' I say, for what other word captures the mood?

'Just leave it for a few minutes. It'll cool down.'

I'm suspicious of her confidence, but say nothing. Not even a sarcastic 'she'll be right, eh?' She opens the bonnet. We wait in the heat, squatting in the small amount of shade offered by a compact car's open doors.

'I wish I had a little bit of butter and an egg, just for experimental reasons. Reckon if you couldn't fry something up on the car bonnet, the expression's an exaggeration,' I say, demonstrating that I'm as capable of staying cool in a drought in the middle of nowhere as she is.

'We've got bread and cheese. We could try Welsh rarebit.'

'Is that really what you call it? I've never heard anyone actually say that. I thought it was some kind of joke among milkbar proprietors.'

'We always called it that in my family.'

'You never called it that around me.'

'You should have made cheese on toast more, and I would have.'

'I apologise for not having made enough cheese on toast during our relationship.'

'Apology accepted, with reluctance.'

I decide against asking for an extension to make amends for the shortfall, and also decide against initiating a discussion (that is, correcting her erroneous proposition) on the nature of radiant and reflected heat in the grilling of cheese on car bonnets. Instead, I opt for the seemingly tamer, 'It's lucky we're in no hurry.'

I'm in no hurry and I try to gauge from Maria's face how anxious she is to be in Adelaide. I wouldn't ask her, because to ask her would be to invoke in her mind an image of her boyfriend waiting at the other end. He's probably already by the front door, standing there nameless and undescribed, but still somehow attractive, knowledgeable, apprehensive, thoughtful, personifying stuff.

Maria's smile is perfectly calm. I remember this about her. She is a very good person for crises. She was always the one who knew where the torch was in blackouts, had a friend with a gas cylinder when the stove broke down or my gas was cut off. She knew where the all-night pharmacy was, or knew the right phone number to find out. That said, being good in crises is not a wholly positive character trait. It's only worth having if there actually is a crisis. Otherwise, it counts against.

'We'll get there eventually,' she says. She opens the back door, pulls out her camera. 'Better shoot this before it stops steaming.'

'Is there much call for car breakdown pictures?'

'Not yet.'

'Oh, how interesting. Art or commercial?'

'Jack, I promise you, you won't be able to open a magazine without seeing images of your car in the middle of nowhere.'

I follow her around to the front. 'Get this then.'

I take off my shirt and wrap it around the radiator cap, turn the cap one notch anticlockwise. The radiator hisses and sprays hot liquid downward through the small gap. Not good. I turn the cap rapidly and jump back. There's a brief green fountain of steaming coolant. I hear the camera's motor drive.

'Got it,' she says. 'And the blur which is you.'

'Just as well, because there's no more coolant.' I pause for dramatic effect. 'But fortunately there's a bottle of water.'

'Phew,' she says, mock-relieved.

'Yeah. Because I hear beer's really bad for radiators.'

'Would photograph well, I bet.'

She takes a couple of closer shots of the gasping radiator opening, then puts her camera away and gets out a novel, sits back in the shade. I find a change of shirt in the boot, open a beer (which is very warm and almost but not quite undrinkable), then squat down and scratch cartoon characters in the dust with a stone. After fifteen minutes or so, I refill the radiator. No sign of a leak, so that's one good thing.

I start the motor, we drive. The temperature's still above halfway and there's an ominous slap, slap, slap. The temperature rises visibly. Slap slap. We watch the needle move into red. I stop the car, open the bonnet, pull out the remains of the fan belt.

'Fuck,' I repeat. 'How far do you reckon we are from the nearest servo?'

Maria hands me the map. 'No idea. But I don't think blowing the head gasket's a very good idea.'

'Nor do I. And, of course, as much as I'm enjoying your company, I agree that saving my car so we eventually get there is a good idea. Which direction do you reckon we should hitch?'

'It's not going that badly, you know, Jack. Bad start, maybe. But I can tell you're enjoying this trip, being out here. I'm starting to take your move-to-the-country plan half-seriously.'

'Yeah, right. But I'm collecting some great dinner-party anecdotes.'

We're leaning over the map, pointing to little bits of empty road, guessing where we are, wondering whether there might be a service station at a nearby crossroads.

'Looks like it has to be Balranald.'

'I think so too.'

'I want to lock some of this gear in the boot,' says Maria. I toss her the keys and she reorganises my luggage, slams the boot, grabs a little sports bag which I guess contains her camera.

We stand beside the car. The bonnet is up, the radiator steaming. The sun has gone, though the sky is still light. I'm holding up a busted fan belt and trying to think whether thumb or finger is the approved method out here, but I've never been here before, so don't know. I consider tossing a coin. Maria holds out her thumb. A couple of cars pass. One driver stares ahead, refusing to see us; the second points to the right, meaning 'I'm not going to pick you up, but I'm going to give you a reason you can't understand.'

I say, 'If this car next doesn't stop, I won't hold the fan belt any more. I'll assume it's being misinterpreted as "Stop here so we can garrotte you." '

'That's a lovely thought,' says Maria.

The third driver stops. I get in the front and Maria gets in the back.

'Fan belt, eh?'

This is a very, very good sign, I think, as I'm holding a broken fan belt on my lap and my car is undriveable at the side of the road. I'm hoping we can have inane conversation all the way to Balranald. It would be a pleasant change from every conversation so far on this drive, with the exception of a couple of light-hearted exchanges with my ex-girlfriend. The driver's question gives me hope that, for the next forty-five minutes or hour, I will receive no advice or information on how to fall in love, how to be in love, how to resuscitate love, how to cope with the end of love, how good sex is, how good sex is with a certain person, how often sex is had or how many people sex is had with.

'Yup,' I say, putting as much comradeship as I can muster into my voice. 'That's exactly right. You live round here?'

'Kind of,' he says. 'Now that's a story. Live round here. Live! Ha! I've got to tell you, you people are bloody lucky to be travelling together like you are. I'm no judge of these things, believe me, and maybe you two've been married since you were sixteen, or maybe you're living in sin. Or maybe, for all I know, you've each got five other lovers in Sydney. From what I've heard, that's what Sydney's like, don't tell me if I'm wrong, 'cause I like to think there's somewhere like that. Doesn't bother me at all. Cities have to have some purpose, don't they, considering they're the least useful places on earth for anything else.

'I'll tell you what though, seeing as you'll be spending longer round here than you planned: you don't want to be a single man coming through this part of the country. It's been hell here for ever for single men, or since the English declared the beginning of time, which is for ever as far as the white people around here are concerned. Out here, and I tell you this from personal experience, they guard their daughters like you would not believe. Frankly, and I can tell you this only because anyone can see you're not from round here — you are from Sydney, aren't you? — frankly, they're mad in these parts, and I'm mad to stay here myself.

'But there's this girl, or she was a girl when I met her, hardly out of school. She's much older now, and so am I, but that's how it goes. When we met, I didn't have any part of a car, not even a busted fan belt. I was just a young traveller looking for a new experience, and thought I'd find it round here. In those days no one drove cars. Everyone was jumping on and off trains, saving bus fares, hitchhiking around — on purpose that is, not like you two — except for the car drivers that is, and half of them were flogging vacuum cleaners. I must have been the only intentional holiday-maker for five hundred miles.'

'So,' I interrupt, realising the danger: this bloke was about to launch into something. 'You're a farmer now, or a — what do you call it? — pastoralist? Do you grow things? Oats and beans and barley? Cows and meadows and sheep and corn? Is it a good year for growing things?'

He laughs. I'm hoping Maria will help me here, perhaps talk about rural opportunities for photography.

'Mate, I couldn't grow a pimple in a chocolate factory.'

I have the strong feeling that this will be my last chance to avert the almost inevitable story. The only way is if I do the talking, try and steer the conversation in any direction away from his 'personal experience' of daughters of the land.

'Ha ha ha,' I force-laugh. 'That's a pretty funny expression.'

'That's what this woman always liked about me, I think. Out this way, they pride themselves on being laconic. It means you can fit in an extra drink or two, but it doesn't help much with conversation. I wouldn't want to boast about it, but to be honest, I have a bit of a way with words.'

'So do I,' I interrupt again. It's going to be harder than I'd hoped. 'You know shish kebabs?'

I am aware that I am not behaving like a proper hitchhiker. I have been a proper hitchhiker in the past and I know that

215

the proper role of the proper hitchhiker is to allow the driver of the car to say anything at all, to approve of whatever the driver has said, or, at least, to be silent in a way which could be understood as approval. For example:

'You know how the moon got there, in the sky?' a truck driver once asked me.

'How?' I said.

'Bits of cosmic dust rubbing up against the earth's atmosphere, building up, adhering to each other, gathering together on top of the stratosphere like a snowball, then the whole thing floating up a bit and there it is.'

I said, 'That's really interesting.'

'I tried to tell that to a professor in the university in Perth and he wouldn't listen, threatened to call the bloody security guards even.'

'That's too bad.'

'You'd think these professors would want people to come to them with ideas, wouldn't you?'

'Yes, you would think that.'

That is the proper attitude for hitchhikers to take. Here, though, the steady accumulation of confessions along the Mid-Western and Sturt highways is getting to me. Maria's ironically expressed fear that our relationship would be spread along fourteen hundred kilometres of major Australian highway is looking like not too bad a guess. The only difference is that she thought she'd be the one to suffer from the tales, whereas so far it's me who's copping it. Everything seems to reflect on me being dumped, hopeless, lonely, unwanted. I have to stop it.

But what am I going to say to this guy? Don't tell me about your fraudulent love adventures. Don't tell me about the women who have begged you for one more passionate night, the models you have glimpsed naked through gaps in the curtains — who have then seen you and not minded at all — the nymphomaniacs who a single accidental touch in passing would make yours for as long as you wanted, the rich and beautiful older woman who taught you everything when you were a teenager, the bosses you cuckolded, the bosses with nymphomaniac wives who were older, rich and beautiful models who found you irresistible, and you so young to lose your cherry that none of your mates would believe you so you have to find travellers standing beside the road waiting to reinforce your confidence in your abilities as lover and story-spinner. Mate, shut your trap.

'She could cook well too, like me,' he continues. 'Or not at first. At first she cooked like everyone else out here, like her old man. Her father was an arsehole. That's what I was going to tell you about, but we have time so I'll come back to it. That's what there's plenty of out here. Time. Plenty of time, but not much cooking. The food is generally terrible, unless you're a sabre-toothed dingo with a taste for charcoal. There are no recipes, let alone recipe books. Out here, they think you kill an animal, cut a piece off it, toss it on something hot for a while, and there it is. That's your food. They might add a few potatoes. But you asked and yes, I do know what shish kebab is. It's the same as what they eat out here, only more cut up.'

'I agree,' I nod, managing to combine the hitchhiker and the deferral of stories momentarily. 'I'm no shish kebab defender. I cooked them every week for a year. After a while you really stink of it, crap meat, spitting fat, onion juice. I quit my job and went vegetarian for a while,' I tell him. 'Except that I also avoided onions, which had become tainted by the experience.'

'You're really lucky it's me you're telling this to,' he says. 'Anyone else would beat the crap out of you for saying that. You've got to be careful what you say and do in these parts. I'm a doctor. I know these things.'

He's started on the advice. He's decided I am the hitchhiker. My moment of agreement may have been an error. I wish I was sitting in the back with Maria, that we'd made out we were so in love as to be inseparable. I wish Maria was sitting in the front instead of me. She's gazing out the window with a completely tuned-out expression on her face. The driver is perfectly happy about this, because he is going to tell me a bloke anecdote and if Maria were in the conversation he'd have to make asides and mightn't be able to play up his eventual victory with the bravado I am already dreading. I make another attempt at diversion.

'A doctor, eh? You a GP?'

'This is what she asked, that first afternoon,' he says. '"Have we met somewhere before, city doctor boy, or do you have a feel for the way people think round here?"'

I've asked the wrong question, and like a defeated grand master in a chess tournament, I know I am gone. All that remains is bluff. I could try to swamp him with the personal, but that could be too bonding, could lead to an exchange of stories of women we have known. We're already bonded more than enough. I've mentioned a life experience, pointless as it was, and now will have to endure one of his. I could claim to have contracted a rare disease, but Maria is bound to make snide comments. So far she's shown herself entirely unhelpful in holding back waves of excessively relevant narrative.

What can I possibly do to appeal to his sense of decorous silence? I have the sense he's winding up to a long story. We would have been better off waiting by the car till nightfall and driving towards Balranald at ten kilometres an hour.

'Don't worry,' says Maria, but she's addressing him. 'He's not going to ask you for medical advice.'

'I was, actually,' I say, grasping at straws. 'What exactly is lumbago? Are there any diseases specific to this area? Will you write me a few prescriptions? What do you prescribe for truck drivers who want to make it to Perth without stopping?'

'You're a joker!' says the driver, very pleased. 'This'll amuse you, then.'

*

I never liked to imagine the father who would disapprove of this doctor for his daughter, if she were to luck out on such a farm-escaping opportunity, but such men exist.

Picture the daughter smiling after me as though the only thing my fingers were guaranteed to treat was her lack of love. Healing is obviously pouring out my fingertips. Doctor's touch, that could have been my slogan. I wasn't about to volunteer to cure common colds or skin conditions, no menorrhagia, non-specific viruses, diarrhoea; there were none of the usual complaints in my waiting room, at least not in her view.

She and I stood there listening to the approach of the four-wheel drive. Over-revving: that's how they learn to drive out here, I'd guess. Soon, the front door admitted a farmer, a big fellow, as they all are. His daughter and I had met about twenty-four hours before, felt like old friends now, so she said my name to the old man, and 'this's my dad' to me, and she didn't look at either of us. Daddy and I pronounced each other's names as we shook hands. I remembered to get a grip before he did. They like to squeeze a doctor's fingers, these father farmers, they have to be superior in some way and that's the way they generally go for, sometimes commenting on the soft skin of my hand, thinking, humph, this one wouldn't have done half a decent day's work in his life, wouldn't have peeled a carrot. Might even say something like that, like, 'Ho ho, he better be careful going into pubs round here for what people might make of a man with soft, never-worked hands, heh-heh, a "kept man" maybe,' question mark or wink or asking, 'Were you very close to your mummy?'

As this father went through the expected rigmarole, his darling daughter was sucking in her lower lip to stop herself from laughing — Daddy was thinking, isn't my honourable, familiar daughter sweet, making a face so as not to laugh at this spongy city doctor who might be hurt, so vulnerable are his emotions, and a guest too. But I knew it was so she didn't crack up at the charmless old man.

When the soft hands routine had no effect — and the point of his darling's secret knowledge of my soft-handed manliness and mine of Daughter's hard-handed womanliness was to be *secret* — he tried something else, as fathers do.

This one boomed out: 'You wouldn't know too much about haymaking, would you, eh? Why don't you come out on the tractor tomorrow? You ever drive one? That'll shake your bones up pretty damned well.'

I laughed with as much jollity as Daughter was displaying meekness, and overpolitely refused. I reckoned I knew how close dear Daughter and I were to an understanding on shaking bones, but I wasn't about to disclose the details to the self-deluding old bastard. He'd been at his other farm overseeing his men when I arrived the previous day and so lovely Daughter did all the looking-after by herself, picking me up from the bus depot and getting to know me. She'd spent some time with this city doctor during those last twenty-four hours and we would understand each other a lot better yet before my bones, my hands and I found ourselves back in the city, bloody oath we would. This daughter had heard something of city men whose appearances belie their abilities, and she'd as good as said as much. 'A good-looking doctor like you, beautiful smooth voice.'

'You ever milked a bull?' is one more this witty country father asked, this inquiry after his delicate daughter had left us to extract conversation from each other. This was one question I carefully shouldn't have and didn't laugh about too loudly or ignorantly. Instead I asked about his stud bulls which he must be famous for round these parts. Why, possibly even in the city — what had he called his entry or entries at the Royal Agricultural Show in Sydney last year? Right, that's it, New Shropshire Prince II. I couldn't understand how a catchy moniker like that slipped my mind. And it's funny, I thought I'd recognised the name of this station from the bulls' enclosure up at the Show, though of course I'd been much too polite to confirm that with his daughter, her being probably too ladylike to talk about electrodes up bulls' arses, rubber-red bull dicks shooting off into beakers. Nice young lady, if he doesn't mind me commenting. New Shropshire Prince won then, did he? No? Must've been robbed of his rightful ribbon then, and no doubt by Hunter Valley judges who wouldn't know shoulder musculature from post-operative scar tissue. Obviously not the kind of gentlemen who attended medical school alongside me.

Despite my poofy hands this father might even have taken a liking to me. Would have been the major achievement of the year, mine (withholding sarcasm just long enough to become likeable) or his (to recognise humanity beyond his own sun-ruined nose). Me, I could tell he was despicable.

'Anyhow, we'll find something useful for you to do in the morning,' were his last words to me that day. 'You being a doctor.'

Daughter, whose name became 'the Spunkrat' the more I thought about her and what would happen between us, had installed me the previous afternoon in the lace-and-goosefeather guest room they called 'The Barn' (there's still a sign saying so). It used to be a barn, too, but they had made the interior all pastel fabrics and rustic bare wood. The bedding was supposed to look hand-quilted but it was too evenly uneven and had been machine-made, a label went on to inform, in South Korea. No doubt it also simplified making up the bed, which was what the Spunkrat was doing when I returned to my room after her father had done with aggressing at me and I'd finished parrying. I was trying to think of a name to do justice to him. 'Pizzle-puller' was not bad. 'Bullrout' would have been poisonous enough, but too marine. Besides which, he looked as though he'd never seen the sea's cooling breeze. I needed a name which condensed the idea of midday sun shredding his hide.

I smiled at the Spunkrat, who gave the pillow a last pat and stood to face me.

'This window doesn't shut too good, so I hope you don't mind if you find me climbing through it some time in the middle of the night,' she reported, matter-of-factly, indicating an aluminium-framed sliding window on the side facing away from the main house.

'You climb however you like,' I answered. 'I suppose you know what you're doing vis à vis the old man.'

'Don't go worrying about Dad or his big shotgun. He's like a dingo with an aching jaw, wants to bite someone all the time. He can be a nasty old coot, but he's really good at sleeping too,' Spunkrat soothed.

'Well then, that's all right,' I said.

I tried to sound surer than I was. HomeFarm Pty Ltd, through which I'd booked myself three nights of 'experience the real Australia' — which was what brought me out here — hadn't mentioned anything like her, though why would they? I was probably the only professional person who'd been within two hundred miles of this 'retreat'. The only guest at all, most probably, certainly the only doctor whose window Spunkrat had ever promised to crawl through.

For her father's membership of HomeFarm Pty Ltd, I'd say the company must have guaranteed him some number of guests as a minimum. No other way to explain the agency doing the hard sell on me: 'Definitely worth the drive or easy train trip; believe me, there's no landscape like this anywhere in the world; mate, it shits on Ayers Rock and all that Alice Springs crap, makes the Olgas look like haemorrhoids; I was out there myself for three weeks last year and didn't regret a day; I ended up trying to convince the old farmer to part with thirty to forty per cent but he wouldn't have a bar of it, not after five generations in the same family. I would've put my own home in hock for the chance, my family still inside, I really would've,' claimed the slicked-back Kirribilli boy at HomeFarm Pty Ltd's glass-walled Sydney office.

My second day in holiday wonderland, I followed Spunkrat's directions to a dry creek bed and turned left. That is, I walked to where a few trees stood in line. The sun was directly overhead, for bloody hours it seemed, and I made my way along the deep red floor of the gully. Dead tree roots sectioned a deep blue sky. From the train I'd seen small red rock formations not much bigger than pebbles about two kilometres away. When I reached them, I pressed myself into a small arc of shade at the base of the largest, emptied the contents of my plastic water bottle down my throat and ate the tasteless and stale cheese sandwiches the Spunkrat had made after I'd declined tinned beef. I tried to play out the tourist role I'd been promised: I stood on a small rock and looked in every direction over the red landscape. Sure thing it's likely that visitors from every continent will come running to see this. I followed the creek bed and its column of brownish trees back towards New Shropshire Stud. I was parched. I sat in her kitchen and drank more water.

The Spunkrat had arranged three or four more sachets of sugar and instant coffee into a small basket on the sideboard though I hadn't touched those already there. I described city-boy holiday salesman to the Spunkrat, who recalled no such person.

'Then am I your first guest?' I asked.

'Well, we've had a few friends staying here before,' she replied and wouldn't say anything else because she sensed I had a devious reason for wanting the information, and she was exactly right. Later on, though, it struck me that her reticence could have been because mister-refined-fast-talking-holiday-seller received the same hospitality she offered me. Maybe, maybe not. Made no difference to me wanting to lay my palms on her lovely, country-muscled arse.

'No,' she instructed. 'You go and tidy yourself up, have a wash or something, and then come into the house for supper. I'm going in there now to get some food ready for you.'

I undressed myself and turned on the shower. My own 'pizzle' (telling myself little farm jokes now!) was definitely more than half-interested in the evening's promised activities, my stomach not so much, as it indicated through the slight nauseous sensation associated with mild sunstroke, and my head was saying: 'What the fuck are you doing here anyway? This is your idea of a holiday, is it? You like some little country girl just because she admires you, oh mighty and educated man?' and generally assailing me with self-sarcasm.

I stepped under the shower and immediately became less nervous. Creeklets of red clay ran towards the drain. New Shropshire's shower curtain was decent and heavy, did not arch inwards, did not stick to my legs. Farm grit was replaced with the usual generic squeakiness of this well-maintained, healthy body. Good, I was content. When I was dry, I put on clean underwear and a fresh shirt. The cool evening would not do to me what the heat of the afternoon had done, dampening clothes and making a person drowsy. Yes, the day had been something like Ayers Rock, but in that aspect only.

The Spunkrat was a hearty cook and heartier still provider of alcoholic beverage. A piece of cow stretched from one side of my plate to the other, and they were not small plates by a long shot. Potatoes and peas waited in further bowls until I'd eaten space for them on my dinner plate.

'My father already ate,' said the Spunkrat, sitting at the table with me and matching me fork for fork, gulp for gulp, as we headed towards china and bottle bottoms. 'He likes to eat early, sleep early and rise early again the next day.'

Father sounded fascinating, but it's her dad so I added nothing to her description of him.

'Good appetites here,' I commented, and only that.

'You know it,' she smiled, taking the empty plates and beer bottles and nearly done bowls and bringing back pudding, as she called it, which was apple pie, and also two mugs of port. After this, she sent me home.

'Go and read your textbooks for a while,' she suggested.

I settled into my soft bed under the soft duvet and stared uselessly at the in-focus, out-of-focus letters on page after page of books and magazines provided for the comfort of The Barn's guest or guests, no doubt as recommended by HomeFarm Pty Ltd. There was a glossy volume of Hitchcock movie stills; my fuzzy, sun- and alcohol-affected eyesight shared responsibility for the poor reproduction with some no-name printer. A photograph of a shower curtain arched and flattened, arched and flattened. That last swallow of port anaesthetised my lips, I thought. A dull, yellow guest-room light shining in my eyes could not counteract the combined hypnotic effect of cool sheets and warm bed covers, the secure weight of Hitchcock face down and open on my chest like shield. I slept until I felt a body move on top of me, her night hands stroking my face. Brain said nothing, nor stomach. Hitchcock jumped.

'So thin,' the Spunkrat whispered, grasping my upper arms (I couldn't have said the same of hers, all muscle, solid, surprising), but then she said 'ooh!' and nothing else in words until — I could hardly believe it myself — 'Thank you, doctor.'

'Thank you too,' I replied, with single 'ha' of laughter, and then we both relaxed too much.

We were woken by beating on the door and yelling.

'Oh shit,' said Daughter, already out of bed, 'you're in for it!' and she leapt out the window.

'Who's there?' I called. I acted normal. That was the first plan to mind, despite the sound of New Shropshire's guest-room door cracking and the easily visible scattering of the Spunkrat's clothes all round the room. There was no verbal response, only the solid shoulder hitting the door and the door complaining.

'No no no no no. Wrong idea,' figured my brain, rushing to overtake my mouth and control my part of this early morning's new direction. 'This is not a knock-knock joke; Plan A needs superseding.'

'Coming!' I called, this being the next option to mind, which I knew to be the oldest delaying tactic in history. 'No need to break down the door!'

I too dived out the window.

I landed in an empty flower bed and stood up. Cool, pre-morning soil was under my bare feet. There was no sign of the Spunkrat I could see. Ahead and to the left, the sky was the palest grey, and there was no colour for the land yet; it was all silhouette, trees and low hills, with faint patches of mauve in the clouds to my right. Everywhere was still except behind me. All noise concentrated on the guest-room door. Father's thumping and shouting. I did the commando bit, keeping low, made myself think, 'Serious, this is bloody serious' as I heard a loud crash from behind me and the hammering ceased. I was crouch-running for the front gate. A light in the guest room went on, the slightest tinge of yellow rose touching the dry lawn behind me. I stubbed my toes one by one on fist-size rocks as I headed along New Shropshire Stud's private clay track towards the tar.

'You sneaky, slimy, Sydney bastard,' shouted Daddy. His footsteps were coming for me; my brain said, 'Don't turn around.' I was over the gate and turning right, turning east, already out of breath but accelerating hard on bitumen as the first effulgent pinprick of orange transgressed the horizon.

*

'That ought to be the end of the story,' says the doctor, 'but it isn't.'

'That's okay,' I say, defeated but struggling to prevent further damage, further stories of our driver's invisible attractiveness. 'I don't expect to know your whole life from one short car ride. Maybe you could email me the rest?'

'I like you!' enthuses the doctor. 'You're very funny. There aren't that many funny people up here. Round here they think "clown" is an insult. You don't want to call anyone a clown or they'll take a shotgun to your front windows, not a pretty sound at three in the morning. I've attended the aftermath in my professional capacity. This is not the place for understated behaviour. I'm talking from experience.'

'Sure,' I acknowledge, an acknowledgment I'd intended as somewhat dismissive but which he interprets as assent to continue his tale.

'You may have noticed,' the doctor makes some kind of twirling gesture with his left index finger, 'that I'm still here. Her father likes to pretend not to have warmed to me, but I'm still here.

'The old bastard growls at me and orders me off the property, fires shots into the air. He's hilarious too, though in a different way to you, because he's completely unintentional. He puts up signs threatening "Trespassers including those with medical training" with everything from prosecution to electrocution. But as the years have passed, he's become more lax. Nowadays he'll ask me for a diagnosis of his injuries or breathing difficulties before sending me away at gunpoint. He'll allow me to stay for days at a time before suddenly "noticing" me and calling the police. Years ago, the police used to manhandle me. I spent a number of weekends in the lockup, where the cops mocked my nice city voice and warned me that my "type" was not welcome in this region. I'd inform them that it was government policy to encourage my "type", i.e. doctors, to rural areas, and they'd tell me the government meant respectable doctors, not my "type" of immoral trespassing derelict.

'These days the coppers greet me as "Doctor", talk to me about their children's limps and rashes, ask me to play it cool for a day or two while the old man calms down again. They advise me earnestly to keep my curtains drawn in the guest room, to make my own breakfasts instead of getting the old man to do it.

'The old prick's become very friendly in a legalistic, mean-old-man kind of way too. He's still a vile, narrow-minded man, but he has come to like me a great deal.

'Funny thing is, the daughter won't have a bar of me. She went off to Melbourne to study, came back to pick up her things. Won't speak more than three abusive words to me now. She's moved away, and when she comes here to visit the old man, she insists I vacate the old barn for the whole time. But I've got a lot of friends around here now, so I can stay pretty much anywhere I please. She shouts at me for taking advantage of her father, who all of a sudden she thinks she loves. I'm the one who looks after him, more often than not, with his endless muscular complaints, axeman's elbow, burns, scratches and ant bites. Not to mention other problems, which I won't detail in case either of you has a delicate constitution.

'I don't understand her at all. We had a grand old time for a few months, me sneaking back to see her or meeting down the creek. She was so bloody sexy, you wouldn't believe me if I told you. I made up as best as I could with Daddy, that bad-tempered son of a bitch, and leased his failed tourist enterprise. She accuses me of buttering him up, trying to usurp her rightful inheritance, all kinds of terrible things. Poisoning him. Terrible things. I changed my life all around so I'd be able to stay up here, found myself a bit of doctoring to pay the rent. I even paid him a rental bond. I still pay him, even when I'm not there because of her.

'As soon as it was fixed up that I'd stay, she wouldn't see me any more. I try to talk to her about it, but she just tells me to get off it, leave her alone. It's completely beyond me, the logic of it. But that's women, I guess.' He looks briefly over his shoulder towards Maria. 'No offence.'

'I'm not offended,' says Maria, smiling a little maliciously. 'I understand perfectly where you're coming from.'

'By the way,' says the doctor, 'there's not much point in going all the way to Balranald for a fan belt when I know a bloke who's probably got one, and he's not far from here, fifteen miles, twenty max. I'll give you a lift back too. No, don't thank me. I've really taken to you, mate. You're very funny. If you lived around here, I reckon we'd get through a few beers together, would we what!' He turns briefly to Maria. 'You're okay too, darling.'

'I appreciate it,' I say, 'but please, don't go to any trouble. We'll be right from the town. We'll probably get a lift back with your father-in-law, who'll tell us the truth about your bullshit.'

The doctor laughs loudly. 'That's a risk I'm not about to take.'

'I'd be happy to go to Balranald too,' interjects Maria, at last taking some responsibility.

'You can drive there yourself later,' dismisses the doctor. 'That is, if the fan belt's your only problem.'

He steers off the road; the back of the car slides around and he corrects and straightens out.

'Otherwise you can walk!' He guffaws generously at his own joke. We're now heading down a bumpy clay track with nothing in sight, certainly not a mechanic's, only low, sparsely grassed hills, occasional earthworks from eroded rabbit burrows, a waterless creek.

'One thing is, be careful what you say. This guy's had a pretty rough life, so he's kind of delicate.'

Maria leans forward and pats me on the shoulder. Her first apology of the journey.

After a time, we pass between two hills and suddenly come upon a huge rectangular building, like an aircraft hangar, built entirely of corrugated iron. The doctor stops beside a stretched chicken-wire fence about three metres tall. Behind this ugly enclosure is a small, intensely green lawn, about the size of an inner-city garden. The lawn is punctuated by a number of tiny trees in cages.

The doctor cooees and almost immediately an old man steps from the barn.

'Hello, doc,' he says. 'What's wrong with your fucking car this time?'

'Good to see you too, Fish. This is a couple of friends of mine I just met up the road. They've snapped a fan belt. I've rescued them and brought them here. My car's fine.'

I dangle the fan belt at him.

'Aren't you a fucking hero then?' he says to the doctor, and to me, 'You'll be lucky if that's all that's wrong.'

'Do you have a fan belt?' I ask, all customer now.

'I really doubt it, but I'll look. Pig's chance in an abattoir frankly. Come with me. At worst I'll be able to fix you up with a towrope, but then you'll be stuck with that fool for the rest of the week while he figures out where to tie it. You'll be better off walking. Burke and Wills would've refused a lift with that fellow. Come on then.'

Maria and the doctor remain standing in the orange, perpendicular sunlight. Maria staring at the lawn, the doctor turning to face her as if about to start a conversation or (more likely) a monologue.

'What's with the wire?' I ask the mechanic.

'Rabbits still,' he says. 'The virus got most of them, but in drought they'll still ringbark a tractor if you give them a chance. I'm proud of that garden. I've actually grown trees from seeds round here, and that's saying something. My trees are the only surviving large vegetation planted since myxomatosis in this area.'

'Impressive,' I say.

'Thank you. I'm proud of them, but it's nice to have someone objective appreciate it too.'

We enter the hangar, where the mechanic begins opening and shutting drawers in search of a replacement fan belt. My eyes gradually adjust to the darkness of the shed, which is lit only by pinpoints of light coming through bolt holes in the iron. There are a couple of old cars on blocks, but the space is dominated by an impeccably painted fishing boat, ten metres long.

'Beautiful boat,' I say. 'Funny to see it out here.'

'Guess it would be, but no joke once the floods come.'

'Floods! Is that why you're called Fish?'

'No one calls me Fish except for that idiot,' says the mechanic. 'He thinks it will help me. He thinks it's a therapeutic name. Can you believe that?'

'Oh,' I say. I can believe that and so suddenly feel extremely non-rural.

'We'll have the inland sea of legend back within a month, once the real rains start. Burke and Wills and the rest, they might have been a few score years too early but they weren't wrong.'

'I see,' I say. 'But I didn't mean to pry.'

'That's all right, son,' says the mechanic. 'I appreciate someone who shows himself ready to listen. All that imbecile can do is talk. My feeling is that he must have smoked some of the funny baccy back in the 1970s, and it's still affecting him. That's why he's been stuck here for the last twenty-five years. That and the fact that he can't shut up long enough to pack his things and leave.'

'He is talkative,' I agree, 'but he's been quite helpful to us.'

'You're not much of a talker, are you?'

'I suppose not.'

'And you're a modest bloke too. That's commendable in a young man.'

'Thank you.' What else could I say?

'Let me tell you something I haven't told anyone else in this district. My life hasn't been the easiest, though you mightn't guess it from my lovely garden. It's been tough. I didn't grow up here. I guess I escaped to here, in a way. Perhaps my story will help you make the most of what you have: that beautiful young woman, the freedom to travel, a sympathetic manner. I'd give a lot to be your age again, son.'

I'm nodding as if grateful, hoping he has a fan belt.

'You don't really have to tell me your story. It sounds as though it may be too personal for a stranger,' I say. It's pointless, isn't it? I can't stop any of them.

'It's a lot of responsibility, being young, though it may not seem it at the time. Do you feel it?'

I nod once, then again more emphatically.

'You're probably thinking about starting a family, building your lives together. I was too, at your age.'

I keep very quiet, remembering the doctor's warning, remembering too that my attempted intervention had not stopped the doctor from telling me about his seduction.

'You're right to listen carefully,' says the mechanic, 'because I can picture you out there in your boat, thinking you can rely on people like me. But you can't.'

'Um, I don't have a boat,' I say.

'Hush now,' he says. 'I know who you are.'

*

I knew about duty, but mine was ripped out to sea. The matches, the meteorological skills, my techniques of illumination went with it. I could not kindle the lamps; I could hardly try.

There were reports about me then, about my failures, as once there had been reports of my courage. I have the old clippings. Here he is, immersed up to his chest, and the boy in his arms will breathe again. Here he is, alone on the headland where only yesterday he had stood to throw the lifeline. Here he is. The later stories were not published, unless as clipped whispers one was incapable of tearing from a page and sticking in a shameful scrapbook. This much is true: I am no longer commendable. Also: I ask for no commendation.

In the east there was nothing to see. And so I stared at nothing. I remembered nothing, not how to be myself, not as I had been. Forty metres below, intentionless white-capped black rocks supported me in that place, sure they did, and with as little care as I showed approaching shipping.

There were pale flashes on the horizon; they were coming between your boat and me. Soon after, I would fail once more. I felt the mood of a storm coming on, overtaking the horizon, passing your boat, overwhelming me. My advice to you would have been to seal the portholes and decant the rum, and it was the last advice you'd receive. The last rum too, unless your luck had stayed better than mine.

The wind changed direction. I sensed moistness in the air. It became cooler. The air tasted different, as though it had lost its oxygen. I may have blacked out; I may have fainted, and come to later, when the sky was blue and the only sign that a storm had passed was that the seaweed had reconfigured and was aligned to the east.

My telephone rang all you wanted, your calls and, the day after, those of your shorebound colleagues, and every day after that. I would not pick it up. Between their snide tales of hardship and well-being, the scandalous evening newspapers for once might have reported my recalcitrance. I didn't read them.

These mean-nothing rocks were more dangerous than sea vipers and that night I did not warn you of them. I did not care for you or me or anyone living. All other times I was as human as 'good morning'. On nights as that was, I became the churning storm clouds doubled in my dead wife's eyes. My wife, who fell into the sea.

My vocation was erased. I forgot my skills, my reflexes and my charity. I knew only the midpoint between my room and the horizon. There was the storm, there followed a blacker night, unevenly punctuated. Water beat against that metal tower. In its centre I stood, tearing the skin from my face.

Sure, you tapped out your coordinates: at a certain moment they were those my wife once occupied. In my mind, I saw her breathing in, but it is water, she's inhaling water, she cannot call goodbye. Every night I close my eyes and this is what I see. The boat collapses; its rudder snaps, planks unpick, plastic bottles and life jackets scatter like teasing cats. My wife falls into a cleft in the ocean, and continues to fall. I cannot help but see her.

The matches might as well have been soaked in brine. I couldn't light a pipe, let alone... The storm was like a prison at night in countryside, its inaccessible flickers amid dark clouds. Green reflectors embedded in the road seemed as bright. The distance across dry hills to the prison was immense, then I was too suddenly upon it. Searchlights were conical spires filled with insects and surmounting high stone walls. But no, then it was different, for my lighthouse was solid, its supports unlit and patternless, and the flashing clouds approached me, not I them. Instead, this later storm was a ship bearing prisoners across the lampless sea. It came.

With the first flash, a portrait began in monochromes and formed my dead wife's face; with the second I was falling towards her, across the hemispheric room. That night the photographs across the diameter of my house burnt only for one second, but then in negative behind my forehead until the next lightstrike. Nothing can rid me of her image though I press the pads of my hands hard against my tight-shut eyes. Every flash felt as though it was the last, as though nothing more could touch me. That is how I read the history of my life. The leadlighting could have been my wife in silhouette against the uncurtained window. I reached out, with hands palm-upwards, but she vanished. The sound of thunder was in darkness, halved behind weatherproof glass. She was gone. And repeat. And repeat. My prayers, if they were possible, were for erasure. If only I could fail to recognise her face. If I could have screamed loud enough to silence the storm. If my shrieks had drowned the sea.

On your ship which I would not protect, you were welded and bolted behind wrist-thick iron plates, and warm because the rocking was gentle, the rum strong and you could not know the end of your journey would be as unexpected as the shape of the next wave. You had company and dancing. There were card games. There was chance.

My dead wife's tourniquet fingers gripped my forearm. She led me towards the water. That way. Over there. I was gulping like kelp around the reefs. When her portrait on the mantel flared, I remembered my dead wife's lips were deep, deep red. It was as though the blood moved visibly through her body, arteries contracting and dilating, capillaries like momentary coral. Blood pressed through her fingers which snatched but could not catch hold of the surface of the sea. I saw the hands opening and closing. I could have kissed my dead wife's lips in the count from the flash to the grinding thunder and it would never have been enough.

Rain dragged the ocean up around me. I was surrounded by my dead wife's mementoes which on these nights become mine as well. Once they contained cities, they stood in for journeys, they might have held her thoughts of me. Their familiar shapes were as ghostly as tides. This was how they lodged in me: by shifting me whole, to and fro.

You were forgotten. No gauge of iron could protect you. If I could have brought light to the beacons, the lightning would have lost the determinate shape of my dead wife. But I could not strike a match with these cold fingers. My dereliction was like a diseased soldier's rattling war memory: dangerous, invisible, constant. I should have been the one to die and now can never be alone. I was too cowardly to cheat my dead wife's alternating claims on me, her impossible entreaties to remember her and to join her.

I prayed for dismissal from that vocation. Come on, take me from here. Every clear dawn begged for my continued employment, but I beseeched you to pay no heed, not to wait for the rupture of metal, the tearing of bolts.

When my wife was falling for me and I for her, the sky was blue or black and I was three fluent brushstrokes on the calfskin of the world. We promised each other every object and every thought we could imagine. I gave up order for her, and of all that is stolen or fled or drowned I do not miss that. We promised each other vertigo and the seaweed scent of gentle rain. If I could make promises so easily again, I would laugh all night with my eyes straining open.

I would no longer hear my dead wife's arms slapping the surface as she drifts out to sea.

*

The mechanic is out of sight, crouched down behind a counter. I hear a loud slapping sound then the slam of a drawer. He stands and turns to face me. He is very pale and his eyes are red.

'This ought to do the trick,' he says, handing me the thick rubber loop. I look at the broken fan belt, which seems much longer than its replacement. I feel I should confirm that the new belt will be long enough to fit the car. It's hard to ask him anything, upset as he is. I should also say something comforting, but can't think what.

'I guess the old one stretched a bit?'

'Reckon it would've.' I suspect he's grateful I haven't tried to administer sympathy. 'You'd better get going or it'll be dark. Especially if that fool's going to run you back. He'd get lost following a road up a hill, he's that bright. If you have any more car trouble, come back here. You know where I am now, and I'm not going anywhere.

'Ten dollars will cover it, by the way.'

I pay him. We step into the remaining light. I see Maria patting the doctor's shoulder as he wipes away tears.

'I guess it's that kind of day,' the mechanic comments.

We stop, hold back to allow the doctor to recompose himself. When the mechanic judges enough time has passed he tells the doctor, 'You'd better get going, or they won't get back till midnight. And then they'll end up stuck in a little, wheel-less caravan on a small plot shared by a madman and his mad former father-in-law.'

'As long as I get them away from you by dark, they'll be fine. Wouldn't inflict you on anyone for more than fifteen minutes, charming as you are.'

Maria and I say our farewells as though the old mechanic has put us up for a week. We drive off.

'Very, very sad,' the doctor says. 'I guess you heard about his wife?'

'Mm.' I try to communicate that I won't be gossiping, that I've been told in confidence. The doctor responds with a laugh, as if I've expressed disbelief.

'He tells that story to everyone, and always claims he tells no one. The old-timers say he moved up here fifty years ago with the same story: lighthouse, the wife disappearing, his guilt. How he's prevented from assisting whoever he's telling. No one knew then if it was true, and no one is sure yet. They say it wasn't in the newspapers, but who knows where he came from? He could be from the far north or anywhere. He has a bit of talent for boats. That one in there is a beauty, not that it's seen water, and he built it from the ground up. I reckon that even if his story wasn't true fifty years ago, he believes in it himself by now. I've tried for years to convince him to get psychological help, see someone, talk it through. Out here they just won't. They're all terrified of mentioning mental health, let alone mental illness. I do what I can, and to be honest I've helped him a lot. He wouldn't thank me for it though, wouldn't admit it, not for anything.'

'That sounds like a terrible story,' says Maria.

'Yes,' says the doctor. 'Sometimes he'll say out of the blue, "I miss her so much." He groans it out, and I don't reckon he's conscious he's said anything at all.'

The doctor's lips purse exaggeratedly and his eyes momentarily water. He continues to drive in silence. There's no way I can start a conversation with him, even if I'd wanted to. I'd have to ask, 'And what about you? Why are you crying?'

When we get to the car shortly after, the doctor waits with his headlights on as I fit the fan belt — which is the right size — and refill the radiator.

'I've written my phone number down, so if you get stuck...' he says. 'A night in a barn won't trap you for ever, not necessarily.'

The doctor and I shake hands. I wish him luck. Maria offers to shake his hand too; the doctor tries to kiss her cheek and there's a slightly awkward pause as Maria decides to allow this.

'I wish I'd met you two decades ago,' he tells Maria, then to me, 'Excuse me. You're a lucky man.'

'I was just out of kindergarten,' says Maria gently.

He waits for us to start the car. I assume he's checking it will start before driving off himself. In the rear-view mirror I see he still has not yet begun to move as we ascend a crest, then we're on the road west again, less than two hours later, driving straight towards the last strip of pale daylight.

*

'What was that doctor bloke so upset about?' I ask Maria. 'That was really weird. I came out from hearing this mechanic's awful story and the two of you are doing the same thing.'

'He didn't say much more about his girlfriend, just asked me what I thought.'

'What did you think?'

'I tried to be gentle, but I told him the truth. Anyone could see. She's finished with him. She's a city person now, and he only reminds her of where she came from.'

'Jesus. That's a heavy thing to tell a bloke.'

'He insisted on me saying it. I couldn't not say it.'

'Do you think he'll be okay?'

'I told him to visit friends and he promised me he would. I asked, "Are you the kind of man who keeps his promises?" and he said he was.'

'You might have ruined his life, Maria.'

'He must have known it at some level. That she was never coming back to him. She couldn't have been clearer. Hopefully he'll do something new, something other than waiting. He might even reconcile openly with the old man.'

'I hope so. I hope you did the right thing, but I doubt it. What a thing to say.'

By this time it's too late to make it to Adelaide tonight. I feel light-headed from a succession of heart-breaking conversations with strangers.

We're still about six hundred kilometres from Maria's destination, that gridded city which might one day be hers, the boyfriend moving along its well-planned paths on his unnamed transport: bus, perhaps, or bicycle, which would account for his inability to collect Maria from Sydney himself. There he waits, nameless and undescribed, certainly lascivious yet still somehow attractive, perhaps apprehensive, perhaps alone in his room, or in his partitioned portion of a large office, perhaps (I might think, reflecting on Maria's capacity for cruelty towards me) a mere figment, a man who cannot wait for lack of body to still or with which to pace. But, no — and I sense this and know this. Despite her many other faults, Maria's not one for imaginary men. She would not drive me to Adelaide and drive me away for a figment.

Maria's travels are measurable to the centimetre. Who knows how far I am from my own endpoint? The answer seems simple if only I ascertain it in this literal and direct manner: turn around in Adelaide and drive back to Sydney. This is calculable. I am two thousand kilometres from the finish, just one-third of the journey behind me.

And yet, can it be said that a return to the beginning is the same as attaining a destination, especially a return to a beginning deprived of half its personnel, and with the deprivation of Maria so insistent, her emphatic absence from the second half of my journey? We have met people whose trajectories start and end unpredictably, who veer inexplicably north or west, who meander, who stop and

do not move again, who stand by roads in the middle of
the night hoping for movement, who stand in towns for
decades waiting to intersect with the trajectory of another.

I stretch out from Sydney, test the elasticity of my
communications with Maria, check our thin bond over
the heated terrain, and after I have dilated all that
remains between us from one city to another, will be
sucked back to the first, slowly returning to my earlier,
unexpanded state.

Humans customarily designate that transformations
take place at invisible hours, at times when unnatural
effort is needed to observe them. The changes from
Friday to Saturday, from week to week and old year to
new year, take place at midnight, well past our natural,
diurnal bedtimes.

At sunset we were on the highway, heading west. We
had truckstop sandwiches to hand and bottles of sweet
carbonated liquid. We consumed these and maintained our
velocity. Now, in darkness, nothing's changed but the
mileage and fuel indicators on the dashboard, which have
risen and fallen respectively. And Maria and I have
switched positions. Seesawing dials, metronomic drivers.
At sunset she was driving, the sun visor lowered, Maria
sitting up straight to keep the sun out of her eyes, moving
the visor to the front and to the side and to the front again
as the road swerved more westerly and more southerly
and then west northwest. The sun disappeared soon
enough, and I drove through the twilight, visor raised,

eyes relaxed. Then she drove again. Now, she pulls over and we stretch our legs, drink a little water from a bottle. I drive.

The headlights shine into my eyes, first a pinpoint slowly amplifying, a flare on passing, gone, amplify, flare, gone, amplify, flare, gone, flare, flare, flare, gone, gone, gone, flare, gone, a kilometre or fifty metres between cars, amplify, amplify, dip, flare, gone, flare, flare, gone, gone, amplify, dip, amplify, gone, black, pinpoint, amplify, flare, gone, flare, gone, amplify, flicker flicker flicker through trees, amplify, flare, gone, amplify, flare, gone, amplify, flare, gone, amplify, flare, gone, flare, flare, gone, gone, flicker, flicker, bright, dip, flare, gone, pinpoint, black, pinpoint, amplify, bright, dip, gone, weak tonal changes repeating and repeating Doppler's thesis, high, low, high, low, pinpoint, amplify, amplify, flare, flare, gone, gone, as I try to keep my eyes down, looking down and to the left, away from the oncoming headlights which begin as a pinpoint, amplify, amplify, flare and gone or amplify, amplify, highbeam, dip, flare, gone, bright, dip, gone, flickering through trees, gone, the black empty road silent but for the sound of my car, tyres on road, the engine high-pitched and steady, amplify, amplify, bright, bright, amplify, very bright, gone (arsehole), black again, a pinpoint on the horizon, amplify, motorcycle monobeam (is it?), amplify, (it's not) one good, one failing headlight, pressure to orient relative to the centre of the road, amplify, amplify, flare, gone, seems like this for hours, pinpoints on the horizon, slow, slow amplification, black, visible as they come over the crest, divide into two headlights, brighter, high beam, dip, flare, gone, amplify, flare, gone, amplify, flare, gone, flare, flare, flare, gone, gone, gone, and I'm beginning to feel it in my temples and on the crown of my head, and I'm looking down and left, flare and gone, amplify, down and left, flare and gone, and conscious of my neck, of keeping my neck off centre, of the rising nausea as the cars appear on the horizon, approach, approach, approach, their tone suddenly rising then dropping, flare and gone, flare and gone, telling Maria I feel pretty weird, stopping the car by the side of the road, there's long, dry grass, and the cars and trucks keep passing, the drag as each pair of headlights disappears, flare and gone, I'm kneeling in the grass, vomiting, covering my eyes, perspiring out of proportion to the heat, hearing the vehicles approach, the rise in tone then the sudden drop, the drag, the long grass rustling slightly and I'm vomiting while Maria brings me a T-shirt soaked in water and I think I can taste petrol but that's impossible and I lie down in the long dry grass as cicadas shriek in the black carless night.

After some time, I wrap my head in the damp T-shirt and get into the car. Maria drives us to a motel by the highway.

'Where are we?' I mumble through the tepid cotton.

'In Euston, near Robinvale. But you don't have to worry about the names of places,' she soothes.

249

Maria goes into the office to negotiate.

She returns and says, 'They've only got a double room. We'll have to share a bed.'

'Whatever,' I mumble.

'I hope you've finished throwing up.'

So we're finally in this motel, Maria and I, this room with one double bed and barely enough floor either side for a pair of shoes. I'm not quite in the celebratory frame of mind I would have predicted at this theoretically promising moment. Maria carries our things in from the car while I strip off and turn on the shower. The water flows a rust-tinted yellow but is cool enough. I sit on the shower floor. The water runs over my head. Maria brings a couple of headache tablets and a glass of water. This latter would usually seem excessive, as water is streaming all over me, but the water Maria brings seems clear and I drink it all even though I'd swallowed the tablets with the first sip. I sit under that shower for another ten or fifteen minutes, until I imagine the tablets are beginning to have an effect, then I dry myself, walk into the main room and climb straight under the cool motel sheets. The room is pleasantly cold but very loud. Maria has the air conditioning on full. I find the noise painful and I ask her to turn it off, which she does.

My photophobia recedes and for the first time I see the room. Our silent TV is bolted into the discoloured wall via a number of metal strips. There's a low wall unit, and on it a small, paper-doily-lined basket with sachets of unbranded coffee and tea lined up like office files, and beside the basket a small electric jug which next morning we will find does not switch itself off. The fridge hums and rattles slightly. I ask Maria to unplug it but she says she can't, that it's wired into the wall.

I close my eyes. I have the sensation that the foot of the bed is rising and that soon I will be flung backwards. I sit up. Maria brings me a third pillow. I lie back and cannot remember anything further of the night.

# DAY THREE

I THINK I WAKE up. I bring fingertips to my temple. Nothing too bad. Feels maybe like a hangover, but I hadn't been drinking. My eyes advise against opening them and I take the advice. I think Maria's asleep next to me. Or she may be as awake as I am. My neck is aching a little. I can't really stretch or do anything much about it as I think my arm is under Maria's shoulder. This is unclear. It's also possible that I am remembering sliding my arm under her shoulder, rather than it being there already.

Maria is beautiful, familiar, the person who has slept beside me all night. For a moment I feel an intense warmth towards her. My eyes water with the emotion. I recall bending my elbow, tightening my arm to draw her towards me. I am liking her, or it could be a memory of the liking I felt towards her which accompanied our first few nights together: gratitude and desire, attraction and affection, permission and custom. I must remember kissing Maria's cheek, her eyes opening a fraction of an inch. It seems as though I may have kissed her lips, once, twice, and that her lips then pressed back. Or perhaps they pressed back after my third kiss. Perhaps, and this recollection is the one which grows, I kissed her cheek and she moved her lips to where my lips were by now in position for kissing. It may have been that we were lying there kissing each other like boyfriend and girlfriend, each having forgotten or not brought to mind that this was no longer true. We are kissing, my arm holding us in that vaguely uncomfortable position for a few moments, then we move towards each other. I put my other arm around her, feel her arms gather me towards her. I cannot recall how long we are there, kissing, but it is some time. I could say that time was swept away in the moment. I could say that I'm not at my most empirical the morning after a large photophobic headache. Either way, time disappears. My memory has a pleasant lip-feeling attached to this kissing event, for as short or long as the occurrence continues, the taste of morning kisses, full of sleep. We kiss, arms around each other, my leg slipping between hers, our legs entwining.

It could be that we both simultaneously realise that this isn't what we want at this time, and both move apart simultaneously. Our relationship, we might both conclude, no longer has room for this kind of mutuality. It could also be that during our long minutes of kissing, Maria hasn't yet woken properly, that she is wholly kissing in her half-sleep, and that as she wakes she realises that this is not what she would have set out to do had she been entirely awake earlier, had she been fully aware that the person lying beside her was a recovering headache victim who is no longer her boyfriend, had she been as fully in control as she usually is and prefers to be.

We cease kissing. She pulls back to her side of the bed and I make an effort to move towards mine. She rolls onto her back and looks at the ceiling. I watch her for a few seconds, then do likewise. We lie there for a while. We're not touching. My stomach has that Big Dipper feeling that something may happen, unreal hope. I consider trying to hold hands with her in a friendly manner but decide against. I don't know what decisions Maria takes. After a short time, a couple of minutes, she says, 'I'm going to get up. Do you want some coffee?'

'Okay. Thanks.' I wait until she's out of bed, then do the same. The room's curtains are more effective than usual for this kind of motel. The digital radio reads ten a.m. My headache has left no traces. I feel fine.

Actually, I am bereft.

We are friendly towards each other afterwards. I am concerned she knows that I believe our kissing to be mutually embarked upon. To this, Maria professes ignorance, refuses to engage in even the mildest recrimination or exculpation.

For her part, Maria worries that I should not be too disappointed by the sudden termination of the morning kiss. She also hopes I understand that our relationship no longer includes kissing. I acknowledge her concern about the former, gently rebut the latter. This sense of fixity she wants me to have, it's funny, this certainty, her kind of certainty. It's not a kind of certainty I could possibly understand.

'Jack,' she says, shaking her head.

'You know, I never really got that thing about people being "hungry" for each other's kisses. Hunger is usually met orally, obviously fair enough, and like kissing in that shallow way, but there the similarity ends. Hunger is a pragmatic need in fulfilment of which the oral is a mere link in the chain. The lips are entirely incidental to hunger and the pleasure of eating. Perhaps not entirely incidental with cloves or chillis. But kissing is so lip- and mouth-centred, so consuming in a non-hunger-related way. Don't you think?'

'You're funny, Jack,' she says, but she doesn't laugh. Still too busy with the certainty idea.

The sense I want her to have is something else: it is that below the simple, regulated surface of our new way of being with each other, this way which includes driving, eating, drinking and short bursts of repartee, she wants me. Given our history, I want her to understand, it is natural that she should. The pile of letters, unwritten, undelivered.

*

*Dear Maria,*

*Fuck me stupid. Root me ragged. Screw me senseless. Fuck my brains out. Fuck me dead.*

*Dear Maria,*

*When we walk along the sand together, I pull you close and feel your warmth through all our clothes as the freezing wind howls from the south, as the sea spray freezes instantly, in mid air, leaving beautiful unlikely ice arcs all along the shore. The only thing that is warm is you, you line the tips of your fingers along my shoulder blades when we embrace, I love the feel of your lips on my neck, your skin against mine.*

*Dear Jack,*

*The language is made for us to whisper. The world is full of space for us to be.*

\*

I'm dreaming this as the car radio does its best with my heartstrings. We are driving west. We have breakfasted and paid for our room without further incident. We have heard no stories, nothing to dilute a kiss and then its ceasing. Maria, it's a pity that we are here. The radio follows us, defining who we are and what we like, allowing us to speak less and be sung for more. We are sentimental gently and violently, smoothly and rhythmically. We are punk and dance sentimentalists. We like sentimentality from the 50s,

60s, 70s and 80s. Our trances and houses are sentimental. We like classically and baroquely sentimental strings and pianos. Mostly though, according to the most tuneable radio station, we like sentimental country.

To this soundtrack, the road turns from grey to red, haze for a corona instead of a persistent water mirage.

The vents exhale puffs of dust and a grey patina forms over my hands on the wheel.

Eventually Maria and I say enough to agree that we are equally sick of gold country classics, sick enough to change stations. A joke can only last so many indistinguishable replays. I know Kenny dies tragically before he gets the chance to tell Ellen he loves her, but when that hawk circles purposefully overhead she gets the message. I know Tracy is too tired after her sixteen-hour shift as a truckstop waitress to appreciate what a good-hearted man Evan is, and that she knows Joe is bad, but she likes bad men, and although Joe can't control his temper he says he loves her, and he cries when he hits her, and when she's dead he will be remorseful as he languishes waiting for the hangman. I twist the tuning dial and we lose all the USA's total export quota of musical sadness. I slide through static of various pitches. A voice emerges which might be current affairs. After the time trap of country music, I could do with some currency, so twiddle back and forth. I turn it up loud. Behind the static is some kind of listing.

'What the hell is that?' asks Maria.

I turn it up further. There seems to be music as well, but it's impossible to determine whether it originates from the same place or whether we are receiving two or more neighbouring or overlapping stations simultaneously. We can hear someone stating immediate activities. There is no explanation.

'More volume,' requests Maria. 'I guess that's as tuned as it's going to get?'

She's probably thinking about photography. Everything, unfortunately, contains the seed of a project, but I do as she asks. The static erases all emotion from the speaker. It is impossible to discern through the noise whether we're listening to a song, talkback radio or current affairs. We cannot tell if the voice is teaching English as a new language, performing, or pleading for help.

*

Away from you, I'm walking up the steps. I'm going to the bank. I'm depositing a cheque. I order a cheese roll. I cycle round the block. I try to mow the lawn. I look out the front door. I'm wearing yellow socks. I forgot to take a bath. I'm carrying a bag. I'm going the wrong way. I'm halting in my tracks. I'm feathering my nest. I'm stabilising fast. I'm reaching out for more. I'm adopting a new pose. I'm standing on a bench. I'm cleaning up my room. I'm remembering the place. I'm loitering with intent. I'm gliding at half speed. I'm appealing to good sense. I order you to stop. I'll find my own way home. I'm straying from the path. I'm letting myself go. I'm refining my beliefs. I'm resigning from my post. I'm wiring up the house. I'm sticking to the point. I'm harbouring a dream. I'm dreaming of the day. I'm carving out a niche. I stay awake till dawn. I empty out the sink. I'm brushing up my French. I drag along behind. I'll crawl under a rock. I'm saving you a place. I'm respecting your desires. I wish to be alone. I rest on my success. I'm combing through the chaff. I'm shaking off fatigue. I'm riding on the crest. I'm proud to be alive. I'm driving her insane. I'm panicking myself. I'm developing a limp. I'm waiting for a train. I'm considering a book. I'm rolling you a joint. I'm walking arm in arm. I'm piercing my ear. I'm putting on a tape. I've got an itchy neck. I'm breathing through my nose. I'm measuring my steps. I'm looking at the sky. I'm selling out my friends. I'm living over there. I'm feeling very stiff. I'm talking in the car. I'm lying on the ground. I'm sending you the prints. I want to know the truth. I'm trying to scare the birds. I'm hosing down the path. I'm revving up my truck. I'm working on my speech. I'm polluted by my past. I'm sending the supplies. I'm flagging down a cab. I'm turning round and round. I'm leaning to the left. I'm holding up a branch. I'm sliding down the hill. I'm brushing back my hair. I'm persuading you to stay. I'm putting up a scheme. I'm breathing slowly in. I join up with the queue. I'm tapping at the door. I'm sitting with crossed legs. I barbecue some meat. I'm smiling with my eyes. I'm sucking on a straw. I'm voting with my feet. I'm holding back my tears. I'm supporting a small child. I'm putting bums on seats. I'm worrying too much. I go against the grain. I'm learning to comply. I don't get that at all. I'm breaking with my wont. I'm watching out for rain. I'll expect to get a call. I have to sneak in late. I'm feeling more mature. I'm flying through the day.

I'm tucking in my shirt. I'm recording every thought. I'm rocking side to side. I'm moving slowly on. I'm compiling a full set. I'm facing up to it. I'm showing off my legs. I'm hurrying to work. I hold the door ajar. I'm ordering a meal. I'm going off the grog. I'm sitting on the fence. I despise you for your health. I'm trying to hitch a ride. I'm finishing my peas. I'm resting on the beach. I'm taking out the waste. I'm picking up my act. I'm linking two ideas. I'm existing through good luck. I'm tacking on some more. I'll explain it to you now. I'm looking good in blue. I'm crying deep inside. I copy what I see. I'm evidently here. I'm feeling every twist. I'm twisting what you say. I'm saying what I mean. I have nothing more to add. I'm burning the last bridge. I'm erasing what I wrote. I calculate the cost. I'm glancing at my wrist. I'm folding all my clothes. I'm vacuuming the house. I'm marking out my space. I'm aching in my gut. I'm dredging up the past. I took another tab. I've realised my goals. I'm practising my scales. I'm leading you astray. I'm cutting out the core. I'm losing sense of it. I'm drawing out the tale. I identify the shape. I'm allaying my guilt. I'm repeating what I say. I'm drifting back and forth. I'm eliminating choice. I'm lying through my teeth. I'm stabbing in the dark. I'm peering through the drapes. I'm circling the earth. I whisper in your ear. I'm calling to a friend. I'm standing in the shade. I'm bearing down on you. I'm peering through a crack. I'm handling a whim. I'm taking off the scarf. I concentrate my coat. I'm starting a new line. I flicker with the dusk. I articulate my lust. I'm taking it real slow. I'm wiping off the smile. I'm selling cars for cash. I'm learning how to swim. I'm improving my façade. I'm atoning for my sins. I'm rejecting your demands. I hear the latest news. I'm using all I have. I'm kicking myself hard. I'm administering funds. I hesitate to add. I register my grief. I reconnect the phone. I'm staring out the door. I'm carrying more weight. I'm questioning the right. I'm stopping for a piss. I'm passing out for thirst. I carry you inside. I'm struggling with a word. I'm filling up the tank. I'm smoking my last fag. I'm playing pool for beers. I'm encouraging the team. I'll go directly there. I photograph the view. I present you with my cheek. I long to weave a rug. I'm reflecting how I feel. I'm saving the best part. I'm alleviating pain. I don't know where you are. I'm changing down a gear. I'm turning on the gas.

*

'Ergh,' says Maria. 'That got really depressing.'

'My song,' I say.

We drive. Sometimes, when it comes to maintaining or sustaining conversation, I say the wrong things. Maria plays with the radio until she finds bad songs and thus restores the status quo: broadcast sentiment, live silence.

Our car nonetheless runs to a different order from that we established as we travelled through the bushfire smoke less than two days previously. An outsider — a hitchhiker, for example — might have discerned a conversational imperative back then, near the coast. Near the coast, periods of silence were soon overcome with verbiage.

Here, in the interior of a car in the inner part of a continent, the next word is not so predictable.

We drive from horizon to horizon. The dust streams through the car, sweeps over the bonnet and roof as though the continent cannot recognise us as separate. We are a low yet mobile mound with a westward trajectory. We may not see ourselves as subject to geological laws, but this landscape does not concede any other status. We loosen the topsoil. We are within the topsoil. Unmissed molecules of this car blow eastward, racing along in the unchanging continental airstream.

In this manner, in personal silence and amidst continental noise, we continue our tour of south-eastern Australia, its roads, war memorials, pubs and trail of rejected lovers.

*

In Mildura there's a government office. Maria's after another chance to use up film — 'There's a newish memorial here I really have to get' — and there are rumoured to be a couple of wineries around here. We just need a few directions to satisfy all our needs. I walk into the office. There's a young man behind a counter, but he's reading a book and seems not to notice we've entered. I clear my throat.

'Okay,' he says, 'I know you're there.'

Without looking up, he holds some paper towards me. I take it, thinking it might be a regional map. Instead, it's a form of several pages headed 'Proposal to Improve or Otherwise Alter Pastoral Leasehold (Western)'.

'If it's clearing you're wanting, tick "Otherwise Alter",' he says, still without looking up. 'I'll officially refuse your request, eventually, then you can appeal. Estimated processing time at present is three months, though I'm working on increasing that.'

'Sorry?' I say.

He raises his eyes, sees us and rather exaggeratedly changes his manner from mechanical to engaged.

'Oh. You're from Sydney. Thought you were another from round here wanting to kill vegetation. What can I do you for?'

'I was actually after a local map, but I think this is the wrong place, after all.'

'I've got a map you can look at, but it's the only one. This is the Department of Agriculture, you know. There's even a sign outside. Is that who you're chasing?'

'I guess not. What's all this about?' I try to pass the form back.

'Keep it, why don't you?' he says. He picks up another couple of forms and holds them out to me too. 'Take these to your friends in Sydney. Then we'll run out of them sooner.'

I give him a puzzled look but hang on to the papers.

He continues: 'You see, how the land-clearing process works in practice is this. This area, up to the north of here and out towards Lake Mungo, is my land, where I'm from. I also work in this office. My job is to look after the land, keep it from being completely destroyed by rabbits, goats and humans. Local pastoralists have to apply to this office to clear land or radically alter land use. They come in here and tell me they want to clear another couple of acres and plant crops, just in case there's any rain, or the cotton farmers up north leave any river flow. They fence a bit off, try to keep the feral goats out. Rabbits are much better these years since the virus, though. It's pretty dry out here most of the time. You can't run a lot of animals.

'You know how they clear land? It's not tree by tree, axe-blow by axe-blow. There's nothing romantic about it at all. I can understand why loggers want to do what they do, why they enjoy the physical pleasure of bringing down a huge ancient trunk. The loggers are wrong but at least understandable. I can't come at the attitude of these farmers. Everything goes down to ground level. They clear land by dragging a chain behind a couple of tractors. I reckon some of them wouldn't mind starting their engines here in this office, then drive to the horizon and to the horizon again, leaving nothing but loose sand. Some of them don't see the point of any kind of conservation, any land management. Most aren't like that, I've got to say, or this job wouldn't exist, because the entire continent would be completely infertile by now, rainforest, desert and everything between.

'This is how I see my role: I say "no". Pastoralists come in here and ask to rip out the vegetation, and I don't let them. They then complain to higher authorities — ask for reconsideration — and usually they get their way, or some sort of agreement.

'I do what I can to convince them that ripping out all vegetation to ground level to plant wheat is not a very good idea in semi-arid and arid lands. But I can't convince many, so I sit here all day and say "no" as often as I can. At least I force them to make arguments in terms of sustainability. At least I make them acknowledge that someone doesn't agree that tearing out native grasses and saltbush and leaving the land exposed to the winds, direct sun and occasional eroding rains is necessarily an admirable pastoral practice.

'I'd like to explain to them what "pastoral" means, but there's no point. It means looking after, I'd say, not just taking from. We don't always see eye to eye. Despite this we get on okay, and mostly understand where the other's coming from. I think they are the other and they think I am the other, and they think that they're perfectly normal with normal destructive aspirations. My girlfriend says it's a wonder of modern diplomacy on a local scale, the work I do and the respect I get for it from my adversaries — or co-negotiators, as she might say. They do what they have to do and I do what I have to do. I consider each case on its merits, but I also consider each bush on its merits. Sometimes I feel as though I'm getting the upper hand. Sometimes I get despondent. My girlfriend's got a degree in international relations from Melbourne University, so there you go, she's got objectivity. What did you want that map for? You looking for a motel? Nice place, this, for a romantic year or two. Either that or for life. That's what my girlfriend says, and I have to agree.'

'No,' I jump in, to proffer Maria's answer. 'The war memorial.'

He points us the way.

'Imagine that as a career,' I comment, once we've left the office, 'a professional brake on progress. I like the sound of that.'

'I can think of more positive ways of putting it,' says Maria.

'It's positive enough. Just need a negative definition of progress. Think of what we've just driven through.'

As we cruise around to the memorial, Maria and I concur with the Agriculture man that the land around here is pretty dusty.

Maria photographs a symmetrical brick monument to wars in Korea, Vietnam and South East Asia, turret-like extensions at either end and central flagpole, the whole structure behind a neat lawn. Two darker, diagonal elements offer the equally symmetrical legend: 'Together Then, Together Again'.

I say nothing of possible interpretations of these words related to our own situation, but only wait as Maria chooses symmetrical and non-symmetrical vantage points, low angles, wide-lensed distortions of the epitaph, close-ups of the brickwork and documentary shots of the memorial in its context.

'Is this a good one?' I ask.

'That's not the issue,' she says. 'It's the cumulative resonance, the entire country a war memorial. This is national memory we're talking about.'

'So what difference does it make what angle you photograph it from?' I ask. 'It's deceptive if you make it look good.'

'I've got to get variation. I'm imagining the total effect, a sense of the country filled with thoughts of the dead,' says Maria, art-talking through slightly gritted teeth.

'Need to space your photos out then,' I say, 'like a hundred and fifty kilometres apart.'

'Despite your sarcasm, Jack, yes, I think the presentation is important.'

'Despite your seriousness,' I mimic.

'Let's go,' she says. 'This is getting silly.'

*

We have both heard enough strangers' stories. It's as though people have been holding on for years by the highway for us to pass, keeping for decades confessions of their immeasurable capacities for lust, for love.

I too have waited. Maria waits. We wait side by side. I wait for her to relent. She almost relented but then pretended she hadn't. She waits for me to say something so she can reiterate what she feels she must reiterate. My mere, transient feelings cannot move her. I say nothing. We battle in this manner.

The new memory of a morning of near-love in a motel adds to the rest. Between lust and love is self-destruction. I can picture Maria's belly moving beneath me, her hair deranged on the pillowless bed. Not a useful image, considering. Plenty of people believe that carnality constrains contentment — entire philosophies of meditation and purity are built on such faith — but I can't say I'm one of them. Bodily needs can only seem a limitation when seeking their fulfilment. Takes a body to point the finger at pleasure, say I. I wouldn't mind these two parameters (carnality, contentment) in invigorating relation.

Maria, who has a body which seems only to constrain me, is content. So she seems. She will not say otherwise. We are moving, which used to content me, will again in the future.

Maria looks out the window, into the distance. I follow her gaze, my eyes off the road at ninety-nine kilometres per hour.

I see an Australian farmhouse, surrounded by verandahs, corrugated-iron roofing gently sloping out in all directions. There's a woman moving across a verandah from the door towards the front step. The heat transforms a field of prickly brown grass between road and woman into glistening, waterless swampland.

'See her? You reckon she's Australia made flesh?'

'She is too perfect. I'd love to photograph her, but I might be disappointed. I might not capture that sense of ultimate irrefutable Australianness. Perhaps I should have a try. She's just so right.'

'I wasn't actually offering to stop,' I say with a short laugh.

Maria doesn't join in. 'Most of our delays haven't been for photographs, mate. You don't mind too much, do you?'

'I know. I know. I'm an unreasonable bastard.'

'You haven't been that bad, some of the time.'

I stop on the verge alongside the homestead. Maria climbs out with her camera halfway raised already.

The woman has stepped from the verandah and is moving towards the road. She walks in a curious side to side manner, her stiff legs never seeming to advance though she is approaching us. The way she moves, she seems two-dimensional. A dog lopes behind her.

Maria is forced to lower her camera. She cannot photograph this woman who refuses to be objectified from a safe distance. Now she's going to have to speak with her. I get out of the car too.

'Flat tyre, is it?' she asks.

'I'm a photographer,' says Maria, 'and I'm doing a series of Australian homestead scenes. People and their homes sort of thing. Do you mind if I photograph you and your house?'

'That's a new one,' she says. 'Usually it's crap painters staring into the sunset. You want me to change or something? The house looks okay, but I could do with some touching up.'

'You'll be fine.'

She folds her arms and waits to see what Maria will do. Maria walks this way and that, going through the 'best angle' routine.

'This bloke a colleague or your husband? Doesn't look much like a journalist if you ask me. Where's your notebook?'

'She's on a working holiday,' I say. 'I'm not.'

'You're just keeping him on a short leash, are you?' she asks Maria.

'He's self-restrained,' says Maria.

'Well, you're doing well then. A lot better than me.'

\*

The butter has separated in the butter dish. I can smell it easily enough, despite which it is not attracting any snake, reptilian or husband. The dog whimpering for no reason, his nose beside a hole in the floor.

'Good dog,' I mumble. I'm too tired to go into more detail than 'good'. 'Persistent' should I say? 'Restrained'? He has left the saucer alone after only one command. I sit myself on a wooden kitchen chair, which scrapes back a few inches and nearly overbalances. I'm a wreck. Another sleepless night: kept awake by a phantom snake and the Duromine, which the six year old had thought smelt like vitamins.

'No, Tommy, they're special tablets. Prescription tablets,' I'd told him, just in time.

'For what?'

'For me. So as I can cook all night and still be awake all day.'

'Can I have one?'

'You want to do some cooking, do you?'

'No.'

'Well then, no. Besides which they'd poison you. You'd convulse all over the floor.'

'Would not.'

'They're not for you.'

This morning (two or three too many of) the little pills keep my bony hands mechanically preparing the children's breakfast, my eyes blinking appropriately, legs occasionally twitching as they fatigue. I can feel occasional electric impulses, that's how it seems. Apparently, this is how stimulants operate on the body. By increasing electrical activity. Very modern. This is also what nerves are made of, says the women's magazine. How to avoid nervous exhaustion: don't get nerves.

My children don't notice any difference in me. To them, my voice always has that half-cracking edge. Nothing's out of place. Breakfast is pretty much the same as always. It's waiting for them on the table. The kitchen smells of bread and dog and rancid butter. Tommy grabs most of the toast and piles it on his plate. I take up the butter dish, concentrated milk curds floating atop the ghee, and tip it down the sink. The dog watches Tommy.

'Was there a snake, Mummy?' the younger child, Jacky, asks. 'Did Croc get it?'

I tell him with my just-for-Jacky reassuring smile, 'No. He didn't. If there was one, it's slithered away by now.'

'Why?' inquires Jacky — who asks 'why?' no matter what his mother says, no matter how well I explain.

'Snakes are like that,' I say.

'Might still be there,' says Tommy, though the dog has wandered off somewhere and the boy knows it.

'No. Eat your breakfast.'

Croc: my husband's bad name for the dog. Big teeth, right? Good one. I address the animal as 'Dog', but permit the children's misplaced affection for their father to endure. It's hard work. The children always have the next question ready. Staying up all night with the dog is the only time I experience silence. Could I have predicted this life? I don't make many predictions: thinking too much interferes with the experience of living, and talking about it is as bad. A bodily, emotional life begins with silence: all the inexpressible aches of the body from backache to unfulfilled lust.

Conversely, the body dies in waves of eloquence. The world is full of eloquence: the radio news cycles through the day, one public figure saying something and another condemning it; the wind roars outside, endlessly promising thunderstorms which never begin; the dog yaps in the middle distance; my children conduct sophisticated diplomatic manoeuvres, out-negotiating each other for my poor affection; all are disappointed.

Dozens of words cover the undeniable: all this noise, and no body to fuck.

Nor, these last two years, has he sent a hope-inducing letter. I have nothing to anticipate, not from him, not any more. Magazines offer me the men of my dreams, solid, non-vanishing, bachelor types, but how would these men find this place and yet maintain their easy appearances? How do you meet men out here? Only stinking drifters who move across the countryside looking for work, scuffing from rejection to rejection. One or two have been

pretty bloody insistent, but I know how to make my point
of view known: thanks for the offer, darling, but I would
sooner shoot you between the eyes.

In the present, the rabbit fence is keeping the rabbits out
of the vegetable garden, that's something I'm proud of.
And the dog has yet to lose a fight with a snake. I've never
had an animal with such superb concentration. If he senses
a snake nearby, he won't be distracted till he's killed it. Tell
the truth, I would have said the same thing about his two
predecessors. They'd each lost one last fight, first cur to a
black snake and second to a brown. In those days the soil
had been moister, easy to dig a canine grave.

'When you've finished, boy, feed that dog,' I tell the
elder one.

'Yeah, in a minute.' He is holding his breakfast plate like
a steering wheel.

'Tommy. I'm tired today.'

'I said.'

I am being a mother, acting out the role. Motherliness
used to be something else, something other than a set of
behaviours, responses. Now, though, the children irritate
me and I irritate myself. Before — before what? routine?
despair? — motherliness was bodily expression: I
suckled the children, comforted them in my arms,
felt their slowly increasing weight. This home's
different rooms, one hot and airless, one only warm,
were linked not by the hallway's in-between temperature
but by the improvised threads of my song. My body

drew this house together. Now, two attitudes predominate my feeling of motherhood: annoyance and a sense of servitude.

'Tommy,' I say. Or 'No.'

The body acts as emotional conveyance, nothing more. I too could abandon the boys, like my husband, or ex-husband he is really, like he has. I've considered all the ways to do myself in and haven't seriously thought about other ways of leaving them, journeys from here in which I too remain alive. That's not among the alternatives.

My choice is methodological, and still underpinned by duty. For example, I could hang myself, but where? Not in the house, where the children would discover me. I could take a room in some hotel somewhere. Cheap or expensive. I've thought about that rifle. Load 'er up and let it go. I probably wouldn't do it that way, I've read of attempts gone wrong — the firearm slips at the moment of firing, the bullet damages the brain, and what would happen to me then? How would Jacky react to a mother unable to talk or move? The head in the oven is a favourite in town, with the advantage of necessitating less technical preparation, but, once more, the most convenient oven is in the house.

I would excuse my husband's absence if he were dead. Whatsisname. Tommy asked: 'What's Daddy's name? Like yours is Mary?'

'Whatsisname.'

'Really?'

'Yes.'

'Really-really?'

'Yes.'

The human body is so weak it needs sleep to balance wakefulness, food to compensate for activity, self-deception to counteract all the needless punishments inflicted by farming, marriage and motherhood. Me, my body, needs time to recover from time. This is the cycle: exhaustion, recovery, expenditure, recuperation. I feel spent. Do you know what that is like?

I promised myself to let the dog do its job, and the boy — who's competent for his age, easy limbed and well balanced — ought to be trusted too; but with the dog having indicated 'snake', I cannot allow dog or child out of my sight. That dog has to be told to guard the children. The dog with its long memory, perhaps long enough to remember my husband.

If I were to end my life, I've convinced myself, it wouldn't make much difference in the scale of things; I have a body to occupy for so few years anyway. There's the bluff, not far from the property, with a drop I'd estimate at thirty to forty metres, easily enough to kill.

'I'm just going out for a while, boys,' I'll say, half-echoing Scott's young companion Lawrence Oates who (starving, frostbitten and disoriented in the freezing Antarctic) had added, 'I may be some time.'

Instead of doing this, keeping it that simple — you're wondering why I'm still here, I can see it in your cold, city eyes — my version continues in my head: 'Tommy, if I'm not back by dinner, I want you to make toast for you and Jacky. As much as he wants. And telephone the neighbours, too, and tell them I'm running late. I'll leave the number by the phone.'

It will be a strange, slowly revealed sort of abandonment, my presence persisting for hours in the instructions.

At the top of the bluff, I'll look down, see the clumps of sandstone boulders. I'll bend these old knees and prepare to leap. The immediacy of the intention will thrill. Thrill will mean 'terrify'. I'll throw myself forward and hardly feel the rush of air. The sensation of landing will pass in an instant, and I'll no longer be a mother.

But now I'm thinking about the children's lunch, the dog, the snake, the gaps in the floorboards, the phone calls to make, balancing income and expenditure, the time to mulch the vegetable beds, the crises of encroaching wild animals and wild men, all the little projects that take me into the future, that take me past the story of falling and falling.

That's the thing. I can't be trusted to carry it through. I haven't the guts. Is that what you want to hear, you vultures with your camera, you people who think nothing of driving a hundred miles? English as it's spoken out here hasn't the words to convince me. I'd have to throw English away, abandon the concepts of impact of endings. I could wrestle the language out of my consciousness, lose the words that connect me with this land, this property, with my children and the vague idea of husband.

That's if you Sydney lot call my language 'English'. I speak English, but it's my language in name only. I don't care about the grammar, about how I sound, whether I seem cultured or ordinary. English is simply the name of a language which engulfs and criticises the one I received. So, what's left? Australian? Is that my language? Do I own the Australian tongue? When I flatten my vowels, avoid taking on the radio accents, let the words spill over — an assembly of short phrases, never completing a sentence — is this my language? Could-bloody-be. Could-bloody-be.

And also, mine is the mother tongue, the language-bond of responsibility for children, intensified by my (former) husband's disappearance. If only he would vacate the children's imaginations, their hopes. But he will not. Uncertainty finds his possibility everywhere. He will be encountered.

'Is Daddy in Australia?' Jacky asks.

'Like who?' retorts Tommy.

'Like I am.'

'How do you know you are?'

'I am,' the little one contends.

'You wouldn't know where you are. You wouldn't know anything,' the older boy states coldly.

Jacky begins to cry.

'I didn't do anything,' says Tommy. I'm going to give him a clip across the head. But then I change my mind.

'I'll get you. Just wait till I do,' Jacky tells him. 'I'll learn karate.'

'I'm waiting. See how I'm waiting for ya? There's nothing else to do.'

What does my husband or ex-husband do that takes so much time, so much time that he's forgotten to explain his absence? Following the cattle mile by mile, and directing them the same: mile by mile. Mapping, pacing the ground, measuring Australia. All endless tasks, all offering infinity as an excuse. What else? Being a wag: insulting his friends and co-workers. Killing animals. Being himself. Making a living. Sheep tearing the vegetation from the ground. A kangaroo collapsing mid-stride and my ex-husband lowering the rifle. Rabbits stewing. My husband, taciturn.

Yeah, that's right. There's nothing particularly national in the national character. Or if there is, the whole world may as well be called Australia. England turns to dust just as well as this place does, given a bit of dry weather and given that its men spend their lives following cattle and black-faced sheep from common to common. People write their histories and graffiti across the land with marks made by ploughs and bricklayers. They drive animals, leave footprints, stir the dust. Add marks to the marks of thousands of others, each mark beginning to fade seconds after having been made, but taking decades or millennia to disappear, the soil blowing off layer by layer.

And even if all the soil of my pastoral land were removed, every cubic inch I or my ex-husband have leased for a hundred years, even if all the earth disappeared from Australia, if it washed away, blew away, were carted off to be tested for minerals, even if someone dug to the molten core of the earth and was incinerated in the (vainglorious) act, the land would still be there. When the wind tears leaves from twigs, the leaves are no longer of the tree but the tree remains, so I've seen. And the eroded, exhausted land, well, it's a different shape, hollow or empty instead of full. The trees reach down and down to touch bottom, the grasses hold together whatever remains to be held, even if all that is only the memory of touch.

My former husband, his marks are everywhere, the axed notches on every fence post. The door, splintering, half-hanging off its hinges, he'd attached that. He built the divider between the rooms, and had a fair part of building the rest of the house. He put me in it (more or less), and after the children joined us, he left. And, as I knew was possible, I managed, sustained the farm, worked in the fields almost all day and kept the children fed and largely out of trouble.

A combination of soil and sun made me the darkest Anglo anyone had seen. Four years ago I pushed out Jacky, assisted only by my Aboriginal namesake (called Black Mary, to distinguish her), who said 'very good, a little girl, she's coming,' or 'push now, and she'll come, push, push, very good,' and finally a boy came, and he lived.

But that was years ago, and now I have a simple choice: a brief meeting with Atropos, the Greek Fate who cuts off the thread of life and whose name means 'inflexible'; or continued atrophy, the Fate's softer, equally lethal double. A sigh, a fading, a soft F sound, resignation. It is that soft sound I feel sometimes when I realise that I am already wasted, wasting away my muscles, my energy dispersed too early in the morning. Everything is so slow, especially this constricted throat, always feels full of the red dust that passes for soil, and I look around the kitchen and wonder if there's anything I could take to fix this, to alleviate the fatigue and restore me. I know I'm not jumping off any cliff.

In the kitchen, too early, I have a human, irrational way of looking at time: wasting and apocalypse at opposite ends of the durational scale, muscular fatigue and revelation. The children, occasionally sweet, promise love and also not to emulate their father. It is not enough. Nothing could be, not after so many years. I might cry now, and continue crying: inevitably my moment of ceasing-to-be will be a small point on a long line of unbecoming.

*

'Not, of course, that I want to interfere with your vocation, dear,' she says to Maria. 'So you can take the shots now. Now that you know what you're photographing.'

'Thank you,' says Maria in a thick voice. 'Is that all right? Are you okay? Are you going to be okay?'

'The boys are a help. The dog too.'

Just then the front door opens and a huge man emerges onto the verandah.

'Tommy!' she calls. 'Want to be in the papers?'

He limps over. I can see that despite his size he's only about sixteen.

'No, I don't. No thanks, I mean. But are you heading west? I could do with a lift down to Desi's.' He has a deep bass voice, probably exaggerated, as teenage boys do.

'That's fine,' says Maria.

'Where's that?' I ask.

'Ten miles.'

'Okay,' I say, pretending to myself that I have had some role in the decision.

'The photos?' reminds Maria.

Tommy and I stand back towards the car while the young woman directs the older one.

'That your girlfriend, is it?' asks Tommy.

'Not exactly,' I say.

'City relationship then, is it?'

I don't answer. Maria is explaining about three-quarters angles giving more facial definition.

'She's all right looking,' says Tommy.

'I guess so.'

'Not really my type, though.'

'Each to his own,' I tell him. I am not going to discuss Maria's body with him.

'Wouldn't mind a girlfriend, but haven't met the right one yet.'

'Mm hmm.'

'Okay, done,' announces Maria. 'Thanks a heap.'

'Never mind,' says the woman. 'At least you got what you wanted.'

'Let's go,' I say.

'Six o'clock, and ring if you'll be later,' she says to the boy. 'I'm eating then.'

'Yeah, fine. I'll have something over there,' he says.

'And help out a little, will you?'

'Yes Mum.'

'She doesn't need extra people who eat everything in sight and leave mess all over the house.'

'Yes, Mum. I always help.'

'Good.'

'Bye-bye.'

We get in the car and drive off. Tommy has cleared a place in the middle of the back seat, his head bent against the vinyl ceiling and his massive legs filling each half of the back of the car.

'Tell us when you want to get out,' I say.

He grunts agreement. In the rear-view mirror is nothing beyond Tommy's massive visage. In the side mirror, I can still see part of the roof of the woman's house. The land is very flat; by now she must be several kilometres back.

We cannot respond to her confession, not with the 'boy' sitting there. It is also unrealistic for me to expect that Maria will turn and confess, as a follow-up to the woman's story of abandonment and depression, 'I am lost without you.'

I do not expect she will say it. The tyres turn very quickly, taking us further from the photo op, this scene which could yet make Maria's fortune, transform her into calendar queen, most-quoted book cover artist, the toast of Australia Post. The tyres account for all noise I can hear. Tommy fills the car but says nothing. I stare at the road for a while, and when I next look in the mirror, the last trace of house has gone. Are we no longer in Australia? We have passed into the space beyond white imagination, space which can only be crossed by us, not occupied. We are winding along a road which carries all there is of Europe between its parallel edges. To the right and left is the inexpressible.

For some reason, I remember the first time Maria held my hand, how she hadn't known what to do with it. She had looked at it, at her fingers interwoven with mine, squeezed it a little, then relaxed. She had stroked it with her other hand, forgot it for a few minutes, squeezed again with renewed attention, but wasn't clear whether to be conscious of it or let it be. She gripped it playfully then possessively, testing our alternative futures.

We speed along this strip of high-technology asphalt. Maria fidgets momentarily, gives off the sense of being about to say something, or this is the sense I extract from her fidgeting. Her lips are working up to speech. I still know her that well at least. Suddenly I seem desperate to myself, am conscious of my need, am surprised at how much I want her anger or sadness or regret.

Tommy cuts in.

'Left here, mate,' he grunts.

I pull off the road.

'Come in. I'll get you some chutney.'

'That's all right.'

'No. You want this chutney.'

We follow him up a path and into a small wooden cottage.

'Aunty Desi?' he calls. 'Some people here.'

'Come through,' calls a voice.

We're in a small room dominated by a huge empty fireplace below a long trophy-covered mantel.

Two sisters are sitting at right angles to each other. Or not sisters, I think, as I have no reason to suppose they're related, but old friends who might have taken on one another's mannerisms, grown to resemble one another. I estimate they are in their middle or late forties. The older, not by much, or only dresses older and has allowed her hair to grey, is pale, bespectacled, looks the more friendly. The other has a sullen expression, looks as though she once had acne, was suntanned once too; she looks healthy in a leathery kind of way. They both fill in time in the same way, moving a knee slowly from side to side. Perhaps they are sisters, after all.

Tommy seems to be waiting for a chance to break into this non-conversation, but I cannot see any change in the situation, any reason why he doesn't say 'Excuse me' or introduce us as his transport means.

The older-looking one leans across from time to time and says something to her sister (or friend). The more leathery never seems to reply, but somehow they continue to sit in their positions, to converse in this one-sided way. It is not possible to judge how much of their relationship is simply habitual proximity, but I would guess they spend a lot of time together.

I look across at Maria until she senses the stare and glances back. She is neither beautiful nor unattractive. She looks only like Maria now, familiar, necessary, her hands held in the usual way, her posture instantly recognisable, her face, features I have touched, studied with love, watched from inches away as she watches me back. Our gazes meet for a moment, but then I allow my eyes to drop. Maria, who outstares me at will, with ease.

'Can I get these folks some chutney, Aunty Desi?' asks Tommy, finally. 'They give me a lift here.'

'Through the pantry, Tom. You know where.'

'Come on,' he tells us and we go with him.

'Desiree's good,' he says. 'A bit funny, but good. April's good too.'

'Okay,' I say.

'I've learnt to understand their ways. They're very quiet.'

'So they seemed.'

'But underneath it, they're very good.'

He was obviously not capable of being more forthcoming.

'I can't actually find the chutney here, so please go back and wait in the lounge room. There's more in the cellar. Don't worry about Desi and April. They'll be right.'

*

We find ourselves sitting in two armchairs to Aunty Desi's right. April is further away. Desi smiles at us inclusively.

Desiree despises the season: 'I do not like this hot weather,' she says.

April sits quietly. Perhaps she hadn't heard.

'She doesn't hear me,' Desiree whispers to Maria and me. 'She chooses not to.'

\*

To Desiree, April often seems distant these days. She tries to remember the last secret April confided in her, and cannot. That was when they were sixteen or twenty-six, Desiree decides. She is always the forthcoming one.

'Are we the friends we were?' she whispers.

They are no longer the friends they had been. It must be clear to April as well. Their differences now seem pronounced, where before Desiree thought they had complemented each other nearly perfectly. In the past, Desiree believed she was unassertive and that her unassertiveness was a problem. April appeared to do as she felt, to be self-contained and confident in the quiet way of self-contented people, as though it never occurred to her to display self. Desiree is unsure her years in therapy in Adelaide had helped.

She whispers, 'But I continued to go, week in and week out.'

Previously she had been nervous; now she is nervous and self-conscious. This does not help her conversation. April must find the silence as comfortable as Desiree finds it terrible: 'terrible' is one of Desiree's therapy words. Before, Desiree had been uncomfortable with silence. She now understands that silence is unbearable, but that she lives through it, has learnt to possess her feeling. Previously, she felt indifferent towards her friends, unable to love them to the extent friendship requires. Now, she describes her indifference as pain, the pain of being separate, of knowing that two people becoming one is impossible.

She delivered these conclusions to the therapist in her toneless, what-happened-today voice, hoping that, if nothing else, at least she could be an adequate patient.

'Is this okay?' she wanted to know from time to time, each few weeks or months of meeting in that blank office with its contrived features. Was she making progress? The therapist would look at her, eye to eye, encouragingly but enigmatically, friendly, professional, uninterpretable. These sessions may have indicated progress, if that word had currency, but Desiree would recognise it only when she had arrived. A look. As a patient, then, Desiree was not abject, anyway not to the degree that her therapist requested she discontinue.

'I tried to talk with April about the therapy, but these conversations were not successful,' she whispers.

April, it seems, could not understand her need to speak of 'issues' for an hour, would not consent to speak of the speaking of for a further time, albeit diluted with tea or white wine.

'It is what I am doing now,' Desiree would explain. 'It is what I am thinking about.'

April would not participate in these conversations, would or could not join Desiree in trafficking such terms, allowing this language to replicate and disperse.

In the room, the windows are open and the heat rises through the still air from the concreted footpath in front, falls upon them in waves. Desiree says to herself: April is thinking something private. Her friend's forehead is slightly damp in the heat, and seeing this, Desiree touches her own forehead with fingertips.

'Oh. I'm perspiring too,' she confides in us.

April is unreadable, Desiree reflects, and then thinks about the length of their friendship, if that is the proper word for what endures, and the new friends each has made, friendships which often lasted exactly the length of a job or a particular leisure activity or involvement in a cause or course of study, and she muses on their insurmountable differences of belief in the value of self-expression, which further leads her to think about certain self-expressive practices Desiree herself has rejected and the reasons for her rejection of them.

'People attend self-assertion courses to gain new peer groups with strict and easy-to-follow rules,' Desiree tells April, tells the ceiling, allows us to hear. 'They are given new environments in which to assert new characters, like taking on roles in a set, say at the theatre.'

April blinks.

Desiree continues, 'In these courses, everyone learns behavioural traits at the same time and the same pace. People know what others' signs mean because they learn them in clear steps. It is reassuring to have that sort of certainty and who's to say it's more artificial than the banal behavioural faults we absorb from our parents, or that they inculcate into us? I don't even wish life were more organic than the lives we live. Artificiality has some purpose, after all. Without it, there'd be more people slamming each other over the head with rocks and so forth. Don't you think?'

April hardly reacts, an almost discernible nod, a bare assent; her lips remain pursed, her eyes fixed on some object outside the room.

'I've never been to one of these courses myself,' Desiree adds. 'I never thought it would calm me...'

She purposefully leaves a space, half-finishing her sentence with a slightly rising inflexion. April seems unwilling to allow any words out at all. Desiree wonders if her friend is interested in her theory and doesn't want to interrupt or if she disagrees strongly or if she is simply elsewhere with her own thoughts. (These days, what would they be?) She thinks to say 'April' or to make some other noise of demand, but then stops herself, feeling a taboo. April had not interrupted Desiree's musing and, because she hadn't, Desiree decides she should leave April to contribute or not as she wishes.

'You know me. If there's a physical manifestation of worry I've sublimated it: dermatitis, backache, insomnia, piles, panic,' she continues, risking that a fragment of that earlier time and relationship wherein Desiree could speak of anything at all with April, the body's pleasures as well as its shortcomings, persists in the growing space between them.

She no longer knows that April knows her. Perhaps the friendship is automatic, April responding consistently to Desiree's fixed range of stimuli in a manner that would be predictable to some independent watcher yet is beyond Desiree's subjective ability to see. Had she seen April silent in precisely this way before? Did Desiree have the capacity to distinguish one silence from another? She thinks about this briefly, and decides that yes, she does. Over her life, she has learnt to recognise a range of qualities of silence; this is based on the observation of context, of the way another holds her body, of patterns of breathing, not all observations necessarily conscious. She watches April for a moment or two. She cannot discern a mood, only April's distinct kind of self-possession, which she might have admired were its exclusiveness not so pointedly affecting her.

Desiree thinks of the responses April could have made to her small, reiterated confessions: 'Mmm-hmmm' or 'you poor thing' or 'that is bullshit, Desi, worse than usual' or 'I don't get you' or 'try not to worry' or 'I try not to worry' or 'I just read an article that really helped me with the sort of thing you're talking about' or 'your shrink is the biggest quackpot in the southern hemisphere'. She completes their various unsaid conversations in her head, her friend now sympathetic, now hostile, now requesting elaboration. In this manner, some of their conversations gain satisfying conclusions. In one, April says that she admires Desiree, wishes she had the strength to face her own weaknesses. In another, her friend urges Desiree to take up an outdoor pursuit, says that exercise and fresh air would do infinitely more to assist clear thought than repose and introspection.

Desiree notices then that April is watching her, smiling towards her, a little sadly perhaps, as if waiting for something to occur or continue. At that moment, Desiree realises she too has fallen silent.

*

'Here you go,' says Tommy in his too-low voice, coming back into the room. 'It's tomato relish, best in Australia.'

'Thanks,' we say.

'You don't get that many trophies for nothing,' he says.

'Thanks, Aunty Desiree too,' says Maria.

'Yes. Thanks, Aunty D,' I echo.

'I'll see you out, then,' rasps Tommy.

'Have a good trip.' He gives me a nod, with a twist of his lips towards Maria, and it means: she's all right after all.

Maria drives.

I find myself thinking that we should have chosen the other route, via the Hume Highway and then turning right, towards the west, rather than this seemingly more direct one. The Hume is actually a few kilometres shorter (and going a third way, via Broken Hill and then south, we would have added an extra two hundred and fifty kilometres), but with its double carriageway, and passing lanes just about the whole way from Sydney to Melbourne, although we would have turned off towards Wagga Wagga only thirty-six kilometres after Gundagai and eventually rejoined our present route, no part of the highway especially distinguishable from any other part, petrol stops offering the same poor, highly processed, fat-rich food selections and over-controlled air temperatures, the alternative road may have destroyed memory whereas the route we have chosen seems to trigger it.

I think to accuse Maria of participating in a cover-up, of furthering misrepresentations of Australia just as directly as if she had put about more photos of happy bronzed men in red and yellow hats: almost the entire country dedicated to losing its past and she portrays it in memorials of historical events. History is the whole trouble here, in this country, I could tell her, or its definition as a series of commemorative monuments. What about the 'memorials' to forgetting, Maria? Irrigated fields to the horizon, as though this was the way the landscape had always been; rabbits' eyes suddenly green by the side of the road — or, for that matter, cats' eyes reflecting car headlights — appear as natural as swollen wombats lying stiffly on the Sturt Highway's clay verges.

I picture my accusation and Maria's response: of course she had considered my point, did I think she hadn't thought her ideas through before putting them into practice? She was of course drawing attention to the constructed nature of the memorial, not merely naturalising it. Maria's response: she's thought of everything, and dispensed with everything but art.

I decide not to raise the point with her again. It is a difficult position, for one ex-lover to criticise the art work, or as Maria might have it, art practice, of the other.

\*

I drive. Outside: countryside.

There are people, and I know some of them, who are unable to leave the cities, who become disconsolate, depressed, don't know what to do with themselves as soon as they leave the urban environment. I know people who refuse to go the country, who find a day in the Royal National Park — convenient to Sydney and well-kiosked as it is — to be at the limits of endurance.

Maria and I are sitting in a car. We're travelling at around ninety kilometres an hour. We've had the windows open. The city air has gone and has been replaced by a succession of non-urban atmospheres. Smoke, dust, the beating of wind through the car as we ruin the designers' aerodynamics concept. We are wilful in this way.

Sheep graze here and there on the gentle brown slopes either side of the road. We traverse. The land fails to subsume us. The car, having dislodged Tommy, is an urban bubble. I stop beside a large eucalypt.

'What's up?' asks Maria.

'Look where we are,' I say. 'We're nowhere. I want to stand in it.'

'Okay.'

Maria reaches behind and finds the plastic water bottle. We stand beside the car by the side of the road. It's one of those intensely hot, dry days that reminds you of what semi-arid means. Maria opens the bottle and drinks, passes it to me. I think I can smell sheep, but I'm not sure, as the only context in which I can recall ever having smelt sheep before is barbecues. Perhaps at the Easter Show's agricultural exhibits, but I could be confusing the sheep smell with that of the cows, or maybe it's the grass itself. I sneeze. The cicadas are louder than I've ever heard them before. A semi-trailer passes, and we feel its drag and the wave of dust which follows it. I open the back door of the car, bring out a packet of salt and vinegar chips and my second warm longneck of New South Wales beer, with the intention of sitting under the tree to consume them — after all, it is lunchtime — but there's a nest of red ants which begins to divulge its inhabitants as soon as my arse hits the ground. I stand and eat the chips (Maria takes one, refuses more), moving my feet around to discourage the ants from crawling up my legs. Maria, sensitively, refrains from laughing at me. The beer tastes even worse than yesterday's. I invert the bottle and let it drain away.

'This isn't exactly what I had in mind,' I remark.

'It would have been a strange thing to have in mind.'

'But the heat's good. It's distinctive.'

'No sea breeze,' says Maria, with a hint of patience articulated.

'Not really the weather for it, I guess. It never is out here.'

I realise I'm waiting for a sense of being here, of something happening to me, of this verge without a house in sight acting on me. We've driven over a thousand kilometres and I'm only now starting to comprehend where I am. People stand stock-still in paintings of Australian pastoral lands. In stories they slowly kill themselves, trying to make the land viable. They run or fight or ride their hearts out till they die, heroic for ever. In the financial pages, they are impoverished, abandoned by their children, hoping for one bumper year which will enable them to retire in Sydney or, I suppose, Mildura. City people, with our shorter-term plans, are supposed to come out here and feel either lost or free, overwhelmed by the scale or opened up by it. I feel neither. In a few minutes I know we will return to the car, continue to follow our selected, well-marked route (depicted on my passenger's lap at a very manageable 1 cm = 20 km), a set destination ahead of us. It's as though we're not on this land at all, that we've brought the city with us, never left it: it's enacted in our relationship in the car, our bubble of urban life with these hills ('Australia!') like an arbitrary backdrop. It would make no difference if our car were depicted scudding slowly across the low-gravity surface of the moon or slaloming between giant ice creams in an advertisement. Slide the stage doors apart and there will be a skyline.

We nod to each other that it's time to get back in the car. She drives.

I switch the radio on and, to Maria's moderate annoyance, find a cricket match. For once, the tuning is clear, the words audible above the usual static hiss. I once enjoyed listening to cricket, I remember, the pace of the game, its endless pauses. It seems like a pleasure separation from Maria makes possible.

'It's this or nothing,' I say, referring to our recent lack of success in tuning.

'I guess, but do we have to listen for the rest of the day?'

'I'll just get the score,' I lie.

'Who's playing?'

I don't know. I bluff, 'Australia and Pakistan.'

The commentator gives the score that moment — we're listening to a lesser fixture, between Tasmania and Victoria — and announces lunch.

'Should be the news,' I say, but the commentator immediately undermines this statement as well.

'We'll take a few calls,' he says. 'We have David in Wilcannia. Hot enough there?'

'Hello, yes, my thermometer's telling me it's cracked forty-eight degrees today, so I'm not moving too fast, no further than the fridge, I'll admit, though the thermometer's never been right before.'

The anchor laughs and so do I. 'What would you like to say?'

'I'll keep it short. I just think Mark Waugh has had enough chances and that someone else should get a good go.'

'Thanks for that. Pete in Melbourne.'

'Hello?' asks Pete through millions of miles of telephone cable.

'Yes, you're on the air.'

'How are you?'

'I'm fine.'

'This is so interesting,' interjects Maria.

'Like war memorials,' I have to say.

'That's good. I'm enjoying the coverage on ABC radio, as always,' says Pete, as if determined to use his full allocation of air time.

'Good to know. You wanted to defend a maligned cricket participant. It's not Mark Waugh?' encourages the radio anchor.

'Yes, we're always hearing that critics should respect the difficulty players have, but what about some respect for the critics?'

'Pete, I couldn't agree with you more.'

'Do you, as an artist, agree?' I ask Maria, sardonically.

She shakes her left hand dismissively.

Pete from Melbourne confesses.

'My girlfriend's a critic, and I love her. She criticises all kinds of books and other art objects for all levels of media: my girlfriend has a rare talent for judgment. She never lets self-interest or arbitrariness interfere with her objectivity. She always contextualises her subject historically and in terms of its genre. She verifies all her facts and if a fact cannot be confirmed she attributes it to its source or states clearly that her commentary is hearsay. Her research is impeccable.'

'Thanks for that, Pete. It certainly sounds like she puts the work in.'

'That she does. As she sits at the kitchen table crosschecking her references and footnotes, I make tea in two cups, using teabags. Meanwhile, my girlfriend has filled two notebook pages with shorthand and read another several chapters of her current subject, a critique of a recently published biography of the wily old legspin bowler Clarrie Grimmett. This revisionist history claims that Grimmett's "wrong 'un" wasn't so much a wrong 'un as what we would now call a "flipper" or, perhaps, a variation on his "toppie".'

'A controversial point, Pete.'

'Very much so. That Grimmett took wickets is indisputable. That he was born in New Zealand in 1891, likewise. That it was his arm ball that did the batsmen, without a doubt. All else, the traditional critic or cricketer might argue, is vanity. As I hand the steaming teacup to my girlfriend, I see she is frowning.

'My girlfriend was born in 1964. Like most of our generation, her schooling was liberal, the emphasis on method rather than information. Nonetheless, she has a brilliant memory. She is able to quote verbatim selected passages from Kurt Vonnegut, Knut Hamsun, Simone de Beauvoir and Peggy Glanville-Hicks.'

'Pete, this is sounding very impressive, and I'd like to take a few more callers on the subject of Grimmett. What would you like to say to wind it up?'

'Thank you. My girlfriend's reviews, essays and articles are characterised by epigraphs and quotations from these writers and illustrations from the Pre-Raphaelites or, less frequently, from the Primitive Schools of thirteenth- and fourteenth-century Florence.

'Accompanying her Grimmett critique, she chooses Giotto's rich narrative painting *Saint Francis Receiving the Stigmata*. In the work, rays project from a hovering Christ-figure to the kneeling Saint Francis, connecting each of Christ's hands with the corresponding hand of the saint's, foot with foot, heart with heart. Golden haloes surround the figures' heads, as if each head is fixed in eclipse, tiny personal suns showing glowing chromospheres. As I prepare a tray of Florentines and mustaccioli, I can see my girlfriend smiling at the ironic juxtaposition of the painting with this essay: Giotto's ancient linear perspective, sharp angles, clear geometric shapes; Grimmett's flighted parabolas, perfect length, enigmatic turn. The essay is developing very well and I am privileged to observe its progress. I know my girlfriend feels the love I project towards her.'

The announcer cuts in: 'Are you reading this out?'

'I'm just getting to my point. Picture this. The kitchen is now punctuated with columns of cricket books: Lance Gibbs's *The Art of Spin Bowling*, *The Bamboozled Batsman and Other Stories* by Derek Underwood, volumes by Jenner, O'Reilly and O'Keeffe, Bishen Bedi's *Encyclopaedia of Over-Arm Bowling*, histories of sport and sport criticism, of the development of cricket, photographic collections, technical manuals on criticising and playing spin bowling. Each book has dozens of slips of scrap paper protruding, on which my girlfriend has noted internal contradictions, references to other volumes, controversial or poetic quotations. These piles of books tower over the table, cast long shadows across the kitchen in the reddening afternoon light. And still my girlfriend works on.'

'Thank you, we'll be returning to the cricket shortly.'

'By dawn,' Pete continues, unruffled, 'the research and note-taking phase is complete. The loose heap of bibliographic notes on the kitchen table matches and, as an art critic might put it, "comments on" a mound of coffee grounds in the sink. The dozens of books are no longer piled up; they carpet the tiles, each book open to a marked quote. My girlfriend looks tired but also satisfied. She knows all that is knowable about this subject and is deeply ready to evaluate the re-evaluation of CV Grimmett.'

'Hooray,' says the announcer, resignedly.

'And then my girlfriend begins the writing proper. My girlfriend takes each book from the floor in a pre-organised order and transfers the note, comment, reference or quotation to the rapidly growing essay on her word processor. Thousands of letters move up the screen. She does not pause until she attains the length of review commissioned by the sports or literary editor of the relevant publication.

'Does Grimmett's re-evaluator make his arguments? Does he use language with such precision as to make one draw breath with unusual sharpness? Is he of a class of writer equivalent to Grimmett's cricketing stature, such that he is worthy to attempt this biography? Is there a particular anecdote which might have shed more light on Grimmett's adolescence than the anecdote chosen by the writer for that purpose? Is my girlfriend convinced that Grimmett asked for and was denied two further overs at Edgbaston just when England looked vulnerable? Is the book's index inviting and accessible? Is the writer's "wrong 'un" theory a right 'un? My girlfriend's answers flow up and up the page.

'Mate,' Pete concludes, 'I can only put the kettle on, lean against the kitchen bench, and admire.'

The announcer puts on his best wrapping-up voice: 'Thank you for enlightening us on that subject.'

'And, one other thing while I'm on air, I'd just like to pop her the question, if I could?'

'You want to what? You go right ahead!'

'She's just going to pick up the other phone. Hang on a second. You ready?'

There's some crackling and rustling, and a woman's voice says, 'Hello everyone.'

'Hello. Well, will you marry me?'

'Yes, I will.'

'There you have it,' says the announcer. 'Cricket romance, live on air. Certainly no time for other calls now.

And now, back to Bellerive Oval, in Hobart, for the afternoon session between Tasmania and Victoria.'

No surprise, I suppose, for love to seep out of the radio at the strangest moments. We hear it every time we switch it on, and rotating the tuning dial, we hear its expression in each of the styles available on today's airwaves. Love is in the background at all times, for the loved as for the lonely. For those feeling the effects of the end of love, seeking relief from constant thought, there are reminders at every moment, notes left under windshield wipers, classified advertisements in every newspaper, movie posters, the promise of satisfaction revealed in telephone numbers. Country towns are not exempt from this; it's the opposite: offers of lust or fidelity stand out the more clearly in these less commercial-looking zones.

Maria attacks the radio, changing channels with a flick. We hear:

> This bleached-bright real
> machine-cast cylinders,
> rushes from loneliness.
> Eucalypt tops will be drifting bombers
> blowing barrage veiled
> under khaki nimbus.
> The weather paints patiently
> acres of old marriage listen
> to the inexhaustible sky.

'That's better?' I ask her.

'I guess not,' she concedes, switching it off as we come to a five-kilometre marker for Berri.

\*

Berri, in the heart of a famous fruit-growing district, lies about two hundred and thirty kilometres east-northeast of Maria's destination. It also sits, I am beginning to realise, approximately, near enough to twelve hundred kilometres west of mine. I am beginning to prepare myself for the return journey. I will spend a night in Adelaide to overcome my fatigue (from Maria, of course, not this relaxing country drive) and then will face my car towards Sydney and start the engine. I have resolved to speak to no one for the entire trip back. Maria is looking at the road guide, which points up Berri's numerous attractions for the unwary, many of them connected with a river. There are also several walking tracks, some of which offer splendid views. I don't know why Maria bothers to read this out, as there is no way she'd consider spending the afternoon doing a walk, not this close to nameless and undescribed, the lascivious, attractive man who waits, apprehensive, thoughtful, knowing, who is in all likelihood wetting himself with the sense of her nearness.

'Would you like to do a walk?' I suggest.

'Well, I would, but we're several days late already.'

'No, no, Maria. You are late.'

'Yes.'

I notice the bypass sign, but deliberately ignore it and drive into the heart of the town.

'This is a very well-known wine-growing area, so I was thinking of stopping for a beer,' I announce.

'Fine,' says Maria.

It seems that so close to her destination, with the certainty that I will in the end succeed as a means of transport, Maria will allow me some temper, a touch of huffiness. In return, I'll have to grant her the right to martyrish poses.

We stop near the Royal and enter. The public bar is crowded: there are a dozen or more men in cricketing whites, and a match on the pub screen.

'Tony,' says one of the live cricketers to another, holding out his hand for the cursory handshake. Tony is looking miserable from causes beyond the heat.

'Glad to know you,' says the second.

'Let's go through to the lounge,' I say.

'Okay,' says Maria. 'I'll follow you.'

We make our way around the bar and reach a wall and a sign pointing downstairs to the toilets.

'No lounge bar.'

Maria shrugs. The pool table has been taken by the cricketers, pushed back against the wall and piled up with kit bags. Tony is sounding off in an aggrieved way.

'I think we've picked another dud pub,' I say.

'No, no. You've picked,' she responds vengefully, in a tone I find preferable to the long-suffering one she was beginning to adopt.

'Mea culpa. A beer? What do they call them here, pots?'

'I'll have a large one.'

'Consider yourself implicated,' I say, moving to the bar through the sticky shoulders of the cricketers. I'm served immediately. 'Two large beers.'

The bartender raises his eyebrows in a way I know to mean 'Sydney', but fills the glasses without resorting to actual words.

I say, 'Beers coming through' and the cricketers part, one making the compulsory joke: 'Just park them in front of me, mate.'

Tony seems to have cheered up, perhaps because he has been allowed to speak without much interruption as the fellows around guzzle their drinks. Tony's glass, a large one like ours, is already empty.

The cricketers have left one small table against the back wall, but no chairs. I put the beers on their coasters and Maria and I squat beside.

'Hey, you blokes! Chair for the lady!' calls a cricketer and two chairs are overhanded to our corner.

'Thanks very much.'

'You're right. No worries.'

'This beer's okay,' I say to Maria, who nods.

'Frank is such a prick,' says Tony to no one in particular. 'Captain Fucking Hat.'

'Why's he called "Hat" anyway?' asks another cricketer. 'I s'pose he wears one. But so does everyone.'

'I'll tell you,' says a third. 'It's a dick joke. A chick at a party told Ron that the head of Frank's penis is three times wider than the shaft.'

'That's foul, Brett. Deformed,' says Tony. 'Sex with him, too.'

'Maybe there's another room,' says Maria.

'Don't worry about it,' I say. 'We'll just have this beer and then go.'

Tony and two others have red cricket caps embroidered with 'The Goats'. Brett is still wearing his. The other cricketers have blue caps with a town name 'Loxton' and the grade 'D'. Tony is drinking with the enemy.

'Good of you blokes to invite us here,' says the last redcap. 'Saves spending more time with Frank.'

'Where are they drinking?' asks a Loxtonian.

'Barmera. The Oaks.'

'Bad pub.'

'Bad company,' says Tony.

The Royal's video projection screen shows a one-dayer — South Australia versus New South Wales. The latter has lost three early wickets and is doomed. These are the most predictable matches ever devised, but the bowlers' rhythms and the punctuating advertisements after each over maintain cricket's ineradicable beery fascination. Tony is staring at the game, occasionally dropping a pinch of peanuts onto his part-extended tongue.

Brett is telling the Loxton team how much he dislikes their Oaks-drinking team-mates, who are sledgers and otherwise less than pleasant. Hat is the worst of the lot, can't keep his fuckwittiness to himself. He constantly tries to put off batsmen with sharp remarks: 'Didn't see that one, eh? Want some specs?' or 'You play like an idiot, mate.' What's almost as bad, those guys mostly live in or near Renmark. The pits. Various Loxton players are recounting earlier unpleasant encounters with the Goats: Hat once threatened to punch an umpire for turning down his appeal for a catch behind.

'It was nowhere near the bat,' says the player, 'and he went off his nut. The man's a psycho, no bullshit.'

Tony purses his lips and nods freely. Brett points twice (jab-jab) at the guy.

'Psycho's the word,' he agrees.

'Or "Dickhead". That's fairly accurate too,' says the third Goat, waving a corn chip for emphasis.

Tony's explaining: 'I'm not saying I'm a great bowler, but with a bit of seam left on the ball, my arm action's pretty high and I can generate a fair amount of in-swing.'

He tugs the paper napkin from under the peanuts, screws it up and demonstrates his grip. 'For the slower ball I tilt my wrist back like this and run my fingers back along the seam.'

'Sounds reasonable,' says one.

'If this Hat guy won't even give you a bowl, why bother to play? He's not that good himself, from what I've seen.'

On screen, South Australia heads towards victory. Steve Waugh will not save New South Wales today. He is elsewhere, with Australian captaincy duties.

'Steve Waugh and I share a birthday,' says Tony, apropos of nothing. 'And Mark too, if you didn't guess.'

'Well, mate, your form couldn't be worse than his at the moment.'

Maria's gulping her beer, but I'm sipping and have more than half left.

Tony has dropped out of the conversation and is fixating on the screen. New South Wales bats slowly on for pride and percentage, no doubt hoping to last out their full allocation of fifty overs.

'You're right,' Tony suddenly tells the Loxton player who had advised him to leave. 'I should definitely take your advice there.'

'Mm.'

Tony gets up and walks away from the other cricketers. New South Wales continue their collapse.

At the rear of the room, near us, is an old piano, which we soon learn to be well out of tune. A woman in a white blouse sits and begins to play some variety of ballroom dance music, little minuets and polkas perhaps, with an exaggerated elegance in the posture of her thin wrists which, during the course of one somehow recognisable tune, she crosses several times over the piano's discoloured ivories.

'Do you know "House of the Rising Sun"?' calls out a wag, perhaps one of Tony's remaining team-mates.

She indulges them with the opening chords of 'Advance Australia Fair', drawing a round of prematurely drunken applause.

'Let's go,' says Maria. 'This is starting to get a little too cosy.'

'I'm prepared to defer my second beer in the interests of your musical sanity,' I agree, draining the first. What does she expect in a pub? *Nixon in China*?

As we cross the pub, the cricketers, one by one, call: 'Bye. Nice to meet you.'

\*

We leave the pub and drive west. Neat well-irrigated lines of fruit trees stretch up from the road at odd intervals between semi-arid scrublands. I'm hungry — we have not yet managed to eat lunch — and we have only drunk one beer. I am unconsciously humming the national anthem, the white-shirted woman's catchy pub piano tune, and Maria draws this to my attention by joining in with a loudly sung chorus. We don't know any more verses, so start again together. I follow this up with 'God Save the Queen' and Maria then sings the opening of the Marseillaise. We are so relaxed together we are actually having fun. Fun is the point of nationalism. I point this out to Maria, who laughs.

'I've got to eat,' I say. 'I'm starving, but I don't want any more sandwiches. We have to avoid sandwiches. Sandwiches are a bad food. They should never have become important within meals. They should always be regarded as aberrations.'

'What about fruit?'

'That's dessert.'

We soon arrive in the next town, Barmera, where I'm keen to avoid the cricketer known as Hat. There is a restaurant and at Maria's suggestion we go into it. It's Chinese, still open despite it being after two-thirty (oh sweet fortune) and licensed to serve alcohol. This is ideal.

'Look!' exclaims Maria delightedly as she reads the menu. 'Chicken with cashews. And for dessert, fried ice cream. I haven't had this stuff since summer holidays with Mum and Dad.'

The six people in the restaurant glance across at us, one holding his stare at Maria for quite a while.

'I think you've made another friend,' I comment.

This guy across the room keeps looking up at Maria in an almost neurotic way, as if afraid she'll leave without saying goodbye. The meal itself deserves no comment — unfair: it is filling — though the beer is fine and cold.

We're sitting there finishing our drinks after the meal. After a time, the guy gets up and edges over to us, again rather strangely, pretending to have conversations with both waiters along the way, as if he needs to prove he knows everyone in the restaurant. Finally he reaches us.

'Excuse me for doing this, you being in a private capacity, out for dinner or on holidays with Mr S or whatever.'

'I don't know—' begins Maria.

'It's just that out here, you never get a chance to try anything out on you people, so I kind of feel I must.'

'I'm not—'

'It'll only take a second and then I'll go back to my table. Here's my card, so you can call me when you've thought it over.'

'What are—'

'Okay, it's set in a restaurant, an upmarket, all-chrome fish restaurant, but it's a fish restaurant with a difference.'

'Mate—' I try to intervene, attempting firmness also.

'One minute,' he says, without looking at me. 'Painted fish.'

'Look—' says Maria, hopelessly.

'Or decorated. Really painted-looking though, with big naive smiling faces, or landscapes or whatever. And there would be this running joke among the restaurant staff, "I think that one's still alive", which they'll say about a skeleton or a fish head or about any old pile of fish bones to try to make each other lose concentration.

'It's a small restaurant, but busy, so you'd have four regular staff. They'd be the continuing stories, as you might guess. The two owners are husband and wife, incompatible as anything, so their family crises would lead to many comic arguments. The younger waitress and chef's assistant are secretly in love. They get slowly closer to the first kiss throughout the series, but something always gets in the way: kitchen fires, burglars, giant soft decorations falling from the ceiling.

'And the restaurant structure allows you to get in different guest stars every episode, as I'm sure you recognise, so for the pilot you'd have two or three big-name visiting Americans in, and one of them would get the last word of the episode, which would be about a whole snapper painted with a big smile or, you know, decorated with poppy seeds or whatever in the shape of a smile. I can picture it, him saying in a low kind of Italian-American voice, really deadpan: "This fish just spoke to me", and then it'd freeze with the chef in the background beginning to double over with laughter.'

'I'm sure that's a very good idea—' I say.

'Thanks very much. I think it would work. Not too much laugh track though, because I want it to be funny enough that people will actually laugh themselves.

'As you seem interested, I'll send the pilot script tomorrow and it'll be on your desk when you get back from holidays, or location scouting, or whatever you're doing in our town. And thanks for the encouraging words, Mr S, because it's very hard to find encouragement out here. I really believe this project would work.

'And now I'll sneak back to my table. This is truly great. I watch all your series, first run and then repeats. Have a nice stay in Barmera, which is the most hospitable town in Australia, I can promise you. Goodbye for now. Thank you again.'

He's backing away as though Maria were royalty.

'You do lead a double life, don't you?' I whisper.

'I'd be curious to see this script, actually. Do you think I should tell him my real address?'

'You'd have to come clean. As it stands, he'll write a cheeky covering letter: thank you for letting me pitch this to you. And whoever he's writing it to might think "Do I remember this conversation?" and might even read a page or two. So, in a way, you might have just helped make his inevitable fortune.'

'You really can be an arsehole, Jack.'

'What do you mean?' I protest. 'You're the one thinking of concealing your identity to trick him into sending you his life's work. Anyway, this idea could be a goer. It'd be better than most restaurant dramas, that's for sure. Who do you reckon he thinks you are?'

'I could be anyone, Jack, such is my potential.'

'Yeah, right. Anyone starting with S.'

I call for the bill. It's the most expensive meal of our journey so far, mainly because it's the only one which hasn't consisted of chips, fruit, bad coffee or sandwiches. Maria insists on paying. A reflection of her new mythical status, perhaps, or a sign that she regards it as a farewell meal. I cannot say which, but it makes me edgy.

We return to the car. I drive. We're nearing Adelaide. Occasional road signs make this knowledge inescapable. I'm waiting for something from Maria, who says nothing. The radio advertises pesticides. I switch it off. We drive for fifteen minutes without a word. Having touched it at larger towns further back, the Murray River now follows the road along, parallel strips of green and dark grey on a red background.

I swerve to avoid a lizard and nearly lose control of the car. The rear swings right and left before straightening again. I pull off the road to rest for a few moments and catch my breath.

'A bit fast that time, I think,' I say, though I was driving well below the speed limit. 'Sorry about that. I didn't want to hit it.'

This grey strip covered with smears of red.

Maria offers to drive, but I insist on continuing to the next town, Waikerie.

'I'm having too much fun to stop,' I say, without intonation.

A billboard on the approach to Waikerie advertises a restaurant one thousand kilometres north. 'Dig Coopers Creek Eatery. Delicious fresh and preserved meats at roadhouse prices.'

'Detour?' I ask.

'Next time,' she says.

She's thinking about it. She's thinking. Maria the Certain is having doubts. I hold my tongue. I do not indicate motels. This much I have learnt in the space of one corner of Australia.

We stop in Waikerie to switch drivers. The garbage bins are in the shape of oranges. We are stopping frequently. I am calling for a change of drivers every fifty kilometres, supposedly to avoid fatigue at this late stage of the journey. We switch in Blanchetown and in Truro. We play with the radio. Maria is complying, though with what complicity I cannot guess. She does not protest, but I cannot ask again if she's wanting to delay her reunion with the boy. Cooper's Creek, Maria? A return journey? What is she thinking? Maria the Uninterpretable. Her stated destination is ahead, iconic, nameless and undescribed, knowing, apprehensive, waiting, still or moving, interspersing his thoughts of Maria's approach with other thoughts at which I have not the background to guess.

I know that my delaying strategy is transparent, but cannot change it. Near Nuriootpa I want to stop for a coffee. There is nowhere open. We drive on.

We are still about three hours from sunset. The journey will not stretch to more nights together. Some of the roadside stalls are shut for the day, but the more persistent market gardeners remain with their tables or marquees. Maria, with what I sense to be a little embarrassment at her insensitivity, asks that we stop so she doesn't arrive in Adelaide empty-handed. That is, so she doesn't arrive at the boy's place empty-handed. This is not good. It is too forward-looking. We are not yet in Adelaide and should still be doing our journey, not thinking to future scenes. I could make plenty of comments about this: no over-ripe pineapples in my car. What about the wine you haven't shared with me? I decide to keep Desi's tomato relish.

We stop at a very large stall, practically a circus tent, city-like in its size and range, with spotlights clipped to its ceiling poles.

'This isn't the grower's, you know. It's just a shop,' I tell her. 'You're better off going to a supermarket when we get there.'

'I won't be long.'

She appears to want me to stay in the car, so I get out.

The small orchard behind the tent appears insufficient to stock the long tables fully. The extensive marquee is surmounted by several excessively prominent Australian flags. I am sure the proprietor has simply popped into town to stock up and the flags are to hide the fact of imported produce.

Maria has taken a basket and makes her way with it up the first of three aisles. I hang at the front.

'You're not going to tell us a story, are you?' I ask the fruit shop guy. 'We've heard that the entire continent is full of broken hearts. Everyone says so.'

'It's funny you should ask,' he says. 'I won't tell you a story, but let me say something about greengrocers. I am a greengrocer, and it's a profession full of skills. It's not like working in a grocery, say, where everything comes in a can. And I'll tell you something else: all the blue stories concerning tradespeople are about plumbers and milkmen and door-to-door salesmen getting lucky with beautiful women. These stories are mostly told by men, and most of these men know someone who knows someone who is a plumber or a milkman. These stories are not reliable. As a profession, greengrocers are by far the greater lovers, and for this you needn't ask them. You can ask women. That's what you should do.'

Sometimes even I regret my tongue. Why did I say anything? Maria is now in the far back corner of the marquee, with no prospect of rescuing me.

'We really have to know our vegetables,' says the greengrocer. 'And I will tell you one more thing about life in the fruit and vegetable trade. It's full of stories and these go back not just tens of years like fencing salespeople, those show-offs. Our stories can be traced thousands of years, and probably millions of years, back to when all people were herbivores.'

'Another greengrocer told me something similar once,' I comment. 'About the love, that is, not the history of vegetarian narrative.'

'Perhaps you have been inducted. Listen, in those days, fruiterers were thought of as wizards and healers and seers. I'm not a superstitious person myself. Or at least not usually. I'll tell you one more thing, okay?'

I begin to say I haven't much time.

'Nonsense!' he says. He hands me a nectarine, and with a loud 'Hoy!' hurls another the length of the tent to Maria, who catches it one-handed. 'My compliments.'

*

Of course it's tempting to see portents in every aspect of fruit market life, and generally I'm not a superstitious person, as I said, but when first a bicycle shows up, perfectly good and new, and I've never found anything in my entire life in Adelaide (I'm not a lucky person either), and then a day later the apple with her face clear as anything in the markings on the peel, I knew it was time to move.

Then, as if that wasn't enough, I was going on with my daily morning routine of emptying the boxes of fruit into their displays and blowed if the mandarins didn't slide into the shape of New South Wales, quite distinctive and identifiable. I even said to Alfie, 'What do you see there?' and he said, 'It's bloody New South Wales, isn't it!' and I said, 'That's what I thought, but I wasn't going to believe it,' and he said, 'Mate, believe it — it's New South Wales all right.'

'I've got to go to Sydney,' I said.

'I believe you do,' he nodded.

Well, I could have been a hero then and there, tossed in the job, picked up the bicycle and cycled all that way, but I'm not a heroic sort of person, so I begged a week's early holiday and booked a bus ticket. If the portents are genuinely portentous, I reasoned, they won't muck around. I'll find her within a week, and if I can't find her, then all that apple, bicycle, mandarin hoodoo must be meaningless coincidence.

Still, I jumped on a bus that night. Best not to let it ride too much, I decided. I dreamed of Violet, as she had introduced herself to me the first day we met at the fruit markets thirteen years before: she was selecting the best

319

celery by its smell. The next day, I found her among the pomegranates. She was balancing fruit on her index finger to assess, she claimed, even seed development. When we parted I said, 'Goodbye, Violet.'

'It's Rose,' she corrected, and every day she told me a new name, because names are necessary but not important. And we were in love for a year and one day she disappeared.

Bus trips are the pits, and I was tired enough to sleep on a bed of cold-store lettuce by the time we disembarked in central Sydney. But I only had six days left to find her, so I checked into the Greenleaf Motel and began to search.

I'm an orderly person, which is why I'm the one entrusted to set up the fruit and vegie displays each day: particular configurations of tomatoes show each piece's best quality. Customers like consistent colour; the ideal presentation makes best use of the available light, not too many uneven shadows, which can look a lot like bruising. Trust me. And when it comes to searching a city for long-lost love, well, you can't just change your natural character, or I can't, so I looked up fruit shops in the telephone book, arranged them by area and divided the city into six parts, one for each search day.

That first day was hopeless. She was nowhere. I described her to dozens of greengrocers and storepeople and cash-register operators. I told them about the portents and I showed them the apple, but as the fruit had continued to ripen her face had faded. If only I'd photographed it/her! Some fruitsellers were sympathetic and some were sarcastic but either attitude produced the identical outcome.

'What's her name, mate?' they'd ask. I'd have to explain that she had a different name every day, and each day I'd try to guess her new name and she'd give me clues — it'd always turn out to be a flower or a fruit tree or an orcharding district in some exotic language or country.

'So you're looking for some mad chick named Rambutan who's appeared to you in the side of an apple, are you?' sneered one especially nasty fruit shop proprietor. 'You'd better hope she hasn't become a plumber, or she'll be calling herself Drainpipe, or S-bend.'

The first day of my search was a day of fruit sitting in boxes, unsold, unwanted.

But I wasn't put off. She'd simply become lost, and I was about to find her.

Day two began more hopefully. I went to the fruit market at dawn, and on three or four occasions thought I saw her. She always turned out to be someone else, someone with her hair, or her way of walking, but I sensed I was getting closer. People seemed more polite all day, though that could be because I no longer showed them the apple, but instead tried to describe her height, build, hair colour — difficult, as I hadn't seen her since she'd left twelve years before. She could have changed completely, but I was still sure I'd recognise her. That day I saw sacks of potatoes, smelling of earth.

Day three was to the south of the city, shop after shop stacked with an astonishing variety of root vegetables and tubers, but no luck. By the end of the day I was footsore but not dispirited. People talk of Sydney Harbour and the various beaches, but the heart of Sydney is diffuse, scattered in hundreds of fruit shops over hundreds of hectares. That's what I feel, even though I'm not generally a person to believe cities have 'hearts'. I saw trays of globe artichokes with borders of giant thistle-like artichoke flowers.

I began day four peering around fruit stalls in the city proper, and walked through Chinatown. A face-painted juggler tossed three butternut pumpkins into the air, caught one in each hand and one on her forehead: a peculiar tilt of forehead which could have belonged to ... but no, it's not her. Pyramids of kiwi fruit.

The fifth day I travelled north, the fruit shops in arcades or beside railway stations, and once more a sense of impending luck but never becoming actual. Rows of berries in punnets, alternating red and black.

My last day in Sydney. I was thinking compensatory comforts to myself: I'd got such a good feel for the city and its inhabitants; I'd visited more fruit shops than ever before; I'd observed some innovative display methods which would make me even more indispensable at work.

To be honest, I'd given up. I'd say my week had been 'fruitless', but it didn't feel like a joke, believe me. I caught a train back out to the fruit market, well past its closing time. Cowboys in forklifts were clearing away abandoned pallets. A man sprayed at smears of rotten tomato with a high-powered hose. The scene was the opposite of everything I loved about fruit-selling: it was a distasteful combination of waste and pure function. I turned to leave, to catch the night bus south.

At that instant, I saw a second figure wandering, doing nothing in particular. Surely not? But it was her.

'Hello,' I said straight up. 'It's me.'

She hugged me to her as though it was afternoon and we'd seen each other that morning, and I told her about the bicycle and the mandarin map and the face in the apple, and she said she'd seen my face in a bus window and took that as foretelling good luck, and although I'm not often a spontaneous person, I took the return bus ticket from my pocket and I let it drop.

*

'We moved down here about five years ago, and are set up pretty well, as you see. Best fruit in the state by a mile.'

'It looks good,' I agree, for politeness. I don't like to see what happens next. This boyfriend, nameless and undescribed, is to be fleshed out with gifts of fruit as I watch.

Maria presents her filled basket. The greengrocer weighs item by item and packs them into a plastic bag.

'Take my advice. Get yourself a good job in the industry. It worked wonders for me.'

'I'll take that on board,' I say.

Maria pays and carries her boyfriend's bag back to the car. I'm not helping with that, and she makes no comment. It must weigh four kilograms.

She drives.

'These shopkeepers sure know how to talk,' I say. 'And to tally up.'

We pass the Gawler turn-off in silence. I had been a little nervous about the journey's end, and that feeling is growing. Will I see this boyfriend? Will she compare the two of us there at the last stop, me in the car and him on the doorstep? Will she move first one way and then the other, towards me, towards him? A sign promises Adelaide only forty kilometres away. We've driven almost fourteen hundred. I've brought her this far, and she has, I admit, brought me.

I now imagine I would like to arrive at the end of this journey having forgotten Maria, she of the war memorials project, reviver of memories of expired events. Could I remember something or someone instead of her? Can one substitute one memory for another as though exchanging books at a library? The human mind is much too flexible. Forgetting Maria is as unlikely as the car splitting longitudinally and us each peeling off in separate directions.

We pass through Elizabeth now and we are back in the suburban. We switch seats one last time. Life will become ordinary. She cannot be erased, but one day in the future life will become ordinary. I think this as I am driving along the Main North Road, the road which in its name promises Australian interiors, red rocks and road trains, but here we are, taking it south towards its ordinary urban beginning.

This journey is the history, then, of our failure to come back together. Love, grief, hurt, anger, frustration cannot overcome strength of will, determination, fixity. After all these miles I have only arguments left, and she has already rebutted them all. I can still, even now, argue that we would enjoy to be together, but she will not agree. I can suggest we make a further attempt, that we experiment, but she will not do either. I can propose we have mutual unfulfilled desires, and that there is clear evidence in both our behaviours, but she dismisses desire. I might contend that we have been outside our lives, in a space without repercussions, this thin, thin line of bitumen which stretches so far, that we can live within it a little longer, but she will not share this vision.

I do not string these together in words, not now. I have said all I can, have tried every appeal. I have rehearsed my feelings in the creases of my face and the bend of my shoulders, and I have seen her smile and stand tall. I can repeat, I have repeated, but she can and has too, and she will sound more tired than I do.

I have run out of things to say. Maria says things to me now, but practical things: 'Turn here'; 'You will soon come to traffic lights.'

This is Adelaide.

I think I do still love Maria, but I don't know how to tell. Everything I think or do in relation to her is so weighed down. There is no way through. Time together becomes too complicated to solve anything. Time apart is impossible: it goes nowhere. It's like not being anywhere. It's like standing beside a eucalypt looking up a hill with Maria out of sight but still there. I can forget her for an instant, see the sheep and the few birds, a group of resting kangaroos (or they could be boulders; it's hard to discern from this distance) in a shady patch further away. Then there she is, holding out the water bottle. We're silent together. I am silent because I'm thinking all this. Maria may be contemplating our relationship too, or perhaps this land has touched her as it ought to do and she is feeling lost or free or home.

Our relationship and its deterioration are unending. We find ourselves together, travelling as other chaste couples have done in past eras, the changes we have imposed previously on each other submerged.

We have passed through the fertile and arid heartlands of populated Australia and emerged barren. At Maria's command, I stop the car. She jumps out, unloads her bags of clothes and fruit and cameras from the back, leaves them on the pavement and comes around to my window.

'Well, goodbye.'

She leans in, kisses me once on the lips.

'Goodbye.'

I am watching Maria recede.

Maria recedes. She has not turned. She becomes smaller. In twenty years, she will be smaller still. Maria walks away, her camera bag over one shoulder, her travel bags and the rest in her hands. This is the picture I see of her at the end of her journey, the halfway point of mine.

As she shrinks along the concrete footpath, not turning around, not changing her mind, unmoved by our journey, having decided she has said farewell to me, having decided which words will become the final words to have been said, as she moves off at last I realise. We will never be together again.

# ACKNOWLEDGMENTS

For rare writing space in central London, I am very grateful to the Menzies Centre for Australian Studies and its head, Carl Bridge, for a creative arts associateship. Many thanks to Nela Bureu, Carmen Zamorano and especially to Maria Vidal and Brian Worsfold for an informal 'residency' and warm hospitality at the University of Lleida in Catalonia, Spain, to University College Worcester and Jean Webb for the time and space provided by a writer's residency in Worcester and to the Literature Board of the Australia Council for writing time in the form of a New Writing Fellowship. Thanks also to Goodenough College, London for its support.

Versions of parts of this book first appeared in: *Meanjin*, *Heat*, the *Sydney Morning Herald*, *Southerly*, the *Literary Review* (US), *The Thirteenth Floor* (UTS anthology), on public radio station 2SER and in performance at the Art Gallery of NSW. Thanks especially to Ivor Indyk of *Heat* and to Christina Thompson and Stephanie Holt, successive editors of *Meanjin*, for their suggestions.

Thank you to Angelo Loukakis for his faith in the notes-and-a-promise he took on, and to my publisher Linda Funnell for her feedback, enthusiasm and commitment, not to mention patience, during *Hardly Beach Weather*'s slow transformation into a book. I am grateful to my editors Belinda Lee, for numerous constructive and productive suggestions over two years and two and a half drafts, and Nicola O'Shea, for her detailed reading and odometric attention to timing. For generously given help, comments or information, thank you to Susan Pfisterer of the Menzies Centre, Brent Clough, James Storrer, Jenny Millea and David Porreca, and to my literary agent Fran Bryson for friendship and great stores of gentle encouragement.

Deepest thanks to Nicola Robinson for her close readings, close support and close presence, without which ... and to our children Pola and Jo-Jo for being lovely.